Sleet Princess

Book Four of the Sleet Series

S. J. Tilly

This book is dedicated to all my Sleet Sluts.
Thank you for waiting.
And to Jackson Wilder.
You'll always be my first.

Chapter 1

Luke

"You're a prick and I hate you!" my cousin tries to yell at me.

"If *Baywatch* can do it, so can I." I mock back his words from an hour ago.

"It's..." Jacob gulps in a breath. "Harder... than... it looks."

He's always giving me shit about being a professional athlete. Claiming that since I've been naturally good at hockey since we were kids, being a pro hockey player is hardly a challenge.

It's nonsense. And the dying man three paces behind me knows it.

I've been playing pro hockey since I was twenty-two. And for the past fourteen years, I've been working my ass off to keep my place. But I can admit, privately, that it takes me just a little longer to recover nowadays. A little longer for my bones to rattle back into place after a hard hit.

I know the end is coming.

I've accepted that I'll have to retire soon. One year, maybe two.

But I'm not ready to throw in the towel just yet. And the

first game of the season is just a couple weeks away, so... more running.

"Pick up the pace." I spin around so I'm jogging backward. "One more loop, then we'll hit the weight room."

Jacob shakes his head in time with his heavy steps. "No more loops. Weights. I'll spot."

I'm about to argue, but when Jacob stops—stops right there in his tracks—I stop too.

"And you call yourself an Anders." I click my tongue.

"This is supposed to be a vacation!" Jacob collapses onto the sandy beach, sprawling onto his back. "For real. You're not my best man anymore."

"Such a shame," I sigh. "Now get up so we can go to the gym."

Jacob groans and kicks his feet a few times. "Fine," he whines, then holds his arms up. "Help me up."

"Help yourself up."

He waves his hands around. "Seriously, help me up, you fuck face. My thighs are going to be so sore tomorrow that I won't be able to make sweet love to my wife on our wedding night."

I slap at his hand. "Don't talk to me about sex with the woman who's about to be my cousin. It's gross."

He tries to slap at my hand but misses because his eyes are closed.

"*Luke.*" He drags my name out. "What's the point of you getting all jacked this summer if you won't use your muscles for good?"

I stare down at him. "You're making it weird."

When he finally cracks his eyes open, I flex my biceps.

He twists his wrists and gives me double middle fingers.

He's not wrong though. Ever since Jackson, my best friend and captain of the team... and well, Ash, my goalie, and Zach,

2

my enforcer, got married a year ago, I've been spending all my free time working out. And between the team trainers and getting my ass kicked by muscle heads at Atom's Gym, my feelings of loneliness haven't gone away, but I'm more built than I've ever been before.

The guys aren't to blame. It's not their fault they fell in love, one after another.

And I never thought I wanted that. The whole marriage thing. But now...

I look down at my cousin and think about the fact that he's getting married tomorrow.

Now I want it.

I want a girl of my own.

But it's hard to date as a pro athlete.

It sounds backward, but it's true. There are a lot of people out there willing to fake feelings for money and fame. And I don't want to end up with someone who's with me for some sort of perceived lifestyle rather than being with me for me.

I tried the dating app thing. No, thank you to doing that ever again.

And I've tried meeting someone the *old-fashioned way*, but on the occasions I go out with my friends, they bring their wives, not single women. And their wives are all best fucking friends, so it's not like they even invite any other women along. Jackson has a sister who comes around sometimes, but I've known her forever, so she's basically a sister to me too. And I'm not into that particular kink.

So... that leaves me as the odd man out. And going to the gym to pass the time. A lot.

I sigh. "Maybe if I take a picture of you like this, that fiancée of yours will see she's with the wrong Anders, and I can take your spot tomorrow."

"I know you're just fucking with me." Jacob rolls onto his

side, pushing up onto all fours. "But I'm still gonna kick your ass for saying that."

"Gotta catch me first." I shove my foot against his ass and knock him over onto his side.

Then I take off for the resort gym.

Chapter 2

Natalie

"WHAT ARE YOU WEARING?" Heather's face is scrunched up, like my choice of clothing is more offensive than her demanding I join her and her friends in the gym at eight a.m.

I ignore my cousin and her tone and step out of my hotel room.

My overfilled beach bag bumps into her legs, and she shuffles back.

"We're going to the gym," she says, like I forgot why I was awake so early while on vacation at an all-inclusive resort in Mexico.

"Uh-huh." I pull the door shut behind me. I agreed to go to the gym. I didn't agree to do more than *be there*.

At eight a.m.

On my vacation.

The bridezilla huffs before she mutters something under her breath and spins away from me.

"Come on." She waves over her shoulder at me. "The other girls are waiting for us."

The other girls are waiting for us, I mouth behind her back.

5

It's juvenile.

And satisfying.

Heather is... a nightmare. And if it wasn't for my dad, I wouldn't put up with her. But her dad is my dad's brother, and they're close, and blah, blah, so here I am at a beautiful resort in a beautiful country, dealing with her bullshit when all I want to do is move from my bed to the ocean and back.

My sandals slap against the stone floor, in contrast to Heather's silent sneakers, as we reach the end of the hall.

Her trio of twittering friends are standing in a huddle around the corner.

One of them rolls her eyes when she takes me in.

Girl, same. I also find this ridiculous.

Last night, Heather texted in our *super fun* group chat that we would all go to the gym this morning so we could all get one more *good sweat in* before she says I do.

Her obsession with body image has only gotten worse during this whole wedding planning process, and all I can be thankful for is that after she says those *I dos* tomorrow, I'm removing myself from the group chat. As in, while they're standing on the beach, exchanging rings, I'm slipping my phone out of my dress pocket and blocking everyone.

Maybe her friends wouldn't be so awful under other circumstances, but I'll never know. And I highly doubt it.

We turn down another hallway, and a glass door ahead of us leads to the resort gym.

I hitch my bag up higher on my shoulder.

I only have to get through an hour of this, then I can get a coffee and bring it down to the beach.

Chapter 3

Luke

"I'm not gonna do it now." Jacob pants when he finally catches up.

"Not gonna do what?"

"Kick your ass."

"Ooh, right, that." I widen my eyes. "Thank fuck."

He narrows his eyes. "I'm still going to do it. I'm just going to wait until you aren't expecting it."

"Uh-huh, sure." I lift the collar of my T-shirt up over my face, wiping the sweat off as we approach the outside door for the resort gym.

Jacob rolls his neck out. "Alright, so what, like ten minutes of this shit, then we're done?"

"Yeah, ten minutes." And by ten, I mean forty.

My cousin shakes out his arms. "Alright, I can do it. Make me strong enough to carry my bride across the threshold."

I just shake my head and pull open the door. "That's not how this works."

Jacob veers straight for the water station, telling me he'll grab one of the little paper cups for me. But I'm not listening anymore. Because my blood is suddenly no longer concerned with my nervous system and is instead surging to my dick.

Several people are in the gym. Four girls are using the treadmills and ellipticals in front of the window facing the beach. A guy over on the leg press, another couple guys using the free weights... But I'm not looking at them. I'm looking at the goddess draped across the weight bench in the far corner of the room.

I was planning to start with a few sets of squats, really wear out the quads, but I'm having a change of heart.

Clenching my abs in an attempt to stop my dick from betraying me in these shorts, I stride across the large room.

The woman isn't working out.

She clearly has no intention of working out.

And fuck me, I don't blame her. I wouldn't change a thing about her.

She's lying on her back, one leg straight, one leg bent. And...

I clench my stomach harder.

The lacy blue cover-up she's wearing is bunched at her hips, draping down over the sides of the bench to the floor, exposing all of her legs. And clearly visible under the cover-up is a bright pink bikini. It's not a super skimpy bikini, but it doesn't have to be. She attracts the attention all on her own.

My eyes follow the line of the bare leg closest to me, the one that's bent with her foot flat on the bench.

And *goddamn*, her skin looks so soft. From her knee, down the back of her leg, to the curve of her ass.

I bite the inside of my cheek as I look at her lush ass framed in that bright pink fabric.

Halfway to her, I drag my eyes up her frame, up her soft stomach covered in that lacy fabric, to a pair of tits that are begging to be sucked on.

I clench my butt cheeks as hard as I can while still walking.

I'm going to have a full fucking boner by the time I reach this woman if I keep looking at her. But I can't stop.

That damn cover-up is so low cut I'm not even sure what the purpose of it is. Because it's not covering up shit. It's a peepshow.

My eyes take in the flashes of skin through the lacy fabric, spotting a tattoo peeking above the band of her bikini bottom at her hip.

As someone who has become well acquainted with the art of tattoos, I appreciate that she made the commitment to some ink.

Just a few feet away, I finally do the gentlemanly thing and look at her face.

She's reading some sort of e-book, holding it directly above her head, so I can't make out her eye color. But I can make out her plump lips and the dark brown hair bundled on top of her head.

Her fingernails are painted a pale pink, and they tap a random pattern against the back of the device in her hands.

She looks like she can't be bothered with society.

Like she couldn't care less what's expected of her.

She looks like fucking royalty.

She looks fucking ripe.

And if we were alone, I'd step one leg over her and lay myself directly on top of her body.

But we aren't alone.

And dry humping a stranger isn't really my style.

So I take a different approach.

Chapter 4

Natalie

"MIND SHARING, PRINCESS?" A deep voice comes from above me, jolting me out of my story.

My fingers twitch from the surprise, and the e-reader slips out of my hands.

I squeeze my eyes shut and brace for impact.

I've dropped it on my face before. I know this isn't going to feel good.

Except nothing happens.

Slowly, I open my eyes.

Then I open them the rest of the way, because standing beside me is... a man.

I swallow.

He's just a man.

A man of flesh and blood.

And muscles.

And sweat.

And tattoos and arm veins and muscles.

Good grief, the muscles.

From my reclined position, I can't tell how tall he is, but his thighs are...

Right there.

And his shirt is clinging to...

Good grief.

And his large arms are attached to large hands. And one of those hands is wrapped around my e-reader, making the device look like a deck of cards.

My eyes drop back to his thighs. And his navy blue shorts. And his... bulge.

Get a hold of yourself.

I snap my eyes up, ignoring the thin white T-shirt and ignoring his sleeve tattoo.

There will be no drooling over this man.

I try to focus from his neck up, but my eyes are stuck staring at his neck, which is also covered in ink.

He's just a muscled-up, tattooed dude.

He's just a man.

A man reading my book, a little voice reminds me.

Oh god, my book!

Remembering the scene I was in the middle of is enough to snap me out of my daze.

I sit up and twist toward the man so I'm facing him when my sandaled feet hit the floor.

It's a mistake, though, because now my face is level with his stomach, and my eyes are back to focusing on what's inside his shorts.

And I swear it just twitched at me.

A throat clears.

Inwardly, I wince.

Outwardly, I lift my gaze as though I didn't just get caught staring at a stranger's junk.

But he's not looking at me. He's still reading.

"Um..." I start, but that's all I manage.

What is happening?

Men don't fluster me.

They don't.

And I'm not going to think about him calling me Princess.

Even though I was lost in my story—right at the part when the scarred knight throws his wife over his shoulder after she shouts that she doesn't love him anymore—I still heard the way he said it.

Princess.

I've been called it before. Quite a bit, actually, because of my family's wealth. But it's never sounded like that. Like... a compliment.

Completely composed—on the outside—I look up at the man who's still reading my book. "Would you care to switch?"

Whiskey-colored eyes glance at me over the top of the device, then he goes back to reading. "In a minute."

In. A minute.

"I'm sorry, what?" I can't have heard him correctly.

"Shush." The man shushes me.

He, honest to god, shushes me.

My mouth drops open.

His eyes dart to my lips, then back to the story.

I watch as the edge of his mouth pulls up.

This man thinks he's being cute.

But when I take in the rest of his face, it's clear this man is beyond cute.

His facial hair is too thick to be cute. His cocky little smirk is too confident to be cute.

His hair, the same rich brown as his beard, is too sweat soaked to be cute.

Top to bottom, this specimen is too fucking manly to be cute.

I shift to try to stand, but he's in the way, so I can't.

The man, still reading, makes a noise in his throat and raises his brows.

Okay, that's enough.

But before I can reach up and take my book from him, he turns and sits on the bench next to me. So close that our arms touch.

His skin is warm against mine. And I should pull away.

I should, but I can't. Because having this stranger so close, *this close*, is doing something to my senses.

My core clenches as a wave of desire rolls through me. And the hummingbird that resides inside my ribcage flutters to life. Shaken out of stasis by this man.

The message is clear. I need to get away before my body betrays me further.

I reach for my book.

But as I reach, he shifts the device to his far hand and stretches his arm out, holding the book out of my reach.

I turn toward him, not caring that my knees bump into his thigh. "Are you serious?"

The man turns his head to face me, our noses only inches apart.

"This is very serious." He shakes the device in his hand. "I need to find out what happens with Lord Kentigern and his lady wife."

I narrow my eyes. "If you're about to insult my book, I suggest you think twice."

His mouth pulls into a crooked smile, exposing bright white teeth. "I would never. This"—he shakes the book again—"was my sex ed."

I don't drop my suspicious expression. "What does that mean?"

"Means that after my mom caught me, uh, expressing myself, she left a pile of her romance books on my bed and told me to read them. Said if I was old enough to buy porno magazines off the neighbor kid, who stole them from his dad, then I was old enough to read from the other perspective."

I huff out a laugh, surprised at his story and the fact that he shared it. "She had a point."

"That she did. And I'm nothing if not a good student." The man winks.

Winks.

I roll my eyes, hoping my cheeks aren't blushing, even though I know they are.

"Sounds like you have plenty of your own books to read, then. So..." I hold my hand out.

The man pulls his arm back in, but instead of handing me my book, he taps the screen.

"How do I find the title on this thing?" He taps the screen again, turning the page instead of finding what he wants.

"Just give it here." I reach for it.

He twists away from me, causing me to bump into his shoulder.

I stop reaching and glare at the side of his face. "I'm going to ask this again. Are you serious?"

"Princess, you can keep asking, but it's not changing the answer." He swipes his finger on the screen, bringing up the settings menu. "I'm going to need the title." He taps the screen. "Why isn't this working?"

I grip the back of his sweaty shirt and tug.

He's obviously strong enough to resist, but he doesn't.

Instead, he lets me pull him until he's leaning back, then I stretch across and snatch my device from his hand.

"Aww, Green Eyes, don't be like that." He looks up at me, his gaze glinting with humor.

Green Eyes. I really need to get away from this man.

"It was just starting to get good." He grins.

I let go of his shirt, and as I stand, I wipe his sweat off my palm by smoothing my hand down my cover-up. "If you're clever, you'll be able to figure it out."

I keep my back to him as I pick my bag up off the floor.

"And how about your name?" he asks with a smile in his voice.

With my bag hooked on my elbow, I glance at him one last time over my shoulder. "Princess is good."

Chapter 5

Luke

I WATCH HER WALK AWAY, trying not to feel like a creep while I stare at her ass, but also not quite able to pull my eyes away.

Princess is good.

Oh, she's good, alright.

Jacob drops onto the bench where Green Eyes just was. And I heave out a breath when she pushes out the doors and out of view.

"You say you want to date, but then you let that girl just walk away." He makes a sound of disagreement. "It's no wonder I'm getting married first."

"I don't think following her out of here like a stalker is the way to go."

"I'm just saying." Jacob hands me a little cup of water.

"Just saying." I mock him since I don't have a better come-back. "Alright." I down the water, then stand and move toward the weights. "Let's get this over with."

I need to get out of here so I can bump into Princess again.

Chapter 6

Natalie

I HAVE the tiniest twinge of guilt for leaving the gym without saying anything to Heather, but I'll see her tonight at the rehearsal dinner.

"Nat!" my dad calls.

Holding back my sigh, I turn to see him striding down one of the many pathways, his hand lifted, in case I wouldn't see him twenty feet away.

I slow to a stop and trail my fingers gently over a flower while I wait for him to reach me.

Heather might have a cactus-shaped personality, but there's nothing wrong with her taste.

This resort is stunning.

Tropical plants line the sidewalks that weave between the buildings. The food is good, the drinks are plentiful, and I'm sure the pools are great, but I'm focused on getting my ass in the actual ocean. Because this end-of-September weather is perfect for swimming.

"You guys done with the gym already?" Dad asks when he reaches me.

I nod. "Yep."

I'm done with the gym.

And sweaty shirt man.

"Good." Dad drapes his arm over my shoulders, dressed in swim trunks and a polo. "Come have breakfast with me."

I want to get in the water, but... breakfast buffet.

"Alright," I agree.

I should've known it wouldn't be a relaxed breakfast with Dad. Instead, it turned into both of us on the phone, dealing with one work thing after another. Then my uncle showed up. Then Heather and her cronies. And my auntie. And more cousins.

My phone rings again, and I decide to take the opportunity to escape.

"I'm gonna take this outside," I say, picking up my phone and my beach bag because, for the love of god, I'm getting in the damn ocean today.

Heather rolls her eyes at me as I lift my phone to my ear, but I ignore it.

Her attitude used to really bother me. My dad always told me it was just jealousy and nothing to do with me as a person. Which, as a kid, I never understood. Because it's always been just been me and Dad, and she had a whole big family.

Then, as I got older and started to notice the differences, I realized the jealousy was over money.

But it's not like I had anything to do with my dad becoming filthy rich. And it's not like my uncle is hurting—they are more than comfortable. He just didn't invest the same way my dad did. And he doesn't work nonstop like my dad does. Like I do.

Which is why her continued attitude into adulthood is extra obnoxious. I wouldn't have to work if I didn't want to. But I want to. I want to contribute.

I listen to the person on the other end of the line as I weave through the tables in the massive restaurant and push through a set of doors that takes me back outside.

After setting my bag down on a bench, I dig around with my free hand until I find my sunglasses and put them on.

The white chunky frames float, so if they fall off in the water, I should be able to catch them before they become pollution.

Hiking my bag back up, I make noises of understanding while I trail around the pools, past an open-air restaurant, and onto the sand.

The tiny bits of earth instantly cover my sandals, so I pause and slip them off, slapping them against my thigh before shoving them into my bag.

I keep nodding along, reassuring the director of our New York offices that this new acquisition won't affect their location, as I select an empty lounge chair underneath one of the colorful umbrellas.

Since none of the other beachgoers are near enough to listen, I put my phone on speaker and drag my cover-up off, shoving it into my bag next to the sandals.

The man continues to talk while I pull my hair loose from its bun and twist it into one thick braid before I start reapplying my sunscreen.

I put some on this morning, but since my day got hijacked, it's probably time to add more. Overkill is better than sitting on a plane sunburned.

When the director takes a moment to breathe, I finally cut in. "I promise you, nothing will change in your day-to-day. You just gotta trust me, alright? If you're still feeling this way in three weeks, we can talk again."

He makes a noise of agreement, and I hang up.

I hesitate with my phone in my hand, debating if I should leave it sitting right on top of my bag. If someone wants to steal it and deal with my calls while I'm relaxing in the surf and sun, so be it.

But alas, a stolen phone would only make my life more difficult, so I shove it down below my cover-up.

Then I smile as my feet sink into the warm sand while I make my way toward the waves.

Chapter 7

Luke

I sit up from my reclined position, the pink swimsuit catching my attention. "Gotcha, Princess."

Standing from my beach lounger, I pull my shirt up over my head.

"Yeah, that doesn't make you sound like a stalker at all," Jacob mumbles, draping his arm over his eyes.

I ignore him. And head toward the water.

Chapter 8

Natalie

RELAXING BACK, I let my body's natural buoyancy take over as I look up at the bright blue sky.

My toes peek out of the water, and I float on my back in Mother Nature's bowl of monster soup. My heartbeat just another drop in the ocean.

Part of me wishes I could transform into a mermaid and stay out here forever. Away from the pressures. Away from the phone calls and meetings.

But then a lap of water splashes over my chin, and I remind myself why I do what I do. Why I started working at my dad's company when I was eighteen. Why I decided to do night classes rather than go the route of an on-campus college experience. Why I spent the last fourteen years working more hours than almost anyone, hiring the best in every field, arguing with Dad over decisions I feel passionate about, and forfeiting relationships.

I do it, all of it, because I know that if I achieve my goals, if I can take over as CEO of Wag Corp, then I can make a difference in this world.

So I'll keep working.
But today...
I close my eyes and continue to float.
Today is just for me.
Tomorrow too.
"Hello, again."

Chapter 9

Luke

Princess startles, again, only this time, instead of dropping something, her face dips underwater.

"Shit."

I dart my hand out and place it against her back, helping to lift her head back above water.

She comes up coughing, sunglasses off kilter on her face, looking way too cute as she spits saltwater out of her mouth.

"Sorry." My apology would probably be better if she couldn't hear the laughter in my voice.

Her foot connects with my knee, and another chuckle breaks free from my chest.

She spits again and shoves her glasses up off her face onto the top of her head. "Are you always such a menace?"

It's deep enough here that we have to tread water to stay afloat, but she uses one hand to wipe the water off her lashes, clearing her vision.

Which means she can see me grinning.

Her hand slaps down across the surface of the water, sending a splash into my face.

I deserve it, but it doesn't dim my smile. "Sorry."

She looks at me the same way my teammates do when I make a hilarious joke that they refuse to find funny. "You don't look very sorry."

"I am." I place a hand over my heart. "I just don't know my own stealth, apparently."

She runs her tongue across her teeth, making a face. And I get it. A mouthful of ocean water is nasty.

"Sorry," I repeat, going for a more contrite look this time. "Please, forgive me."

She purses her lips. "I will if you let me splash you again."

I like this girl already.

"I'll do you one better," I tell her as I shift my hand motions underwater. "I'll let you push me under."

Sucking in a big breath, I let my chest expand as I lean back, kicking my feet toward the surface until I'm in the same position she was in when I scared her.

"You are ridiculous," she huffs.

"Aw, come on. It's only fair." I goad her.

"I'm not going to—"

I can't hear the rest of her sentence because she does exactly what she was just about to refuse, and she shoves me under the surface.

Clever little Princess.

If I hadn't laughed underwater, I'd have been fine. But the beginning of her comment had me lowering my guard, so instead of being calm and collected, I get a nose full of ocean.

But the burning in my sinuses is worth it to feel her palm against the bare skin of my chest.

She pulls her hand away while I'm still beneath the surface, but I reach out and grab it.

As I lift my head above the water, I keep my grip on her wrist.

"You're a sneaky girl," I laugh, turning away from her and blowing the water out of my nose.

"I literally did what you told me to do," she argues, but I can hear her humor.

I clear my throat and use my free hand to wipe my eyes before I go back to treading water.

"You gonna survive, Mr. Muscles?"

Mr. Muscles.

She's smiling at me. Full-on smiling. And it fills my chest with a lightness I haven't felt in forever.

"I dunno." I try to keep a straight face. "I might need mouth to mouth."

She rolls her eyes. "This is Mexico, not *The Sandlot.*"

I smirk. "Every time you open your mouth, I like you even more."

Chapter 10

Natalie

EVERY TIME you open your mouth, I like you even more.

What am I supposed to say to that?

And who tells a stranger that?

He finally lets go of my wrist. "Luke Anders." He holds his hand above the water. "Starting forward and alternate captain for the Minnesota Sleet."

My brows go up.

"I know." He smirks. "I'm impressive."

I splash him again.

He snickers and wipes his face off, then holds his hand back up.

Sighing, I keep my other limbs moving and place my palm against his.

That damn jolt of desire spears through me again. Just like when our arms touched this morning.

I ignore it.

"Natalie Wagner." I give his hand a shake. "Ocean lover and director of operations for Wag Corp. Nice to put a name to the startling appearances, Luke."

He tightens his fingers around mine when I say his name, then he lets go. "Pleasure. But please, call me Mr. Muscles."

"Now that I know they're for work…" I lift a shoulder.

Luke narrows his eyes. "Are you saying you're no longer impressed by my humongous stature?"

After the word humongous and before the word stature, I can't help it… my eyes dip down.

When I look back up, he's grinning like a fool.

I flick the surface of the water. "Don't be crass."

He lets out an open-mouth laugh. "Tsk, tsk, Princess. I'm not the one who looked."

I try not to smile.

The water distorts the image of what's below the surface, so it's not like I saw anything other than the bright orange fabric of his swim shorts.

"So… Minnesota Sleet, huh? That where you're from?"

Luke nods, his wet hair plastered to his forehead in a way that should be dorky but is obnoxiously sexy. "Born and raised. Now, let me guess." He narrows his eyes at me. "You're from Chicago."

I gasp.

His brows shoot up. "Really?"

I snort at his reaction and shake my head.

His shoulders slump like he's actually disappointed. "Alright, Miss Wagner. Where are you from, then?"

"Naperville."

He blinks at me. "Where's that?"

I pause for a moment. "Just outside of Chicago."

Luke blinks once, then drops his chin and looks at me like I just told the worst joke in the world.

He looks so put out.

I bite my lip, trying to stop my laugh.

This man, with muscles and tattoos and an interest in romance novels... He's adorable.

He slowly lifts a hand above the water, then dramatically positions his fingers before flicking the surface, sending drops of water my way.

And I can't stop the laugh this time.

My shoulders shake, making it hard to keep treading water, and the harder I try to stop laughing, the worse it becomes.

And he's still staring at me, narrow eyed.

It's like trying not to laugh in church. The more you try, the more impossible it is.

I spin away from him in an attempt to compose myself.

"No, don't turn away," Luke deadpans. "I love it when beautiful women laugh in my face."

I shake my head and smile as I look out at the never-ending horizon. "Something tells me your ego can take it."

"Maybe," Luke replies. "But my heart can't take being this far out." He hooks his arm through mine and starts towing me back toward the shore.

I don't know this man. This Luke Anders, professional hockey player, if he's to be believed. And yet... I don't stop him.

I don't pull away.

I'm thirty-two. I'm not a virgin. And yet, this feels like the first time I've ever flirted with a man.

But maybe that's it.

I've never flirted with a *man* before.

Boys, sure. But not someone like this.

Luke's bicep presses against mine, reminding me that he's shirtless and reminding me how he looked with that T-shirt plastered against his chest this morning.

I focus on sounding unaffected. "This part of your vacation training schedule? Taxiing resort guests through the surf?"

S. J. Tilly

"Not all the guests. Just the careless ones who get too close to the deep parts."

"How very Mother Hen of you." I tease him.

"Hey, now. Caution is cool."

I snort another laugh.

Luke slows, and when I straighten my legs, sand brushes the tips of my toes.

As he unhooks his arm from mine, I take in the flower tattooed on the back of his hand.

Luke's shoulders lift a few inches above the water as he stands in front of me.

I nod toward the hand that has disappeared by his side. "What does the flower mean?"

He shakes his head. "It means Ash is an asshole."

My mouth opens, then closes. "I don't know what that means."

"Ash is my goalie. Sebastian LeBlanc." He lifts a brow. "Ever heard of him?"

I shake my head. "Sorry, I don't know many hockey players by name."

He doesn't look offended. "But you know the Sleet."

"I know enough to know that you're our biggest rival."

He clicks his tongue. "Don't say *our*, Princess. You just said you live in Naperville, not Chicago, remember? Sleet's your team now."

Sleet's your team now.

Why is that hot?

I swallow. "I'm not sure that's how that works."

His rich brown eyes stare into mine, and I feel them everywhere.

I swallow and tip my head toward him. "So, your goalie tattooed your hand?"

"Huh? Oh, no. But the prick is responsible." Luke gives an

30

exaggerated sigh, like I asked him to elaborate, even though I didn't. "It was because of a bet."

"A bet?"

"Yeah. We got a little bored after last season and ended up doing a series of bets. Which, according to his wife and my mother, got out of hand."

Men.

I shake my head. "So you lost a bet and had to get a hand tattoo?"

Luke nods. "Yep. Couldn't see it until it was done, but I wasn't expecting a fucking flower."

That makes my eyes widen. "That's pretty trusting."

"Well, we had a few rules." He lifts a hand and ticks off the list on his fingers. "Couldn't be something that would be in violation with the league, couldn't be someone's name, and couldn't be something considered offensive."

"Still leaves an awful lot of choices."

He holds his palm down over the water, the pretty black flower sparkling in the sunshine. "Mine is still better than his."

"I'm not sure I should ask."

Luke's smile is full of self-satisfaction. "Ash had to get *Live, Laugh, Loathe* across his lower back."

"Loathe?"

Luke cracks up. "That's right."

I hate to admit that it's clever, so I don't.

"How does his wife feel about that?" I ask, genuinely curious.

Luke snorts. "Meghan's a freak. She probably outlines it with body glitter while he's sleeping."

That's a visual.

"But he got me back with this." Luke tips his head back, exposing his neck tattoo.

My mouth drops open. "You tattooed your neck on a bet?"

31

Luke lowers his head. "Joke's on Ash though. It looks awesome. And to piss him off more"—Luke lifts the arm without the hand tattoo, showing me his full sleeve—"I got this."

I will never understand men.

"How would that piss him off?"

"Because he's always been the most tatted-up dude on the team. And it was going to his head."

I shake mine. "This whole story is ridiculous."

"I have no idea what you mean." He can't say the whole sentence with a straight face.

"So it ended there?"

"No."

"Course not. Who lost next?"

"Ash."

I shift my toes in the sand. "And what did you make him get?"

Luke scratches the side of his beard, trying hard not to smile. "His nipples pierced."

My hands automatically move to grab my breasts, but I manage to stop them a few inches before they make contact. "Wouldn't that hurt when he gets checked in a game?"

Luke snickers. "Sure does."

I wince. "So, that ended it?"

"After that, Ash got his dick pierced." Luke winces. "And *that* put an end to it. No way was I chancing him winning again."

I can't help but bite my lip, thinking of the possibility.

I've never been with a guy who had a piercing down there, but I'd be a liar if I said I wasn't curious.

Water splashes my face.

Chapter 11

Luke

Twenty minutes in this woman's presence, and she has me questioning if maybe I do want to get my dick pierced.

I shake my head.

No. No, I don't want to do that.

"Now tell me about your ink," I say, my voice a little deeper than usual. "I saw it in the gym."

Natalie lowers her hand to her hip. "It's a hummingbird."

I can still only see the splash of teal peeking out from under her bikini bottoms, but now that she's said that, I can totally picture that what I saw was a cute little bird's head.

"Why a hummingbird?" I ask her.

She rolls her lips, like she's deciding whether she'll answer. "Did you know they're a keystone species?"

My mouth pulls into an impressed frown. "I did not know that."

Natalie nods. "Everyone knows what a hummingbird is. Knows that they're pretty and that they're fun to watch. But most people don't know how important they are to the world." She lifts a shoulder. "And I just like them."

The shrug is meant to blow off the first part of her reasoning, but I think I get it.

My Princess is beautiful.

The world loves beautiful things.

The world loves to prop up beauty above all else.

But Natalie Wagner is more than just a pretty face.

And I'm thinking maybe the world hasn't told her how much it needs her.

Something twists in my chest, and I resist the urge to press my hand over the ache.

That was too deep for vacation.

My eyes are drawn back to the water. "Can I see the rest of it?"

Her serious expression shifts, and she's back to looking amused.

But she doesn't answer, and I can't help it when my hand reaches for her.

The waves distort my view of it. Of her. And I want to see everything.

I reach out slowly, waiting for her to stop me, but she doesn't.

My fingers brush against her skin, just above the material of her swimsuit.

Swimming is such a funny thing.

Playing in the pool, floating in the ocean, it seems so innocent. But we're essentially naked. And standing here, having moved a little closer to shore, the waves dance across the top of Natalie's tits while I touch the bare skin at her hip. And it's hardly even considered inappropriate.

Her breath hitches, and I move a few inches closer.

Natalie places her palm on my chest.

"Why are you in Mexico?" she whispers.

"My cousin's wedding," I whisper back.

"I'm here for my cousin's wedding too."

"Name on three?" I offer, slightly worried that I'm having dirty thoughts about someone I'm related to.

Natalie nods.

I take a breath. "One. Two. Jacob."

"Heather."

A small laugh bubbles out of Natalie.

We don't have the same cousin.

And we're not here for the same wedding.

She starts to smile, but I'm already moving.

Chapter 12

Natalie

Luke's body crashes into mine, dislodging my toes from the sand.

He wraps his arms around me, low on my back, and then lifts me until we're eye to eye.

My hands clutch at his shoulders.

It happened in a heartbeat. And that's all it took for my pulse to start galloping.

"Luke."

My blood courses through my veins, every nerve ending lit up.

And I close my eyes.

Chapter 13

Luke

I CAN FEEL the change even as I see it.

Her body softens, her lids lower, and she leans into me.

I close my eyes too as my mouth finds hers.

Our first kiss.

Standing in the ocean, with the sun beating down on top of us.

She's so warm and so soft. So comfortable in my arms.

So calming.

I tighten my arms around her and slide one hand down until I'm gripping her ass.

That goddamn ass.

And then she does it.

Her arms go around my neck, holding me tight, as she lifts her legs and wraps them around my waist, pressing her warm core against my already throbbing dick.

I almost lose my footing. Almost send us into the depths.

I pull her tighter against me, my grip on her ass potentially bruising the soft skin.

But she doesn't flinch.

She does the opposite.

She tilts her hips.

The movement increases the pressure between us.

We both moan.

Natalie opens her lips for me, and I tilt my head as I slide my tongue into her mouth.

She meets me, her tongue seeking mine.

We both taste like seawater.

But I don't want to spit out the salty flavor.

I want to consume it.

And I want her to swallow it.

I want her to take me.

Fingernails scrape up the back of my head.

"Fuck," I groan against her mouth.

"Not in the water," she pants.

And it takes me a second.

Just a second.

Then I picture it. Dragging her out of the water onto the sand. Ripping that suit off her. Claiming her.

I tip my head back and groan. "Christ, Green Eyes, are you trying to embarrass me?"

I'm so close to coming in my shorts that it's not even funny.

Clearly knowing what I'm referring to, Natalie's body vibrates with a silent laugh.

I flex my fingers against her flesh as I lower my gaze back down to meet hers. "You laughing at me, Princess?"

She widens her eyes. "Me? Never."

Her thighs flex against my sides, and I want to do more.

I want to ask her to dinner.

Want to walk her right back to my room and barricade the door so I can ravish her body.

But... I've always been more of a pest than a romantic.

I let my knees give way and drop us both below the surface.

Chapter 14

Natalie

I HAD JUST enough time to close my mouth before we went under, and I have to fight the urge to laugh.

But instead of pushing away and trying to find my way up, I just wrap myself around Luke even more.

I hug him tightly, my legs squeeze his hips, and I tuck my face into his neck.

Then I bite him.

Chapter 15

Luke

TEETH SINK INTO MY NECK, and I swear to fuck, I come a little.

Needing to get her off me before anything worse happens, like attracting a school of fish from jizzing in my shorts, I plant my feet and push off.

We only went under a foot or so, but I mix my momentum with digging my fingers into her ribs. And sure enough, when we break the surface, she retracts her arms, slamming them down to her sides to stop me from tickling her more.

Later, when I'm alone and no one is around to read my thoughts, I'll think about this moment. And how I, a thirty-six-year-old man, tickled someone today.

But none of that stops me from doing it more.

Even as my pretty Princess kicks out, her foot glancing off my side.

Dropping my hands from her sides, I reach for her ankles, catching one right before her foot connects with my junk.

Her other heel lands in the middle of my thigh.

"Mercy!" I shout with a laugh and drop her ankle.

She swims backward a bit before she stops. "Such a quick surrender." She shakes her head. "And I'm supposed to switch my allegiance to the Sleet?"

I start to move toward her. "Oh, it's gonna be like that?"

She opens her mouth, but before she can speak, and before I can pounce, someone shouts her name.

We both turn toward the shore, and a woman is standing near the water's edge, waving our way.

"That your cousin?" I ask.

Natalie sighs. "One of her minions. If she's looking for me, that means it must be time to start getting ready for the rehearsal."

"Probably means I should get out too," I reply, and we start moving toward the shallower water. "Wonder how many weddings they have here at once."

Natalie has to swim for a moment before her feet touch again. "Four, according to their website."

"Huh." The water recedes around my shoulders, then my chest, then my waist.

Then I stop.

I was going to walk her out. Maybe walk her to her building so I could find out which one she's staying in...

Natalie stops a few steps ahead of me, then turns around. "What—" Her eyes drop down to the front of my shorts. "Everything okay, Mr. Muscles?"

I take a step back into the deeper water. "Everything's fine, Princess. Just realized I haven't done my water stretches yet." I lift one arm straight in the air and bend to the side.

"Water stretches?" She fights a smile.

I nod. "They're good for relaxing the body."

She shakes her head, causing other things to shake, and my eyes trail down to her glorious cleavage.

Whoever engineered that swimsuit deserves a damn award.

I've always been a fan of thick girls, just like I've always been a fan of big tits, and hers are practically begging to be in my mouth.

Water hits my face.

"Bye, Luke Anders."

I blink the water free and watch Natalie's backside as she walks out of the water, exposing more and more bare skin as she goes. "See you later, Natalie Wagner."

Chapter 16

Natalie

As MY FEET sink into the sand, I don't think about the way my ass looks from Luke's viewpoint.

I don't think about the way the material of my bikini top digs into the softness at my sides.

I don't think about the way the backs of my thighs aren't perfectly smooth.

What I do think about is the way Luke's hand felt on my ass.

How good his arms felt circling my back.

How nicely my legs fit around his waist as he held me close.

I think about the hardness that was wedged between us.

I'm only here for two more nights.

I need one of those nights to be with Luke.

Chapter 17

Luke

I'D FORGOTTEN ALL about the woman who called Natalie's name until I look past my Princess and find that woman's narrowed eyes on me.

Turning away from the image of water streaming off Natalie's perfect curves, I wade deeper into the water.

I'm pretty sure this is an adults-only part of the beach, but that doesn't mean I want to walk out with a half chub tenting my shorts. Especially with the way wet fabric clings to everything.

Something bright catches my attention on the surface of the water.

I reach out, snagging the white sunglasses.

My fingers twist around the earpiece.

Natalie said she had a rehearsal dinner tonight, same as me, so that means she's here through tomorrow night at least.

I put the glasses on, dimming the sunlight reflecting off the water, and then I stretch out, floating on my back.

If I can't find her again tonight, I'll find my Green Eyes tomorrow.

Chapter 18

Natalie

As HEATHER PRACTICES walking up and down the aisle, I pull out my phone.

There's no wedding party. Which I think is cool, because why bother? But I'm sure Heather chose it because she wanted all the attention on her. So I have nothing better to do than search online for Luke Anders.

Sure enough, his cocky grin stares back at me from my screen.

It's not that I didn't believe him, but a girl has to be sure.

I click on the top link, which takes me to the Sleet home page, and pull up his bio.

Veteran on the team. Starter.

"Let's just start with one team, yeah?" Dad whispers as he reads over my shoulder.

I click back to the home page.

"Just some friendly research." I turn my phone off and set it on my lap.

I felt a little weird when Luke said he played for the

Minnesota Sleet. And then, when he confirmed he lived in Minnesota, I started to feel a little more weird.

I didn't lie.

I do live in Naperville. I've spent most of my life in Illinois.

But I didn't mention that my dad and I, and a group of Wag Corp employees, are moving to Minnesota before the end of the year. Because Dad has decided to finally invest in the one thing he's always dreamed of.

Professional sports.

Sitting here next to my dad, I send up a silent thank-you for the fact that he loves football above any other sport. Because it will be awkward enough to tell Luke my dad is about to buy Minnesota's professional football team, the Biters. I can't even imagine how uncomfortable it would be if my dad was buying his team.

But I'll wait to tell him.

There's no need to tell Luke I'll be moving to his metro area unless we're somehow still in contact when I make the move.

Until then, why make it weird?

Dad leans into my side again. "I did have a nice chat with the owner the other day."

"Which owner?" I whisper back, thinking of the couple that currently owns the Biters.

"The Sleet owner."

Oh, sweet Jesus.

"Dad, I—"

"Don't worry, he wasn't offering to sell. I know one team is enough." Dad pats my knee, misunderstanding my reaction. "He invited us to a game."

"Oh, well, that's nice." I try to think of something else to say. Something other than *Oh, that's funny because I was practically humping one of their star players in the ocean this afternoon.* But I can't think of anything, so we just settle into silence.

Turning off the bathroom light, I head into the main part of my suite.

I took a quick rinse-off shower after our outdoor dinner. And now my hair is up in a bun on the top of my head, and I'm in my pajamas with my nighttime lotions slathered all over my body.

I flop onto the bed.

The TV is playing reruns of a show I'm not familiar with, but I like the background noise, especially when I'm staying in a hotel room alone.

With no one here to look over my shoulder, I prop myself up on my elbows, pick up my phone, and resume my search for information on Luke.

His Instagram is one of the top hits, and I click on it.

I'm not going to pretend that I'm better than this. That I won't snoop through any of his public profiles. This is reality, and a girl can never be too careful.

As I scroll through his posts, I'm a little surprised at how tame his photos are.

Maybe I shouldn't be surprised, but in my interactions with him so far, he's given off a *cocky jock* vibe. I've seen him in just swim trunks. I've seen him in sweaty, clinging clothing. He's always grinning and smirking.

But these photos of him are all fully dressed.

And there are some with him in a suit before a game, but most of them are just ones he's taken himself of regular life stuff.

He has one with him holding an orange cat, their faces pressed together cheek to cheek, Luke smiling at the camera.

I tap the heart below the picture, then scroll to the next photo.

My fingers freeze.

Shit.

I scroll back up.

I didn't mean to heart that.

Fuck.

Do I unlike it?

Will he still get a notification that I liked it?

Would he even see it?

He's got—I click back up to his profile—a ton of followers. His notifications must be out of control.

He probably won't see it.

My phone vibrates, notifying me that I have a new message request.

From Luke's account.

I drop my face to the bedspread.

Caught.

I wallow in embarrassment for a heartbeat, then lift my head and open the message.

Chapter 19

Luke

IT WAS FATE.

My expression is smug as I type out my message to Natalie.

I was already on this app, wading through all the hits for Natalie Wagner and variations of that name. But none of the profile pictures matched. And half the pictures weren't even of the person.

But then a notification for a new like popped onto my screen.

It's a shortened version of her name. But it's her. I know it is.

> Me: Hey Princess. Looking for pictures of my muscles?

It takes almost a full minute for her to reply.

> Natalie: Were there muscles in that picture? I was just liking the cat.

Her sassiness brings me so much joy.

> Me: Mr. Peter is pretty awesome. So I'll let the slight slide.
>
> Natalie: Your cat's name is Mr. Peter?
>
> Me: Technically, he's my mom's cat. But I named him.
>
> Natalie: How old were you when you named him?

I grin at my phone and roll onto my back.

> Me: Twenty-five. His full name is Mr. Peter Peter Pumpkin Eater.
>
> Natalie: I... don't know how to react to that.

I laugh.

"What's so funny?" Jacob looks at me from his bed. "Why are you smiling like that?"

I crane my neck to look across at him. "None of your business."

Dropping my head back onto my pillow, I type another message.

> Me: Remind me why I agreed to room with my cousin.
>
> Natalie: Because you're a fool.
>
> Me: It's true. Just because his soon-to-be wife doesn't want to spend the night with him, I don't know how it became my problem.
>
> Natalie: You're a better cousin than I am.

I wonder...

Me: Does that mean you have a room to yourself?

Natalie: Of course. Not a fool, remember?

I smile at the phone.

Me: Need company?

Me: I'm a great roommate.

Me: Promise I don't make a sound. I can even sleep on the floor if you want.

Natalie: My dad doesn't allow sleepovers.

I snort.

Me: I can be your daddy tonight. And I'm fine with sleepovers.

Chapter 20

Natalie

MY MOUTH DROPS OPEN.
He did *not* just say that.

> Luke: Sorry.
>
> Luke: Was that too far?
>
> Luke: I can tell that was too far.
>
> Luke: Please forgive me.
>
> Luke: My cousin wrote that.
>
> Luke: My phone was stolen.
>
> Luke: I think it was aliens.
>
> Me: You can have the floor.
>
> Me: Room 112.

I drop my phone and bury my face in my hands.
I can't believe I just did that.

Chapter 21

Luke

I STARE AT THE SCREEN.

Did she really...

I roll off the bed and stride toward the door.

"Where are you going?" Jacob calls after me.

I don't answer.

"Luke, what the fuck—"

I don't hear the rest of what he says because the door slams shut behind me.

Chapter 22

Natalie

I PACE TWICE across the room before I stop and look down at myself.

Oh. Right.

I'm wearing white sleep shorts with the word *love* in neon lettering stamped all over. And a coral-colored strappy tank top that does nothing to hold the girls in or perk them up but rather highlights them with a tiny lace bow right in the center of my cleavage.

I glance at the thick robe hanging beside the closet.

Someone knocks on the door.

My eyes move to the door and back to the robe.

There's another knock.

"Open up, Natalie." Luke's deep voice rolls through the door and straight up my spine.

I walk past the robe.

Chapter 23

Luke

THE LOCK CLICKS, and when the handle moves, so do I.

Natalie pulls the door open, and when she stumbles back out of my way, I grip her arm just above the elbow.

But I don't stop walking into her room.

I keep moving forward, using my free hand to swing the door shut, pausing only to lock it.

Natalie lifts a palm, pressing it to my chest, and I stop.

My heart is pounding beneath her touch.

I want her so much; it feels like a need that's built over years, not simply hours.

"Do you want me to slow down?" I ask her, my lungs heaving like I'm in the middle of a playoff game.

Natalie lifts the arm that I'm holding, and I let it go.

She places her hand next to the other one on my chest.

I don't know if she's going to push me away or tug me closer, but the look in her eyes tells me she doesn't want me to go.

"I lied," she whispers, like these words are just for me.

I lean into her touch. "What did you lie about, Princess?"

She slides her hands up my pecs until she's reaching up to my shoulders. "I don't want you to sleep on the floor."

Natalie grips the back of my neck, and I wrap my arms around her, bending to meet her as she lifts onto her toes.

Just like before, we crash together.

And just like before, there's not much fabric between us.

But unlike before, this time, we're all alone.

I part my lips, and Natalie swipes her tongue into my mouth.

She's not holding back.

So neither will I.

Groaning, I grip her ass with both hands and lift her into the air.

But before she can hook her legs around my sides, I toss her onto the mattress.

She bounces once with a yelp, and I follow her.

I want to pull her shirt off.

I want to suck those damn nipples into my mouth. The ones straining against her thin top, screaming for me to give them attention.

But we have all night. And I need more of her mouth.

Natalie widens her legs, so when I crawl over her and lower myself on top of her, my hardness lines up perfectly with her thin shorts.

She tangles her hands in my shirt and pulls me closer.

Savoring the feel of her reaching for me, I oblige.

Our tongues mingle.

She tastes like mint and sugar.

Her hands roam.

My body reacts.

I roll my hips against her.

Someone knocks on the door.

We freeze.

Our lips are still touching, but we've stopped moving.

We stare at each other, eyes inches apart.

"Nat, it's me," a man calls through the door. "I brought ice cream."

Natalie lets out a quiet groan. But it's not the good kind of groan.

"Who is he?" I ask, not pulling away, so each word has our lips brushing.

Natalie closes her eyes. "My dad."

Fuck.

The man, Natalie's dad, knocks again. "Hurry up. It's starting to melt."

I'm too old to be scared of a girl's dad. And yet...

Natalie starts to shove me, and at the same time, I start scrambling off her.

"You need to leave," she hisses at me.

"How?" I whisper-hiss back.

We aren't doing anything wrong. And yet we're both in complete agreement that we don't want me here, a boner straining my lightweight and easily tented sweatpants, when Natalie's dad walks into the room.

She pushes me toward the wall of windows and pulls back the long drapes.

Not just windows.

"Sorry, this is the only way." She pulls open the sliding glass door.

And then I see why she said sorry.

"Really?" I almost laugh.

Natalie pushes me out the door. "I'll owe you."

"Oh, you'll owe me." I step out onto the patio.

There's a girly snicker behind me, and I glance back just in time to see her sliding the door shut between us.

She turns the lock, then blows me a kiss.

I should probably be annoyed, but I still reach up and pretend to catch it.

Natalie shakes her head, then turns away from me and starts back across the room. Which is when I realize that she never shut the curtains, meaning I'm still in plain view.

Sighing, I turn around and accept my fate.

I sigh once more. Because my Princess has a swim-out suite.

So the only way off her small patio is through the pool.

I slide my phone out of my pocket and keep it lifted above the water as I start down the steps, fully dressed.

At least the water is freezing, so I won't have to worry about my visible boner for much longer.

Chapter 24

Natalie

"One sec!" I yell to my dad as I slide my arms through the robe's sleeves.

I tie it, then pick my headphones up off the desk and glance back out the glass doors.

Luke is halfway across the pool, disappearing into the dark, water up to his rib cage, and his glowing phone held near his head.

It's not funny.

I bite down on my smile and pull the door open for my dad.

"Sorry." I hold up my headphones. "I didn't hear you right away."

He shoves one of the glass dishes into my hands. "There's still time."

Glad he's distracted by the melting dessert, I step back and let him in.

And when I turn around to follow him into the room, Luke is no longer in sight.

Chapter 25

Luke

WITH THE BOTTOM half of my white T-shirt transparent, my pants dripping onto the floor, and my slip-on sandals full of water, I knock on the door to my room.

The only reason I have my phone on me is because it was already in my hand when she sent me her room number. But I didn't bring my room key.

I also didn't bring a condom.

I didn't even pack condoms for this trip.

This wasn't supposed to be that sort of vacation.

I knock a second time.

"Yeah, yeah," Jacob says from the other side.

He pulls the door open a little, then all the way. "What the fuck?"

"Don't ask." I stride past him and right into the bathroom to strip off my wet clothes.

My Little Royal is eating hand-delivered ice cream in her suite, while I'm wet and cold in my shared room with my cousin asking me a million questions.

She definitely owes me.

Chapter 26

Luke

"You son of a bitch, you did it." I slap my hand down on Jacob's back, swaying into him with the movement.

He grins at me, his eyes slightly glazed. "I'm a Mr. now!"

We both giggle. Like children. Then we clink our glasses of whiskey together and take another sip.

"I'm happy for you, man." I let out a contented sigh. "I know I give you a lot of shit, but you're a good guy. And she's lucky to have you."

"Nah." Jacob shakes his head. "I'm the lucky one. But feel free to go tell her that anyway."

I snort and take another drink. "I want her to keep liking me, so I'll pass."

Jacob hums as he nods. "She'd probably like you even more if we could go on double dates. So maybe you could go find that girl you've been obsessing over and make her fall in love with you."

"Love is a big ask for one night." I down the rest of my second drink. "But lust..." I take a step away from Jacob.

"Speaking of which." I reach into the breast pocket of my navy blue suit and pull out a little foil square. "I took your condom."

His eyes move to my hand and widen. "That's my wedding night condom!"

"I know." I widen my eyes back. "You really should have brought more than one."

"But—"

"Congrats again!" I wave the condom at him, then slip it back into my pocket. "I'm proud of you, man!" I back farther away from the outdoor dance floor.

"Luke, what—"

"You made a beautiful groom!" I cut him off with a laugh.

"Is that a condom?" one of our teenage cousins shouts a little too loudly.

"Marcus, shut your trap!" Jacob turns to snap at him, and I use the opportunity to slip away.

If Jacob wants to use condoms with his wife, that's his deal. But only packing one... that's rookie shit. It could break. You could want to fuck her in the morning. You could misplace one or have it stolen.

Really, he should be grateful I told him. He has time to find another one. Or three. This one isn't special. And I know neither of them want kids yet, so it's not like it's sabotaged.

I lift a hand at one of my uncles before I set my empty glass on a table and keep walking.

Normally I wouldn't be feeling it so much after two drinks. But that Perro Rabioso Whiskey hits, and I don't drink that often, so my tolerance is low.

I have to wind around a few tables.

The dance floor, bar, and dinner tables are all on top of a large wooden platform that keeps us hovering a few inches above the sand.

It's pretty, and the waves aren't too far off in the distance.

My auntie tries to get my attention, but I pretend I can't hear her.

She's the one my mom lives with, and I know better than to stop. I lucked out with Mom staying home to watch Mr. Peter—they never leave the cat home alone, and it was Mom's turn to stay back. If she'd have come and caught wind of me chasing a girl, she'd already have introduced herself and invited Natalie to Christmas.

Natalie.

With my eye on the prize, I step off the wooden platform onto the sand and start back toward the resort. Dim lights line the path, marking the way in the dark.

Earlier, Natalie mentioned that there were multiple locations for weddings. I have no idea where Natalie's is, but the spot I'm at now is at the very end of the property. The path literally ends here, so she has to be this way.

Chapter 27

Natalie

"You look so pretty." My aunt smiles with her wineglass lifted before her. "That dress is *so* pretty." She takes a sip. "Really pretty."

"Thanks." I accept her drunken compliment as I smooth my hands down the skirt of my dress.

The lightweight material is peacock green with wide straps and a plunging V-neck. The empire waist is elastic, so there are no zippers, which is great. And the floor-length skirt has pockets.

"Here." My aunt grabs a drink from a passing server and hands it to me.

I should say no.

This isn't my first.

But the best thing about the reception is these custom cocktails. And since I don't know what's in them to recreate them, I might as well have another.

The fruity rummy drink slides down my throat, and my belly heats with each swallow.

I shouldn't get drunk tonight.

Or at least I shouldn't get *more* drunk tonight. Because I want to see Luke.

I want to see him, and I want to sleep with him.

I dig my teeth into my lower lip.

Is it rude to check the time?

The reception is firmly in the dance phase, meaning the food and obligations are done.

My dad is sitting off at a table with all the uncles, puffing on cigars like a bunch of dorks, so he won't be looking for me anytime soon. And everyone else... none of them are Luke.

I want Luke.

I'm wondering if I should go look for him when I feel my phone buzz with a notification.

After shifting my drink to my left hand, I reach down and pull my phone out of my pocket.

There's a new message for me.

From Luke.

I click to open it.

Luke: You look fucking stunning.

My eyes jump up to the foliage past the edge of the reception area, and I see him.

He's a dozen yards away, standing in the dark, backlit by the resort a short distance away.

Just a shadow.

But there's no mistaking him.

That's my hockey player.

My aunt is already gabbing at someone else, so I take the opportunity to walk away.

My sandals slap against the wooden flooring—the same platform reception design they have all over the property—as I make my way toward the dark.

Luke doesn't move closer. Doesn't draw attention to himself or the fact that I'm leaving.

My footfalls become silent once I reach the sand, but my heartbeat becomes loud.

This is what I wanted.

What I still want.

But my nerves are going wild.

When I'm a few steps away, I can make out his details. And holy hell... he looks good.

His suit is perfectly cut. His white button-down shirt is open halfway down his chest. And his hair is a bit unruly, like he took the time to dance vigorously before coming to find me.

I bite my lip. He lifts a finger to his. Then he holds his other hand out for me to take. And I take it.

Of fucking course I take it.

Luke grips my fingers firmly and brings me with him as he turns around.

We make our way down the path, with our hands and hips bumping since it's narrow and hard to see the pavers beneath our feet.

He doesn't speak until we get to the first fork in the road. "I'm not sure you're allowed to take those."

I look up to see him looking at the drink in my other hand.

"Oh, whoops." I didn't even remember I was still holding it.

"I'm gonna be honest, Princess. I've had a couple. I'm not exactly drunk, but I'm not exactly sober."

His deep voice vibrates right through my body.

I lift the glass and take a sip. "Same." I take another sip, then hold the drink up for Luke. "I think I'm more on the drunk side than the sober side if you'd like to have the rest. Even us out."

I know it's not great to have drunken sex with a practical stranger, but if we're both tipsy... I'm not going to stress about it.

66

Luke takes the drink from me, his other hand flexing around my fingers. "What's in it?"

"No idea," I answer honestly.

He shrugs and lifts the rim to his lips.

He's about a head taller than me. I hadn't noticed as much when we were in the water, but standing here, he makes me feel the good kind of small.

There's enough light for me to watch his throat bob as he downs the rest of the drink in one gulp.

God, that's attractive.

A small sound crawls out of my throat.

And Luke brings his gaze to mine as he lowers the glass. "Princess—"

Whatever he was about to say gets cut off by loud laughter.

We both look forward, seeing a group of people heading our way on the narrow path.

"Fuck." Luke's grip on my hand tightens. "This way," he whispers as he pulls me off the walkway.

We cut between some artistically shaped bushes, duck under a short palm tree, and take a few more quick strides away from the lighted path.

There's a low row of bushes between us and the path, and a few seconds later, we end up on the deserted beach.

"Luke," I whisper through a laugh as he keeps dragging me forward.

But he doesn't stop. Not until we've found another cluster of trees. Then he halts and pulls me to face him.

"Sorry," he says, with only the moon illuminating his handsome face. "Those were some of my cousins, and they would've held us up forever." He gently tosses the glass into the sand, then lifts his hand to the side of my neck. "And I'm not waiting any longer." He leans in closer. "You're all mine tonight, Green Eyes."

The hummingbird inside my belly is flapping her wings so fast I feel dizzy. But it doesn't stop me from reaching for him. It doesn't stop me from lifting onto my toes.

Right now, nothing could stop me from kissing Luke.

Our lips press together.

And it's softer than I expected.

It's sweet.

It makes my knees weak.

Luke brushes his thumb across my jawline. "Open for me."

My legs sway.

I let go of his hand so I can cling to his suit jacket. Then I do exactly what he says.

I tilt my head and open my mouth, and it all changes.

There's nothing soft about the way he plunges his tongue into my mouth.

Nothing sweet about the way I suck on it.

Nothing gentle about the way I feel about him.

I slide my hands higher, his chest flexing under my touch.

Then I slide my hands lower, feeling that same flex in his stomach. The expensive button-down shirt does nothing to hide the feel of him.

His hands aren't still either.

He grips my hip, holding me in place with one hand, as he slides his other palm down my neck, down my collarbone, then lower. Down the bare skin until the heel of his hand is pressed into my cleavage, between my breasts.

"Tell me I can touch you." His demand spears through me.

"If you don't touch me"—I arch into his hand—"I'll drown you in the ocean."

His lips curl into a smile against mine.

And then, as his tongue invades my mouth, he twists his wrist, his fingers rotating with the movement, sliding beneath the fabric of my dress, beneath my bra, until his hand is cupping my bare breast.

Not just cupping.

Squeezing. Feeling.

Luke pinches my nipple with his calloused fingers, and I groan into his mouth.

"Fuck," he breathes.

Then his mouth leaves mine.

I try to grab his shirt before he can pull away, but instead of stepping away, he leans down.

Luke tugs the fabric of my dress to the side, shoving the cup of my bra down in the process, and the cooling night air ghosts over my flesh a second before his mouth closes over the peaked tip.

My moan is louder this time.

"Naughty girl." His tongue twirls. "You trying to get us caught?"

I reach my hand down and palm his length through his pants.

Luke tips his forehead against my shoulder, letting out his own groan.

I squeeze my fingers around his length, and his size has my core pulsing.

"Naughty boy," I whisper. "You trying to hurt me with this thing?"

"Never gonna hurt you." Luke turns his head and licks a streak across my neck. "Promise you'll like it when I stuff you full of this dick."

Good god.

If words alone could get me off, I'd already be done.

"I'm gonna need a closer look before I agree to anything," I tell him as my other hand joins the first to work on his belt.

Luke's hand flexes against my hip as he closes his mouth

over my nipple.

His tongue is hot against my skin, while his exhale sends goose bumps dancing down my arms.

I tip my head down and close my eyes when his belt loosens.

Listening to the sounds of our heavy breathing, with the waves lapping at the shore a few strides away, I feel like I'm someone else.

This feels like something from a movie.

My fingers work, and I get the button on his pants undone at the same time Luke tugs the other side of my dress over, and the hand that was on my hip is now pinching that nipple. Plucking at it.

A dirty, dirty movie.

When I close my fingers on the tab of his zipper, I open my eyes.

And as I pull the zipper down, I lower to my knees.

The movement dislodges Luke's mouth from my breast, and he lets out a sound that might be disgruntled, but the tone changes when I start to tug down the front of his boxer briefs.

"You don't—" he starts.

But I pull the band down farther, reach in with my other hand, and wrap my fingers around the base of his cock.

Luke says some sort of prayer, but I'm not listening.

It takes a little more work to free him. And when I do...

My body reacts on its own.

I'm pulled to him, like a magnetic force, finally close enough to react.

My mouth opens, and I close my lips around the head of his cock.

He's thick. And hard. And even in my buzzed state, I know I won't be able to take his whole length into my throat.

But I want to try.

Chapter 28

Luke

As HER KNEES sink into the sand, my dick sinks deeper into her mouth.

"Fuck," I hiss.

My legs start to lock, so I bend my knees as I drop my head forward to watch.

Natalie slides back, her lips dragging up my length until her tongue swirls around my head.

I reach down and grip her ponytail.

As soon as I saw her in this dress that should be illegal, the first thing I thought of was grabbing hold of her ponytail. This moment.

Her before me.

My dick in her mouth.

And my hand in her hair, holding her still as I feed her more.

So, that's what I do.

"Relax, Princess." I tighten my hold. "Relax that throat for me."

She licks the tip, and I pull my hips back so I'm all the way out of her mouth.

"Such a bad girl." I reach down with my free hand and trace my fingers over her cheek.

I wish I could see her better.

I wish there was more light.

But I don't need to see her to know how beautiful she looks.

"One minute," I tell her. "I want to control this for one minute. And then I'm going to fuck you."

My voice is strained, basically a growl. But I know she hears me, because she gives a tiny nod. The best she can do with my hold on her hair. And then she opens her mouth.

I push my hips forward.

And she takes me.

In and out.

I slide deeper each time.

Out again.

Her fingers claw at my thighs.

In again.

I bump into the back of her throat.

Out again.

"Such a pretty Princess." I push forward and hit that spot. "Relax."

I pull back just a little and feel her mouth slacken.

When I push my hips forward, I don't stop. I get an inch deeper.

"Look at me," I groan.

The moon glints off her eyes as she blinks up at me. Mouth filled with dick. Throat working to take me.

I drag my hips all the way back until I fall free from her mouth.

But I don't let her hair go. I keep her where she is and bend down until we're eye to eye.

"Such a good Little Royal." I press my mouth to hers in a rough kiss. "Now put your hands in the sand."

Chapter 29

Natalie

W HEN L UKE LETS GO of my ponytail, I have no choice but to follow his command as I collapse forward, digging my hands into the warm sand.

We're on a well-used beach.

Inside the boundaries of a well-attended resort.

Hidden by nothing but the dark and a handful of stout trees.

It's practically public.

And I have to protect my reputation above all else.

Yet...

I arch my back when I feel Luke pull up the back of my dress.

And yet, I'm going to risk it all just to feel what comes next.

A foot taps the inside of mine. "Widen those legs, Princess."

I do as he says, shifting my dress out from under my knees.

When my skirt is flipped up onto my back, I'm grateful that I wore my favorite thong.

Luke lets out a low groan as he settles behind me.

I can't see him.

Can't muster up the energy to lift my head and look over my shoulder.

But I can feel his knees on the inside of mine. Pushing them even wider.

A finger gently traces over my hip. "Such a pretty little hummingbird."

The inked bird on my side stays still, but the one in my ribcage is panting on the floor.

He trails his finger down my hip until both of his large palms smooth over my ass.

His hands are so warm they leave trails of flames behind.

Those flames spread as he slides his hands down the backs of my thighs, then back up between them until he cups my sex.

"This for me?" He presses his hand against me firmer. "Have you soaked through your panties just for me?"

I nod, the movement choppy.

Luke heaves out a breath, and then his hands are on the band of my thong, pulling it down over my hips.

It can't go far, not with my legs spread like this, but he pulls them down enough to peel them from my core.

He wasn't exaggerating.

I'm soaked.

I don't know if I've ever been this ready.

Maybe it's the drinks.

Maybe it's the ocean.

Or maybe it's just Luke.

One finger slides against my bare entrance, tracing my seam, and I suck in a breath. My arms wobble with the intensity of the first touch.

"Natalie Wagner," he says my name like a prayer, even as his hand slips away from me. "I don't think I'm gonna last long inside this slick little slit. But I don't think you're gonna last long either." Clothing rustles behind me, and then his suit coat floats down in front of me. "When you collapse. Collapse onto that."

I lower onto my elbows and use my hands to pull his jacket closer, bunching it up.

Behind me, there's the sound of something tearing.

A condom.

My core clenches around nothing while I chastise myself for not even asking if he had one.

I'm smarter than this.

I know better than this.

But there's something about this hockey player that makes me stupid.

"Remember." He settles one hand on my ass before he slides it around my hip and down toward my center. "We gotta be quiet."

I shift my hips, not caring about his warning, just wanting him to touch me. There.

Luke slides his fingertips lower, and featherlight, he traces them over my clit.

I groan in frustration.

He's not wrong.

I'm so close to the edge that I'm going to combust in moments.

And I don't want to wait anymore.

Something blunt nudges against my entrance from behind, and my brain switches focus to that.

He rubs his tip through my wetness.

I push back.

He presses his fingers hard over my clit.

My mind laser focuses on that feeling.

And Luke shoves his hips forward.

Stuffing me full, just like he promised.

A cry of pleasure tries to escape my lungs as my arms give way and my shoulders connect with the beach.

Luke sinks himself as deep as he can go, and I press my mouth into his suit jacket, muffling my sounds.

"Fuck. Yes. Christ." His fingers are no longer on my clit; instead, they're digging into my hips. He's gripping me with both hands. Holding me in place as he thrusts into me.

He's big.

I knew he was big.

And he feels so good.

"So fucking good," I mumble the words into his jacket.

Luke presses his hips into me so there's no room at all between our bodies, and then he jolts his hips forward.

There's nowhere for him to go. And yet...

I cling to his jacket.

He's so...

"So deep," I moan.

"That's right, Princess." He makes the move again. "So fucking deep in this royal pussy."

He pulls out almost all the way, then slides back in.

My breasts are still hanging out of my dress, and the sand rubbing against my sensitive nipples is almost too much.

I arch my back more.

"Fuck," Luke groans.

We're being louder than we should.

I push back against him.

"Always so naughty." He thrusts again. "So greedy."

He loosens one hand from my hip, and I almost cry out in relief when I feel his fingers near my core.

"Luke." I say his name as a plea.

"That's right." He circles my clit with a fingertip. "Say my name again."

"Luke." I moan it this time.

A noise of praise rumbles out of him, and I swear I can feel the vibrations through his fingertips.

"Please," I beg.

He stops teasing and applies firmer pressure on my clit as his fingers move in quick motions.

My core squeezes.

"That's it, Princess." He moves his fingers faster as his thrusts become rougher. "Come for me."

His words ignite the last thread of control I have, and I once again do exactly what he tells me to do.

My pussy contracts, and I try to squeeze my legs shut as the orgasm crashes into me.

But Luke is between my legs. And when my body tries to jerk forward, the intensity of the release more than I'm used to, Luke tightens his hold on my hip—not letting me go anywhere.

Chapter 30

Luke

Natalie wiggles and whimpers as she comes around my cock, and I can't take anymore.

I dig my fingers into her soft hip and pin her body to mine as my dick starts to pulse.

Each contraction of her pussy extends my own release. And I have to grip her tighter to hold her still.

Jerking my hips forward one last time, I feel the last drops leave me.

"Holy shit," I pant, trying to hold completely still.

Natalie turns her face to the side, her cheek against my suit coat so I can hear her. "Are we dead?"

I snort.

And then I wince. Because my dick is too fucking sensitive now.

Slowly, I slide back.

"Ah!" I choke on a cry when Natalie's pussy gives one last spasm right before my tip slides out of her.

She chuckles, but it sounds more like a moan than a laugh.

Carefully, I slide the condom off, twisting the end into a knot and dropping it next to the discarded glass.

I'll pick up both before we leave.

But not yet.

With nothing handy for either of us to use to clean up, I slide Natalie's panties back up her hips and into place.

I feel a little bad that they're stretched out, but I'll buy her one hundred pairs if it means we get to do that again.

I tug her skirt back down with the last bit of my energy. Then I collapse face-first into the sand next to her.

Remembering too late that my dick is still out.

Chapter 31

Natalie

"Aww, FUCK." Luke's curse is different this time. And when I look over, he's on his back, brushing sand off his cock.

I snicker.

Then I snicker some more.

How can this guy be the hottest fuck I've ever had while also being the biggest goofball?

I sigh, then realize I still have my boobs out. And if it weren't for Luke's clever thinking, I'd have a mouthful of sand by now.

With a groan, I roll over onto my back too and pull my dress and bra back into place.

Sand coats the front of my dress, so the sand stuffed into my cleavage fits right in.

"They always make beach sex look so hot in movies." Luke shifts, and I hear him zip up his pants.

I take a deep breath, trying to slow my racing heart. "I dunno, I still think that was pretty hot."

Luke's big body is suddenly over mine. Hands next to my head, knees on either side of my hips.

Freaking athletes.

Luke bends his elbows, lowering his face until it's just over mine.

"That was very hot." Luke's words puff across my lips. "Until I got sand in my dick hole."

A laugh bursts out of me, and Luke bends lower to bite at my earlobe.

"Sorry, sorry!" I shove at him. Because it's push him away or start all over again.

Luke pushes back and turns his head a moment before I hear the voices.

"I think we can go through here," an obviously drunk person whisper-shouts.

Luke quickly rises to a crouch, then holds his hands out.

I take them and let him pull me up.

We take two steps, then he scoops his arm down and picks up the empty glass and the sand-encrusted condom.

I can't help but pull a face.

In the moment, pretty much anything can be hot. But after... some things just aren't.

We stay low behind the cluster of trees and then start to cut back through the landscaping to the walking path.

Thankfully it's empty when we reach it, and I take a second to help Luke brush off his back.

I didn't notice him picking up his jacket, but it's draped over his arm, and the condom has disappeared into one of his pockets.

A man who doesn't litter.

Luke glances down at me and presses his lips together.

"What?" I ask, still whispering.

"You are... covered in sand."

I roll my eyes. "Well, duh. Some jock just fucked me into the beach."

His grin is instant. "Sounds fun."

I lose my battle against my smile. "It was."

Light bounces off Luke's amused features, and I realize we're already back at the resort.

The path we're on leads right to the center of the complex, where hallways head left, right, and center.

We pause when we reach it.

I'm to the left, but I don't know what wing Luke is staying in.

"I'll walk you—"

Someone shouts his name.

"Anders," another male calls out, in an over-the-top presenter voice.

Luke groans before he faces me fully and places a palm on each of my cheeks. "Go. Save yourself." Then he presses his lips to mine.

I kiss him back, even as I smile at his words.

He releases me and takes a step back. "I'll message you."

He takes another step back. "Send me your number."

The trio of men approaching have almost reached him.

Luke spreads his arms out, glass still in hand, pretending to block them. "Run, Princess!"

"Night, Player." I shake my head, then turn away.

Chapter 32

Natalie

"Will you hold this for a second?" Dad hands me his glasses and a paperback.

"Uh-huh." I yawn as I set them on top of the sweater folded on my lap.

As soon as the plane takes off, I'm going to wedge my sweater between my head and the window and take a nap.

It was not my idea to book the six a.m. flight home.

Dad drops into his seat next to me. "So, you left a little early last night."

I knew he had something he wanted to say to me. He's been acting cagey all morning.

But I also know my way around a negotiation, and I know not to answer when a question isn't actually asked.

So, I just hum a reply.

Flipping Dad's book over, I pretend to read the blurb.

"Wouldn't have anything to do with the guy Heather's friend saw you swimming with, would it?" Dad continues.

Fucking Heather.

And a direct question.

I flip the book over, studying the cover. "I would like to point out that all of your evidence is hearsay."

Dad grabs the book from my hands. "So that's a yes." He settles back, opening his book. "Hope you remembered to use a fake name."

I make a sound that he'll hopefully take as agreement.

Dad isn't trying to be an asshole; it's just the nature of our reality.

But even if I don't know Luke that well, his salary is public information. And I think it's safe to say he's not after my money. Even if I have more.

I slide my phone out from where I tucked it under my thigh and type out a text.

After I got to my room last night, I showered off the sand and promptly fell asleep. So this morning, I opened Instagram to message Luke with my phone number, but he'd already sent me his.

Not wanting to text him at four in the morning, I saved his number but waited until now to use it.

I hit send and make my shirt pillow, all thoughts of the hockey player out of my head.

Chapter 33

Luke

"L<small>UKE</small>." The barista reads my name off the paper cup.

Shouldering through the ever-growing group of family members, I make it to the counter and collect my coffee.

I don't waste any time before I take a sip, the added ice cubes I requested cooling my plain black to just the right temperature.

As an only child, I always wanted siblings. As an adult with too many fucking cousins and second cousins to count, who are all crowded around me, being purposefully obnoxious and blocking my way again, I realize my sibling-less existence was a blessing.

"Would you fuckers move?" I snap out, still a little hungover from last night.

The three dipshits who derailed my plans of walking Natalie to her room last night are in the middle of the group, and they start to push everyone else back.

But, of course, they make a scene doing it.

"Make way. Make way. The famous hockey player needs his space."

I roll my eyes and take another drink of coffee as I push through the path they created.

They follow me, telling our other family members, "*No photographs, please,*" and I swear I have no idea how these three manage to run a successful construction company together.

Jacob already has his drinks and is waiting in the main hallway, so he falls in step with us as we head toward our gate.

"So." Cousin One slaps me on the back. "You ready to tell us about the girl in the green dress?"

Jacob's sleepy features perk up. "You found her?"

"Found who?" Cousin Two asks.

"The girl he was chasing all weekend," Jacob answers helpfully.

We were all too tired this morning to talk during the van ride to the airport, but apparently, that has changed now that everyone has started in on their caffeine.

I open my mouth to argue with his *chasing* assessment, but I kinda was.

Cousin Three bumps me with his elbow. "Based on the *we just fucked in the sand* look, Lukey here found someone to ravage last night."

I shake my head. "Ravage? Really?"

"At least you put the condom to use, I guess," Jacob grumbles.

The rest of the guys start to razz him, so I'm assuming it already got out that I stole his one and only.

I still don't feel bad about taking it. But I try to remember if I took the used one out of my pants pocket.

I take another drink of my coffee.

After this trio found me, I distracted them from going after Natalie by offering to buy them another round. And because no one peer pressures like family, I had another one, maybe two. Either way, the details of stripping down for bed are kinda blurry, so I'll have to triple check my pockets before I send my suit to the cleaners. But at least Jacob was sharing a suite with his new wife last night, so I had the room to myself.

When we reach the gate, Jacob veers away to bring a coffee to his wife. They're going on their honeymoon in a few months, so they're flying back to Minnesota with the rest of the family today.

We're early for our seven a.m. flight, and I've tried to keep an eye out for a head of glossy dark hair, but I haven't seen any signs of my Princess in the airport.

Dropping into one of the uncomfortable chairs, I tug my phone out of my pocket.

"Ya know we're just giving you shit," Cousin One says as he and his brothers fill in the seats around me.

"I know." I roll my eyes. "You idiots just can't help yourselves."

"True." Cousin Two shrugs.

Cousin One nods to the phone in my hand. "You guys exchange numbers?"

I narrow my eyes at him. "Maybe."

He holds up a hand, hunching his shoulders in defense. "Just asking."

"We know you like to think the best of people," Cousin Three adds. "Just want you to stay on the lookout for gold diggers."

"Appreciate it," I deadpan.

And I do. To an extent. Because I do tend to see the best in the people I like, but there wasn't anything about Natalie that struck me as greedy or ungenuine.

She's attractive and funny and fun to be around.

And I think she's into me the same way I'm into her.

Or at least she seemed that way last night.

And in the ocean.

And in her hotel room.

I push my thoughts away from the feel of her body against mine. Because it's not just the tight, hot feel of her as she took every inch of me. It's her.

I want to see *her* again.

With that on my mind, I check my phone and find a text message from a new number.

> Unknown: Have a safe trip home, Mr. Muscles. Thank you for all the times you appeared out of nowhere. I fear this weekend may have been dreadful without you.

Smiling, I save her number.

Chapter 34

The First Text Messages

Luke: It was my pleasure, Green Eyes. I'm at the airport now. Let me know when you land.

Princess: Landed in not-quite-Chicago. Have three hours before my first web meeting... would rather be floating in the ocean.

Luke: Landed in it's-really-Minnesota. Times like these, I really appreciate that I play a game for a living.

Luke: What sort of meetings do you have today, Corporate Princess?

Princess: Canadian ones. I'll wave to your state from the air.

Luke: Tell me the time and I'll wave back.

Princess: Don't you have practice or something?

Luke: *groans* Yes, but I'm pretending I don't because I don't want to get out of bed.

Princess: Such a lazy athlete. You gotta put all those fancy muscles to use.

Luke: So... You think my muscles are fancy?

Princess: (puts phone on airplane mode)

Princess: Saw your face in the airport today.

Luke: Oh yeah? Was I handsome?

Luke: That's a rhetorical question because obviously.

Princess: Someone slapped the magazine barcode sticker across your forehead. So maybe not as handsome as you're hoping.

Luke: Hmm. Good to know. Forehead tattoos were next on the docket.

Princess: Might I suggest something other than a barcode?

Luke: Guess I'm heading back to the drawing board.

Luke: What are you doing tonight?

Princess: Eating takeout in my hotel room.

Luke: Want some company?

Princess: You in LA?

Luke: I'm in my kitchen. But I've heard of this thing called FaceTime. And I'd like to try it.

Princess: With jokes like that, how can I resist?

Luke: I am irresistible. Okay, let me order my own food, then I'm calling.

Princess: So, first game of the season this week. How are you feeling?

Luke: Excited, but in the way where you might throw up.

Princess: I can only imagine the pressure of playing in front of a crowd like that. But according to my friend, The Internet, you're pretty good at what you do. So I doubt you have anything to worry about.

Luke: Thanks, Princess. That's sweet of your friend to say, and I still feel good. But...

Princess: But...?

Luke: I'm gonna be thirty-seven in a few months, and I feel it. I know I'm good for this season. And maybe the next. But I know I need to start thinking about what's after.

Luke: Sorry, I didn't mean to go that deep.

Luke: That's what she said.

Luke: But seriously, I wasn't trying to complain.

Princess. First, did you seriously just do a that's what she said to your own comment? Second, I don't mind you going deep.

Princess: That's what she said.

Princess: But seriously, I'm happy to talk or not talk about whatever you want.

Luke: I respect you so much more now that you set yourself up for that same joke.

Princess: Thanks?

Luke: Distract me. Ask me a question.

Princess: Why do you call me Princess?

Luke: Because that very first time I saw you, you were languishing across that weight bench like a princess in a drawing. Or like those cartoons growing up where the reigning royal was always reclined on a pile of pillows while someone fed them grapes and someone else fanned them with palm fronds.

Luke: I wish I'd taken a picture.

Luke: But I didn't because that would have been creepy.

Princess: Now I kinda wish you'd taken a picture too.

Luke: Plus you looked super hot with your ass peeking out of your cover-up, and I wanted to bury my face in your tits.

Princess: And there goes the sweet moment.

Luke: Morning, Princess.

Princess: Morning, Player.

Princess: You don't need it, but good luck at your game tonight.

Luke: Thanks, Green Eyes.

Luke: You gonna watch?

Luke: Better yet, don't tell me.

Princess: You're going to do great.

Princess: Since the game has started now and you won't see this until after it's over... I'll let you know that, yes, I am watching. Yes, I'm in my pajamas. And yes, I'm thinking about how you got your dick all sandy in Mexico.

Princess: Congrats on the win! And the goal!

Luke: Thanks, Little Royal.

Luke: And thanks for reminding me about the sandy-dick trauma.

Princess: You're welcome.

Princess: I gotta admit, hockey is much more entertaining than I thought.

Luke: I'm pleased and insulted.

Princess: Consider me a convert.

Luke: Does that mean you'll keep watching my games?

Princess: Only if you promise to get into one of those fights. Those were fun!

Luke: I've created a monster.

Luke: Glad you watched.

Princess: Me too.

Luke: Where are you off to this week?

Princess: Flying to Denver tomorrow and finishing the week in San Fran.

Luke: Any chance you want to squeeze a stop in at Vegas on Thursday night? We have an evening game and then a few days off after, so we're gonna hit the strip.

Luke: And by hit the strip, I mean grab some drinks and walk around people watching.

Princess: I might be able to make that work.

Chapter 35

Natalie

MY FINGERS TIGHTEN around my beer until the plastic cup starts to bend.

I was a little late getting here, so I missed the team warming up, but that might be for the best. Because this seat is... right here.

I take a sip of my liquid courage and try to relax.

Luke asked me to come, so it's not like I'm being a weird clinger by being here. And when I looked up tickets and saw this single one up for resale, it seemed perfect. So I bought it. But now that I'm here, I'm having second thoughts.

Not about the game.

About the seat.

The lights in the arena cut out, and the dramatic pregame show starts.

This is my first hockey game, but it's not my first time at a professional sporting event, so I'm not surprised by the over-the-top team introduction.

Since we're in Vegas, the announcers are focused on the home team, giving the Sleet the bare minimum attention. But I don't miss them announcing number twenty-four, Luke Anders, as one of the starters.

I smooth my free hand down the front of my Sleet jersey, my baby-pink nails the best shade I could find to go with the green and blue team colors.

I'm second-guessing everything and wondering if the jersey is a bit much. But I'm set to move to Minnesota next week, and there's nothing wrong with supporting my local team.

I take another drink of my beer.

This damn move to Minnesota.

Almost every day since leaving Mexico, I've communicated with Luke.

Texts, a few FaceTime calls...

Yet, I haven't told him I'm moving.

I'd like to blame it on how busy I've been at work. All the travel. All the meetings. But I'm always busy, so I can't really pull that as an excuse. I just need to clip on my lady balls and tell him.

I take a breath. That's a problem for later.

The arena lights come up, and the announcer asks us all to rise for the national anthem.

Setting my drink in the cupholder, I stand.

I tug up the waistband of my skintight dark-wash skinny jeans. They're stretchy enough to be comfortable but tight enough to firm up all my jiggly bits. And they look good with the jersey.

When the song starts, I shift closer to the glass so I can look at Luke as he stands on the ice.

He really is a handsome motherfucker.

His hair is already damp with sweat, and it just makes me think about the first time I saw him looming over me on that weight bench.

And here we are today.

As the anthem ends and the crowd starts to cheer, I shove my rising nerves back down.

Luke invited me.

I told him I was coming.

He knows I'm here.

And maybe, before the end of the game, he'll spot me.

As everyone starts to sit, I do the same, wedging my ass back into the narrow seat.

Really, it's not unlikely that Luke will see me. Because I'm in the front row.

Right against the glass.

Near center ice.

Sitting in the seat next to the penalty box.

Literally next to the penalty box.

So, no matter what, I'll get some close-up looks at these hot-ass hockey players.

Chapter 36

Luke

PRINCESS IS HERE TONIGHT.

Somewhere in the stands. Attending her first pro hockey game.

She's here for me.

Cheering for me.

I need to give her something to shout about.

And then later, I'll have her shouting for different reasons.

"Let's fucking go." Zach Hunt shoves his shoulder into mine as we skate onto the ice.

Let's fucking go.

A ref blows the whistle and the game starts.

Chapter 37

Natalie

THIS IS FUCKING NUTS.

They're so fast.

I never realized how fast they move on the ice. Television does not do this game justice.

My fingers twist together nervously as I lean forward in my seat, watching the action unfold right in front of me.

A Sleet player takes a shot, but it gets deflected, and then one of the Vegas players steals control of the puck.

He breaks away back down the ice toward the Sleet goal.

The goalie, something LeBlanc, centers himself, bending his knees so he's lowered and covering as much of the net as possible.

How they move so quickly in all that gear, I'll never understand.

The arena gets to their feet.

The crowd is screaming, hoping for their player to score.

I'm on my feet too, hands pressed together in front of my chest, hoping our guy stops him.

And then I see it.

Luke.

I step closer to the glass.

He's flying over the ice.

Catching up to the Vegas player.

I want to yell for him to hurry, scream at him to get there, but an odd mix of emotions strangles my lungs. I can't get a sound out.

There are only feet between them.

They're almost to the goal.

The Sleet goalie is getting lower, moving side to side, preparing.

The Vegas player pulls his stick back to take the shot.

It's one-on-one.

But then Luke is there. And his stick hits the puck before Vegas can, deflecting it to the side.

No shot on goal.

The Vegas fans groan in disappointment, and I have the ridiculous urge to cry.

This is too intense.

A ref blows his whistle for something, and the game pauses.

Dropping back into my seat, I tip my head back and watch the replay of the stopped shot on the jumbo screen above the ice.

Watching it unfold again is just as intense. The camera angle is from above, and the way Luke moves is mesmerizing. And when *replay Luke* darts his stick out at just the right moment, I nearly cheer, the tightness around my throat finally loosening.

Then the camera cuts to a live shot of Luke.

He's sitting on the bench. Breathing heavily. And he slides his tongue across his upper lip.

Sweet mother of hockey.

If I wasn't already sitting, I'd have fallen.

That damn mouth.

I pick up my beer and take a large swallow.

By the end of this game, I'm either going to have a heart condition or ruined panties. Probably both.

Chapter 38

Luke

I squeeze my water bottle, taking another mouthful before the third period starts.

This game has been rough.

The score is still one to one.

Both teams are fighting to get shots on goal, just like both teams are being aggressive with the defense.

I take another swallow.

"You spot your girl yet?" Jackson asks me as we push out onto the ice, ready to start the final period.

"Not yet." I'm not embarrassed about telling him she was coming. I've known Jackson forever. We don't really have secrets.

He turns so he's skating backward. "Give her something to scream about, yeah?"

I grin.

Oh, I'll give Green Eyes something to scream about.

Jackson squares up for the puck drop, and I take my place off to his right.

The whistle blows.

The puck drops.

Jackson hits it to me.

Control.

I move toward the boards, taking the puck closer to Vegas's net.

Breathe.

Vegas players are on top of me.

Zach passes close behind.

I snap the puck to him.

Zach grabs the pass. He fakes to the right, executes a spin, and passes the puck off to Jackson on the far side.

The Vegas players swarm him.

And I'm left open.

My blades slice across the ice as I close in on the goal, mirroring Jackson's position.

He lifts his stick. Vegas moves to intercept his shot. Jackson adjusts his grip as his stick lowers, and he shoots the puck across the ice to me.

Vegas isn't ready.

But I am.

Vegas bodies are turning my way, following the trajectory of the puck. But it's too late for them.

I'm already swinging my stick, anticipating.

My body is still moving, my skates pulling me closer to the goalie.

He shifts.

But I connect with the puck. And I send it flying over his shoulder and into the net.

The crowd isn't like it would be at home.

It's not deafening.

But I smile at the near silence.

Because I know there's at least one Sleet fan cheering. And she just watched me score.

Chapter 39

Natalie

THE MAN next to me spills his popcorn when I scream.

Chapter 40

Luke

It's two to one, and Vegas is pissed.

The next play proves it.

I chase the puck to our corner, wanting control so I can clear it away from our goal.

Too late to avoid them, I see a Vegas prick right behind me.

The moment my stick connects with the puck, he slams me into the glass.

I take hits all the time. Except this time, I'm twisted from flinging the puck down the ice, so I'm not able to brace correctly.

My shoulder hits first, and I feel it tweak on impact.

I clench my teeth, keeping the sound of discomfort in my throat.

Vegas skates away from me, after the puck that I flung down the ice. And I roll my shoulders out as I chase him.

It wasn't a cheap shot, but that doesn't make me any less mad about it.

Fucker is gonna eat glass before the game is over.

But before I can retaliate, the whistle blows.

It's my turn for the face-off, so I line up across from a Vegas dude.

He's already leaned in low, ready.

I match his stance.

When the ref drops the puck, my stick is the first to connect, and Zach is there to snag it.

He's driving through the Vegas defense.

Jackson and I follow.

It's the three of us again, closing in on the Vegas goal.

Zach takes the shot, but the puck is deflected by the goalie.

Deflected, not caught.

The play is still live.

We move in, going for the rebound, when the same Vegas prick who hit me crashes through, hitting Jackson high on the chest.

Jackson goes down. Hard.

And I drop my stick.

Chapter 41

Natalie

H<small>E'S GONNA FIGHT</small>.

I jump to my feet.

Luke is about to fucking fight!

Chapter 42

Luke

"You GOOD?" I call down to Jackson as I move past him.

"Yeah," he coughs out.

My best friend is alive. But this other guy is fucking dead.

Chapter 43

Natalie

I SEE Luke's mouth move. The game is still going, the other players still going after the puck. But not Luke.

The second Luke moves past his downed teammate, he crashes into the Vegas player, fists already swinging.

When his gloved hand connects with the other guy's face, the rest of the arena gets to their feet.

Luke gets another hit in before Vegas Guy breaks the hold Luke has on his jersey.

Vegas Guy skates back a foot, then throws his gloves to the ice.

Everyone around me starts shouting and cheering.

And when Luke drops his gloves, I press my hands to my mouth.

He's facing the other direction, so I can't see his expression, but I watch his tattooed fist slam into the other man's face.

Luke takes a hit, and I can't tell if it connects with his helmet or his face.

I hold my breath.

More fists fly.

A ref finally blows a whistle, but the fight doesn't stop.

Luke dodges a swing and gets Vegas Guy in a headlock.

He's lifting his arm to throw another punch when another Vegas asshole slams into him and takes a swing at Luke.

I gasp.

Asshole's fist connects with the back of Luke's helmet, then a blur of green and blue flies into the cluster.

I yelp.

The blur is the Sleet player named Hunt, and his battering-ram approach dislodges both Vegas guys from Luke as he crashes through the cluster.

Hunt and the newest guy go down in a heap, fists immediately flying.

And the crowd collectively loses their minds.

Everyone is shouting.

The sound is overwhelming.

Even the players on the bench are making noise—banging their sticks against the boards.

It's chaos.

Complete mayhem.

The refs finally swarm in, breaking up the men brawling on the ice, moving to stand between Luke and the guy he was fighting with.

I inhale, trying to calm my racing heart.

The players are all talking to the refs, pointing at other players, but eventually the refs get them to back up.

Luke skates backward, then bends to snag his gloves and stick off the ice.

The Sleet guy who was knocked down first, a guy named Wilder, slaps Luke on the back, nodding when Luke says something to him.

Together, they go to help their other teammate pick up his

gear. And when Luke turns, I can finally see his face. And the big stupid smile plastered across it.

I shake my head, and my shoulders slump in relief.

I know I said I wanted to see Luke in a fight. But I can admit now that I didn't know what I was asking for.

That was stressful.

As the crowd starts to sit, I take my seat.

I don't know all the rules, but I'm pretty sure Luke is getting a penalty for that.

Which means he's moments away from sitting next to me.

Chapter 44

Luke

UNSURPRISINGLY, the refs send Zach and me to the box, both with penalties for fighting.

But the two Vegas pricks are heading to the box too. So... no regrets.

I shove Zach with my elbow. "You were like a fucking flying squirrel back there."

Zach snorts. "Couldn't let you have all the fun."

I open and close my mouth, testing my jaw. "That fucker had it coming even before he hit Jackson. I think he fucked up my shoulder."

Zach grunts, and I recognize it as his grunt that means he might get into another fight tonight.

I step into the penalty box first, rolling my shoulder out.

Shuffling over, I sit at the end of the short bench closest to the crowd, leaving room for Zach.

Neither of us are strangers to the penalty box, but it's kinda nice to be in with a buddy.

The ref starts the game again, and we watch.

"Fifteen minutes to stop them from scoring," I say to Zach, glancing up at the clock.

We're still up by one, and I'd love to just outright win this one.

Zach grunts his agreement.

I drag the back of my glove across my mouth, and movement has me glancing to the side.

What...

I drop my hand from my mouth and turn my whole head to the side.

Sitting right there, right on the other side of the glass separating the penalty box from the crowd, is a girl.

Her dark hair is twisted up into a bun. She's wearing a Sleet jersey over the most glorious pair of tits I've ever had in my mouth. And her amused green eyes are staring back at me.

I found my Princess.

Chapter 45

Natalie

I PRESS my lips together before mouthing *hi*.

Luke's mouth pulls into a giant grin.

He's so handsome it's almost annoying.

Someone behind me asks, "Who's that?" and I assume they're talking about me, but I don't bother answering.

Not that there's an answer to give him anyway.

I'm not Luke's girlfriend. Not really.

We're just... friends. Who had sex on the beach in Mexico.

The player on the other side of Luke leans forward, trying to see what Luke is looking at.

Still grinning at me, Luke uses his arm to shove the other player back.

The other player shoves Luke in return, making Luke's helmet-covered forehead thud against the glass between us.

Luke narrows his eyes, and I can't stop my laugh.

Luke turns away from me to face the other guy and shoves him farther down the little bench. But then the other guy hooks an arm around Luke's neck and pulls his head down so he can look over the top of Luke's hunched back at me.

I lift my hand in a small wave.

The dude, Hunt, beams at me and says something to a struggling Luke.

Luke gets a jab into the man's stomach, and Hunt finally lets go, only for them to shove at each other a few more times.

Men are such children.

I shake my head and turn to face the game, letting them wrestle it out.

Less than thirty seconds pass before Luke taps on the glass between us.

When I turn my head, I make sure to keep my eyes on Luke and not on his teammate, who is still leaning over to look around Luke's body.

Luke points at my chest.

His hand is bare, and I see his glove in his lap, held in place by his other gloved hand.

Those big hands.

My teeth dig into my bottom lip, and I move my eyes back up to meet his.

Luke is smirking, and he twirls his pointer finger in a circle, gesturing for me to turn around.

Realizing what he wants, I twist so he can see the back of my jersey.

The blank back of my jersey.

I debated getting one with his number. Then I debated the humor of getting one with one of his teammates' numbers. But in the end, I decided plain was the safest plan.

When I turn back, Luke is looking at me with a flat expression and shaking his head.

I roll my eyes and point to the ice. "Pay attention."

Chapter 46

Luke

I'm TRYING to pay attention, like Natalie told me to, but she's so close.

And she's so pretty.

I shake my head again, thinking about her wearing a goddamn blank jersey.

I love that she bought one. Seeing her with my team name plastered across her chest does something to me. But I should've bought her one with my name on the back.

I'll rectify that soon. And the one she has on now is going straight into the donation pile.

Zach bumps his elbow into my arm. "This why you've been itching for a fight all night?"

I bump him back. "If I'd known she was sitting right there, I'd have been in here first period."

"Fair." Then he makes a thoughtful noise. "I need to get Izzy seats next to the box."

I snort. "You can't afford to spend more time in here than you already do."

I have to admit, I like how Jackson referred to Natalie as *my girl* earlier. And Zach referencing his wife while we're talking about Natalie makes me feel like they're taking my feelings for Natalie seriously.

As of this exact moment, Natalie might not be my girl-friend, but that's the goal.

The clock ticks down to the final seconds of our penalty.

And I'm pretty good at getting goals.

Zach and I stand, preparing to get released.

A second before the door opens, I look over at my Princess.

She's staring up at me, those big eyes filled with a mixture of warmth and nerves. So, I do the only thing I can do.

I wink.

Chapter 47

Natalie

THE BASTARD WINKS AT ME.

My heart stutters, and I resist the urge to press my hand to my chest as the door to the penalty box is opened and Luke and the other player launch out of it.

Someone taps on my shoulder. "Do you know him?"

I turn to look at the woman one row back and two seats over. She's stretched over her companion's laps, her eyes wide and excited.

Biting my lip, I nod.

There's no point in denying it.

Her smile is wide. "Awesome."

I notice her green hoodie with the Sleet logo. A fellow fan.

She leans even closer. "Tell me he's as good as I think he is."

My cheeks flame at her question, and she snickers.

"Christ, Stacy," the guy closest to her says as he drags her back into her seat, saving me from having to answer.

Facing forward, I try to act as normal as possible as I watch the end of the game.

And when there's a break in the play, and the jumbo screen shows footage of Luke winking at me from the box, I pretend the clip won't be recorded and played on TV.

Of course it will, but maybe some other athlete drama will unfold, and no one will care to figure out who I am.

Chapter 48

Luke

"Hurry up." I pound on Jackson's door.

He opens it, buttoning his shirt, with his phone against his ear. "Uh-huh, it's him." He looks right at me. "Eager as a puppy."

I flip him off.

Jackson finishes with his shirt and moves the phone to his hand. "Yeah, I'll text you updates. Night, Kitten."

He finally hangs up with his wife, and I widen my eyes in the universal *let's go* symbol.

"I don't know why you need me to come with you," Jackson complains. "You're gonna ditch me the second you find her."

He's not wrong. But also... "I want to introduce you."

Jackson lifts a brow.

"And what are we, chopped liver?" someone other than Jackson asks.

I slowly turn to find Ash and Zach standing behind me in the hall.

"Are you fucking eighty?" I ask Ash, the one who spoke. "Who says chopped liver anymore?"

Ash shrugs. "My wife."

I let him see my eye roll, even though I'm not at all surprised that Meghan uses a saying like that.

Zach smirks. "I already got to meet her."

Ash shoves him. "You did not meet her. What you did was embarrass me."

"Me?" Zach rears back. "I'm not the one who was making kissy lips on the big screen."

"I wasn't making kissy lips," I groan, but they ignore me.

"No," Ash keeps going. "But you were crawling all over Luke's lap."

"I just wanted to see the girl who has Luke's panties all in a twist," Zach argues.

"See? You were trying to *see* her. You didn't meet her," Ash argues back.

"Christ." I rub my temples. "Why am I friends with you guys?"

Ash looks me dead in the eyes. "Because we're hot."

"I hate you," I tell him.

"You guys finally ready?" Jackson pushes me out of his doorway.

Together, we head down to the lobby of the Mazzanti Resort.

Some of our teammates are already gathered and waiting in the lounge area, but when they spot us, they all start heading to the door.

When Natalie said she might come to the game, I'd told her where we were staying and where we would meet her after the game.

We're not supposed to share our rooms, but I told Natalie she could check her luggage with the front desk and stay with me.

I'd risk getting caught for another night with Natalie.

I pull out my phone to send her a text.

Me: On my way.

She replies right away.

Princess: Walk faster. I'm awkwardly lingering by some guys who look like they could be hockey players.

I snort.

Me: Keep it awkward. Can't have them getting the wrong idea.

Princess: What wrong idea?

Me: That you're available.

I slide my phone into my pocket and lengthen my stride.

Chapter 49

Natalie

I SWALLOW and shove my phone into my wristlet.

I have no idea how to reply to Luke, so I don't. Instead, I pick up my drink and take a sip.

Luke doesn't know that I booked a suite in the same resort he's staying at. He told me I could sneak into his room, but I wanted a place to change after the game. So, while the team finished up their team stuff, I traded my jersey for a skintight black shirt with sleeves to my elbows and came over here to the central bar at the casino next to the resort, where we said we'd meet.

We didn't have an exact time, so I've been nursing this vodka tonic and reading a book on my phone for the last twenty minutes.

I take another sip.

There is no reason for me to be nervous, for all the same reasons there was no reason for me to be nervous about my seat at the game.

The game.

I haven't gotten any angry calls from my dad, so even if that little scene from the penalty box made it to TV, no one identi-fied me.

Not that the public should know who I am. But certain circles do.

Someone shouts something, and I lift my gaze to see a group of large men approach the bar.

I take another quick sip.

Men walking with that bearing can only mean one thing. Athletes.

Sure enough, the cluster of guys I've been lurking near lift their hands, drawing the new group closer.

A few hollered whoops and cheers ring out as other bar-goers recognize the players.

They're mostly dressed in button-down shirts. But I can't focus on them.

Because Luke is here.

He's still a dozen strides away, but he looks devilishly good in his black shirt, with the sleeves rolled up and the top two buttons open, showing off all that delicious, inked skin.

I can feel it—the moment he spots me.

His lids lower, his jaw works, and his hands flex at his sides.

Heat floods my belly.

I set my glass down on the high-top table next to me.

And I brace myself.

Luke closes the distance between us, not slowing until he's one step away.

He reaches up and slides his hand along my cheek until he's palming the back of my head.

My skin prickles with anticipation as my eyes slide closed and my head tips back.

Luke doesn't hesitate. He presses his lips against mine.

I flatten my hands against his chest, and his other hand spans my lower back, holding me in place.

The kiss is short. Demanding.

Perfect.

He pulls back just a few inches. "Hey, Princess."

I flex my fingers against his body. "Hey, Player."

We stare at each other, both wanting to take more. But not indulging since we're in the middle of a crowded casino.

Luke slides his hand down the back of my neck until both his arms are around me. "Wanna meet my friends?"

I bite down on my smile. "That was kinda adorable."

"What was?" He lowers his brow.

"Just the way you asked." I don't want to tease him too badly, but it sounded just like a kid asking *Do you want to see my room?*

His mouth pulls to the side, like he's reading my mind.

A tall guy with dark wavy hair steps up beside us. "I'm Ash, this asshole's best friend."

Ash holds out his hand.

Luke doesn't release me, so I have to wedge an arm up from between us to take the offered shake. "Natalie. Nice to meet you."

Another guy with lighter hair moves to stand beside Ash. "You're not his best friend. I am." He holds his hand out, and I think I recognize him from the penalty box. "I'm Zach."

Letting go of Ash's hand, I twist in Luke's hold and take Zach's.

"You guys are idiots." A third guy with dark facial hair shoves in between both of them. "I'm Jackson, his real best friend."

Luke groans as I stretch my arm even farther to shake Jackson's hand. "I'm regretting all our friendships."

Ash and Zach gasp.

Jackson shakes his head as he lets go of my hand. "This group is about as dramatic as they come."

"I'm beginning to see that."

Luke sighs and loosens his hold on me. But instead of stepping away, he turns so our sides are pressed together with his arm draped over my shoulder. "Which one of you besties is buying the first round?"

Chapter 50

Natalie

"Let's sneak out of here," Luke whispers against my ear.

I lean back into him.

His arms are wrapped around me, and he's leaning against the half wall behind us for support.

"Okay," I whisper in return, tipping my head back to look up at him.

The motion makes my vision tilt, so I tip my head back down.

Luke helped me finish off that first drink, and we've each had two since.

Or was it three?

Lips press against the top of my head. And my hummingbird sways in my chest, making me feel drunker than I am.

I shimmy my shoulders against him, like I can burrow into his chest. "I like this."

He chuckles, the sound reverberating through me. "Me too, Princess." He kisses my hair again. "Now come on."

Luke drops his arms from around me, and I shift so I'm standing on my own without leaning against him.

A bearded cheek brushes against mine as Luke leans down. "I've been meaning to tell you."

"Hmm?"

A large hand slides down my back until it's gripping my ass. "You look fucking amazing tonight."

My already warm cheeks heat even further.

Luke has only ever made me feel good about my body, so I wasn't too worried about wearing such a formfitting outfit around him, but it's still good to hear.

"Thanks." I turn toward him. "You're not so bad yourself."

Luke gives me a satisfied look, then takes my hand. And without saying goodbye to anyone, he leads me in the opposite direction from where they all came in.

I think I hear someone shout his name, but neither of us turns around.

It was fun to meet Luke's friends. They were all super nice, with Jackson probably being the most *normal* of the bunch, but I can see why Luke gets along with them.

I didn't know what to expect, knowing he was coming over with his teammates, but I kinda figured he would do the introductions, then want to leave. Or, like some guys I've been out with, introduce me, then expect me to stand there silently.

Luke wasn't like that.

We all talked. Mostly about how I felt about attending my first game, but then it morphed into normal stuff. Chatter among friends.

My heart squeezes at how easily Luke included me, and that happiness seems to kick my buzz up a notch.

I glance up at the sexy man next to me and squeeze his hand.

He slows his stride. "Sorry. I'm used to walking with those beasts." He tips his head back, referring to his teammates.

"Beasts." I snicker. But he has a point, since all the players are over six feet tall, Luke included. Then I squeeze his hand again. "I wasn't trying to make you slow down."

"No?" he asks, flexing his fingers around mine.

I shake my head and admit, "I just wanted to."

He flexes his fingers again.

I've been to Vegas many times for work meetings, but I've only been out on the strip once. It was years ago for a friend's bachelorette party. And it was not my thing.

But now, as we weave, slightly unsteadily, through the casino floor—the chimes of slot machines surrounding us—I'm thinking it was the company. Because I'm enjoying every second of being here.

Luke pauses, looking around, then he turns to the right.

I follow along in silence, watching the people as we go and trying not to breathe in the cigarette smoke that billows toward me from a stranger's mouth.

Finally we reach an exit and step outside.

The noise level around us decreases, and I take a deep breath of the outdoor air.

It's cold back home, so I let my intoxicated self revel in the warm temperature.

We keep walking, my hand still engulfed by Luke's larger one, keeping me at his side.

The sidewalk isn't super crowded, but there are people everywhere. All ages. Dressed for all sorts of experiences. But we don't have to alter our path. Because people move over for Luke.

Maybe it's the tattoos. Maybe it's the broad, muscular shoulders. Maybe it's the way he walks. But his presence is *big*.

I love it.

And with both of us dressed all in dark clothing, I have to admit we look good together.

Luke bumps into my side as he adjusts his angle.

"Where we going, Mr. Muscles?" I lean into his side as I turn with him.

He lifts his free hand and points ahead. "First stop, slushies."

I smile. "I've always wanted to try one of those."

Luke looks down at me, his expression matching mine. "Same."

We make our way to the drink stall on the edge of the sidewalk. Behind the employees is an entire wall of slushie machines, each with a different alcoholic drink ready to go.

Luke asks for the strawberry daiquiri, which sounds good, but I have to go with the piña colada. It's not even a choice.

The cups are obnoxious. Over a foot tall, skinny in the middle, but wide at the top and bottom, with a cheap lid and a thick plastic straw that begs to be chewed on.

When I lift my little purse to pay, Luke shoots me a narrowed-eyed glare.

I shake my head and let the purse go back to dangling from my wrist.

If he wants to buy these overpriced drinks, I'll let him.

With the plastic cups in hand, we step out of line and continue down the sidewalk.

We both lift our straws to our mouths at the same time and take our first sips. Luke's hum of approval matches my own.

I lift my cup, silently offering him a taste.

Luke lowers his, and we watch each other take a swallow.

Fruity sweetness hits my tongue.

I shrug. "Guess I won't mind you tasting like that later."

His mouth pulls into a devilish smile. "Why wait?"

I lift my brows. "Because we're in the middle of a sidewalk."

The look on his face promises dirty things, and standing here on the crowded concrete, I squeeze my legs together.

131

Luke's gaze moves above my head, and I watch him tilt his head.

"Let's check that out."

I turn to see what he's talking about and notice a narrow path cutting between two buildings. It's not exactly an alley; it's just a sidewalk that leads to a dead end about twenty yards back. But it doesn't end at a wall. It ends with a door, a glowing pink light, and a bouncer.

"Looks... interesting," I reply, torn between curiosity and wanting to run the other way.

Luke squeezes my fingers. "You up for an adventure, Green Eyes?"

I close my lips around my plastic straw and swallow a mouthful of icy booze. "If this turns out to be some sort of black-market organ-swapping party, I'm telling everyone who you are." Luke lifts a brow, looking amused. "I'm sure your professional athlete body parts are worth more than mine."

"Nah, Nat. You're definitely worth more." He starts to pull me down the path. "But I'll still sacrifice myself for your freedom."

Sucking down more of my drink, I just shake my head.

As we get closer, the bouncer straightens from where he's been leaning against the wall, widening his stance and crossing his arms over his chest.

"Private event," the big guy grumbles out.

But since Luke doesn't stop walking, neither do I.

"Hey, man," Luke greets when we're a few yards away.

"This is an invitation—" The bouncer stops talking, and his mouth drops open. "You're Luke fucking Anders."

I didn't know it was possible for such a big man to look so starstruck.

We stop in front of the bouncer, and Luke lets go of my hand so he can hold it out. "That I fucking am."

The bouncer smiles so wide it changes everything about his appearance as he roughly shakes Luke's hand. "That goal tonight, that was smooth as hell."

"Thanks, man." Luke drops his hand, then gestures to me. "Want my girl to take a photo of us?"

The bouncer is nodding before Luke finishes the offer.

It takes a moment, but I get my and Luke's cups tucked between my forearm and boobs, then I take the man's phone and hold it up in my free hand to take a couple pictures.

The two are about the same height, but the bouncer is wider, and I have to fight the snicker that wants to come out at Luke looking so small in comparison.

When I hand the phone back, the bouncer checks the pictures, sliding through each one, to make sure they're good.

He nods in approval before he slides his phone back into his pocket.

The man glances at the door he's guarding, then back to us. "You two really here for this party?"

Luke moves back to my side, slinging his arm around my shoulders. Then he lies. "Yep."

The bouncer looks at the drinks in our hands. "Okay, but those can't come in. Sorry. The caterer will chew me out."

Luke turns to me. "Race you?"

"What—"

He starts sucking on his straw like he's trying to drink it as fast as possible.

"Seriously?" I laugh, then start to suck my own drink down.

I go until Luke jerks his cup away and scrunches up his face. "Brain freeze."

I stop before I reach that point, knowing I don't need the whole thing anyway.

"You got a garbage can anywhere?" Luke asks the bouncer while pinching the bridge of his nose.

"I can set 'em back here." The bouncer nods to a little podium in the corner behind the door.

Luke holds his cup out. "Couldn't've told me that before I slammed it?"

The bouncer laughs as he takes both of them. "I never said you had to drink it."

"That is true." Luke blinks a few times.

"You gonna survive?" I ask him as he puts his arm back around my shoulders.

"I think so." He tugs me against his side.

The bouncer sets our cups out of sight, and I cross my fingers that we don't forget them. I want something to remind me of tonight.

Then the bouncer opens the door, and we walk through.

Chapter 51

Luke

Music and lights.

My eyes adjust as we step out of the short entryway and into an epic dance party.

I whistle, but the sound is instantly lost in the vibrating noise around us.

Natalie leans into my side as we take it in.

We've entered some sort of DJ show. The musician is up in his booth on a raised stage at the far side of the expansive room. And above him is a light bar shooting out colorful beams across the top of the writhing crowd.

A low wall divides the dance floor from a walkway around the back and sides, with openings at intervals that seem to lead to restrooms and a bar area.

It's chaos.

And enticing.

Before we step onto the dance floor, a server comes over and hands us each a champagne flute.

Natalie tips her head back to look at me, her brows raised.

I tap my glass to hers. "Ready for an adventure?"

Her smile is wide as she lifts her glass. "So ready."

Chapter 52

Natalie

I ROCK WITH LUKE.

My back to his front, his large hands gripping my hips.

It's hot.

His body is hot.

And I'd rather melt into nothingness than step away.

He holds me tighter as we move with the music.

And I can feel him. Like *feel him* against my ass.

The music vibrates through us, and my head lolls against him. My eyes are still closed, like they have been for the last several minutes. Maybe longer.

The hands on my hips move, sliding to my belly. One slides up so it's just under my breasts.

Luke makes a noise that sounds like a groan, and I get it.

I don't know how long we've been here, but the desire to have more of him is itching at my skin.

"Luke." His name comes out as a plea.

A sweaty temple presses against mine. "I think we need to leave soon."

I nod, agreeing.

That slushie, mixed with the champagne, tipped me past my limit. And the haze of pot smoke that filled the room a while ago has blurred the rest of my sobriety.

I'm not mad about it.

Not at all.

Because right now, I feel like the best dancer in the world. And with Luke wrapped around me, I feel like I can take on the world.

He makes me feel safe.

But I know we need to leave this place soon so I can properly enjoy the man, and the length, behind me.

I take a deep inhale, ready to pull away from Luke's grip, when a voice stops me.

"Beautiful people!" the DJ shouts into his mic. "How you feelin'?"

Everyone cheers.

I smile and think the word *good* while Luke whistles.

"It's time."

At the DJ's announcement, the crowd cheers again. Louder than before.

I continue rocking with Luke, who's still swaying behind me, holding me tightly.

The music hasn't stopped, but the DJ quieted it just enough for him to be understood.

"Face your partner."

It takes me a second to understand the DJ's direction.

Maybe this is turning into a line dance.

Luke's still holding me tightly, so I reach down and start to pry his hands free.

"Where do you think you're going, Princess?" His words are thick against my ear.

He sounds the way I feel. Really good.

Heat fills me, and I miss the next thing the DJ says. But then Luke loosens his grip enough for me to turn and face him.

"Keep those bodies moving, side to side," the DJ tells us.

I can't focus on the whole crowd, but the people next to us are doing the same thing.

I press my hands flat against Luke's chest.

"I like this part," I say to him.

Luke leans closer. "What'd you say?"

I tap my fingers on his firm pecs. "I like this part of you."

The man smirks as he flexes his chest. "I like you liking it."

"Tell your partner you love them," the DJ says.

Luke's smirk pulls into a devious grin. "I love you, Green Eyes."

He just says it.

So easily.

Like he means it.

The hummingbird in my chest wraps her wings around my heart and squeezes.

I can feel my blush, but it's so warm and dark in here that I hope Luke can't see it.

He wiggles his brows, his happy expression going nowhere as he urges me to say it back.

I curl my hands into his shirt. "I love you, Mr. Muscles."

The crowd keeps swaying, the synchronized dance easy but fun.

"Now tell them you'll be true. That your ho era is over."

Laughter bubbles across the room.

I tug on Luke's shirt, making him bend closer. "My ho era is over. Yours better be too, Player."

Humor and something softer cover Luke's features. "I only have eyes for you." He slides his hands up and down my sides. "My pretty Little Royal."

We're already closing the distance between us when the DJ speaks again, something more about happiness.

Luke presses his lips gently against mine.

Then the DJ shouts, "Now make out like you mean it!"

There is no time to smile. And no need to be told twice.

Our mouths open, and I slide my hands up and around the back of Luke's neck.

The haze consumes me, consumes us, as his tongue presses into my mouth.

He tastes so good. Like strawberries and champagne.

I love you, Princess.

I hold him tighter.

I want to hear him say it again.

I want him to say it because he means it.

Emotion tries to strangle me, so I open my mouth farther.

Luke groans against my mouth, and I can't stand it anymore.

I need him.

Naked and inside me.

I pull back enough to pant, "Take me to the hotel."

Luke's fingers dig into my side as his hooded eyes stare into mine. "Whatever my Princess wants, my Princess gets."

God, I really might love this fool.

Luke straightens, and with the distance, we both notice all the people still making out around us.

Luke widens his eyes at me. "Probably good to get out of here before this turns into an orgy."

I nod. "That's not really my thing."

He slides one of his hands down and cups my ass. "No one sees you naked but me."

My hummingbird plucks a feather out of her wing and fans herself with it.

Why is possessiveness so hot?
Luke takes my hand and pulls us back the way we came.
My steps aren't straight.
But neither are his.

Chapter 53

Luke

I<small>T'S</small> <small>BEEN</small> a long time since I've been this intoxicated. It's also been a long time since I've felt this... content.

I pull Natalie closer, bending down to talk to her over the music. "The last time I was buzzed was in Mexico." My lips brush against her hair. "You're a bad influence, Princess."

Her laugh is bright. "I think it's you. Normally I stop at one glass of wine."

Someone bumps into Natalie from her other side, causing her to stumble.

I tighten my hold on her hand as she laughs off the incident while the woman who ran into her apologizes.

When we finally break through the crowd, a pair of servers —dressed the same as the one who gave us champagne—meet us at the edge of the dance floor.

One of them has a tray piled with little white drawstring bags, and the other has a clipboard.

I take one of the tiny bags and tuck it into my pocket. Some party souvenir, I'm sure. Natalie takes the pen offered by the other server and signs her name on a form.

She hands it to me, and I do the same.

I've seen this sort of consent forms before, allowing them to post the photos of tonight online. And since we've done nothing illegal, and I want everyone to know Natalie is spoken for, I'm happy for them to share pictures.

Handing it back, I'm a little surprised when both the servers sign the sheet before handing the piece of paper back to Natalie.

Thorough.

Natalie quickly folds the paper and shoves it into her pocket.

"Have a wonderful night!" One of the servers beams, and the other says something as we step past—sounded a lot like *congratulations*.

"Right to the hotel?" I ask, taking Natalie's hand.

She beams up at me. Her cheeks are red, her eyes are a little glassy, and she sways when she nods up at me.

Heat bubbles in my chest, and I give her hand a sharp tug.

"Luke!" Natalie falls into my chest with a laugh, her free hand gripping my side.

I lean down and press my lips to hers.

Once.

Twice.

A third time, and I'm kissing her smile.

"I want you naked," she demands against my mouth.

My cock jumps in excitement over the implication. And I agree with it.

It's time to get Natalie to the hotel.

I pull my mouth away and drag Natalie down the little hall and out of the secret party.

We stop and get our slushie cups back from my new friend, The Bouncer, who congratulates us for some reason. Natalie helps me slip the thin parts of the cups under my belt, so the pair is secured against my side like a pair of slushie pistols and I don't have to hold them. And instead, I rest my arm across Natalie's shoulders.

Natalie leans against me, and I lean against her.

We make it to the street.

We smile when we pass the slushie bar.

We sway as we work our way around the casino we started in.

I hold her tighter as the hotel comes into view.

"I need to get my bag." Natalie bumps into me as she says it.

I press a kiss to the top of her head as we enter the building. "No problem."

When I head toward the front desk, she tugs on my arm. "It's in my room."

I let her pull me in the direction of the elevators. "You got a room?"

She nods, her eyes bright as she looks up at me.

And when we press the button for the elevator, I let myself feel the feelings building inside me.

The need. The want. The desire to be around her.

"I don't want you to go, Princess," I say quietly.

She looks up at me. "I'm not going anywhere, Player. We can spend the whole night together."

"You're damn right we'll spend the night together, Green Eyes, but I meant after this. I hate that you don't live near me." I admit the truth that's been eating at me since we parted ways in Mexico. "I want to see you more often than this."

She bites her lip and looks at me with mischief in her eyes.

"What?" I ask.

She pauses for another moment, then smiles. "I'm moving to Minnesota next week."

I stare at her.

Not comprehending.

My thoughts slower than usual.

I hold her gaze. "Say that again."

Her smile wavers. "My company's headquarters are moving to Minnesota." She lifts a shoulder. "And I'm moving too."

The elevator doors open behind Natalie, and I step into her.

I step into her space, pressing my chest to hers.

The movement is more aggressive than I meant it to be, my impaired balance making my steps heavy.

She moves with me, stepping backward and grabbing my hips as her back bumps against the elevator wall.

"You..." Natalie blinks up at me. "You're okay with it?"

"Oh, Princess. I'm more than okay with it." I press my hips into her. "And I'm gonna show you just how okay with it I am."

My mouth finds hers as the doors slide shut behind us.

She tastes like summer vacation.

I slide my hands to her ass. Loving the way she fills my palms. Loving the way I can dig my fingers into her flesh.

The doors slide back open.

"Oh, uh..." someone mumbles.

Natalie lets out a squeak, and I glance over to see a man backing away from the open door.

With her forehead pressed to my chest, Natalie points to the panel of buttons. "Press the button for the top floor."

Whoops, forgot to select one.

I twist my torso and reach back to press the highest number.

The doors slide shut, and the man never steps back into view. Which is good because my girl looks horny as fuck, with her lips a little pink, her eyes shining with lust, and her hands pulling me closer.

She wants me, so she can have me. But no one else gets to know the dirty side of my Princess.

When the car starts to rise, I reach down and grip her thigh, lifting her leg as I align our bodies and press into her.

"Luke."

My name is a moan on her lips, and it lights my already sizzling blood on fire.

I roll my hips as I claim her mouth.

My dick is painfully hard. Eager to be back inside her.

She drags her fingers against my sides, and I don't realize what she's doing until I feel her touching my bare skin.

She pulled my shirt free, and her hands are roaming.

Skin on skin, and that fire inside me burns brighter.

"Fuck." I hook my hand under her thigh, sliding it up until it's wedged between her legs.

She tilts her hips, increasing the pressure between us.

"I'm taking you in your room. We're not waiting for another elevator ride unless you want me to fuck you right here." I say the words into her mouth.

"Yes. No. Up here." Natalie rocks her hips and slides her hands around to my back, her fingertips against my spine.

We both sway when the elevator comes to a stop and the doors open again.

I glance back to make sure it's the floor we want, then I let go of Natalie's leg and take her hand.

"Which way?" I ask as I pull us out of the elevator. My dick is straining inside my pants, and I hope we don't run into anyone else.

"Um." Natalie bites her lip and looks at the sign showing which way for which room numbers. "One sec." She opens her little purse and finds the room key and the little piece of folded paper with her room number.

I hold out my hand, and she sets the key in my palm.

Checking the number, I take us to the right.

Seeing the right room number, I stop, letting Natalie bump into my back, and hold the key against the door.

As soon as it unlocks, I shove the door open and walk Natalie through.

Chapter 54

Natalie

LUKE TURNS me so I'm walking backward as he lowers his mouth back to mine.

I lift my hands between us and start undoing his shirt buttons.

There is no more waiting.

The sound of the door slamming shut echoes through the room, but we keep moving, Luke's mouth on mine, and his hands on the button of my pants.

He lifts his head, and my eyes slide open.

"What..." Luke blinks. "Where's the bed?"

I turn my head and see the large living room space we're standing in.

"There." I tip my head toward an open set of French doors.

Luke keeps his hold on me, making me walk backward toward the bedroom.

When we reach the room, neither of us bothers with the lights, since the curtains are open, letting in the glow of the strip.

"This room is nuts," Luke says as he pulls my shirt up over my head.

"I know the owners," I tell him as I undo his belt, and our slushie cups fall to the floor.

"Better not be an ex," he growls as he kicks his shoes and pants off.

Satisfaction blooms across my skin at his jealousy.

Luke narrows his eyes at me as he shrugs his shirt off, leaving him in nothing but a pair of bulging black boxer briefs. "Natalie."

I toe my shoes off and kick them to the side. "Not an ex."

I try not to smile, but I fail.

"If you're lying to me..." He reaches for my pants.

"I'm not lying."

"Good." Luke starts to tug my pants down my legs. "Take off your bra, Princess."

I do what he says, watching the top of his head as he grips the top of my panties and pulls them down too.

When Luke stands to his full height, his chest is rising and falling in time with my own. "On the bed."

My eyes drop as his hands move to his last piece of clothing.

His palm grips his length through the cotton, and my core pulses as I watch.

My body sways, the sight of it tipping me off balance.

"Bed." Luke says the word like it weighs a thousand pounds.

I scramble to the center of the bed, but I keep my eyes on his hands.

Luke shoves the band of his boxers down, and even though I've seen it before, my mouth still opens at the sight.

God, he's perfect.

Naked, Luke places one knee, then the other, on the

mattress before he bends forward to crawl over me. But when he puts weight on his arm, he grimaces and drops to his side.

Luke lands on the mattress next to me and rolls onto his back.

"Are you okay?" I lift onto my elbow.

Luke nods. "Forgot about my shoulder. Gonna need you on top tonight, Princess."

I blink at him, then down at his cock that's pointing to the ceiling.

"What?"

Luke pats his chest. "Be a good Little Royal and sit on my face."

Chapter 55

Luke

Natalie rises to her knees, then puts her hands on my chest as she swings her leg over my waist.

"Gotta get closer than that." I grip her thighs and tug her forward.

Natalie moves her knees up until she's forced to lift them over my shoulders.

Her pussy is inches from my mouth, and I'm sick of waiting.

I slap my hands down on her ass and pull her the rest of the way.

Chapter 56

Natalie

When Luke's tongue laps at my entrance, I jolt, slapping my hands against the headboard.

He makes a rumbling sound that I feel *everywhere*, and I close my eyes.

I've never done this like this.

Luke licks again.

It's too much.

I'm too exposed. Too open.

I roll my hips.

It's not enough.

Luke doesn't stop. And he doesn't fool around.

Again and again, he licks and sucks.

His tongue drags over my clit.

He uses his hold on me to rock me over his mouth.

His fingers press into the soft flesh of my ass, and I moan as I let him devour me.

I feel dizzy and lightheaded and so incredibly wonderful.

And when he pushes me back, I go.

And when he tells me to lift, I do.

And when he notches the head of his dick at my entrance, I let myself sink down.

One inch. Then the next.

"That's it. You're doing so good." Luke urges me on.

His fingers trace over my hummingbird tattoo before his hands palm my breasts.

I lower another inch. And when another inch of him fills me, I lean forward and brace my palms on his chest.

I'm breathing heavily.

I'm stretching around him.

I want all of him.

Luke pinches my nipples, and I drop my hips until our bodies are flush.

"Fuck," he groans as I gasp for breath.

I'm so full.

"Ride me." He tugs on my nipples, rolling them between his fingers.

I rock back and forth, lifting my hips and lowering them.

And then I find the spot.

The spot where the base of his dick rubs against my clit. And I stay there.

I press down while I roll my hips. Over and over. The pressure building.

Luke moans as he squeezes my breasts. "That's it, Princess. Take what you need."

I do.

I don't stop.

It's so good.

I'm so close.

And then it hits me. My release.

My head tips back, and my body pulses around him as my hands lose their spot and slide higher up his chest.

Luke makes a sound.

It's deep and full of pleasure, and I feel the tremor of it against my hands.

I blink my eyes open, my pussy still clenching in ecstasy, and see that my hands are pressed to the base of Luke's throat. Choking him.

But when I try to shift back, to pull my hands away, one of Luke's big hands slaps down over mine.

His hooded eyes stare up at mine as he holds my hands in place.

And then he comes.

His body flexes.

His hips lift.

And Luke comes inside me as my hands squeeze his neck.

Chapter 57

Luke

NATALIE'S HANDS slip from my throat as she collapses forward onto me, and I suck in a lungful of air.

My head spins as the lack of oxygen mixes with the alcohol, and I feel my dick pulse a final time.

"Shit," I pant. "That was new."

Natalie laughs against my shoulder, but it makes her body shake, and when her pussy clenches on my sensitive cock, it's too much.

With a groan, I grip her ass and pull her up until my length slips free.

Wetness follows, sliding from her onto my stomach, but neither of us has energy to care.

Natalie wedges her hands under my shoulders like she's trying to hug me, and I slide my hands up and wrap my arms around her back.

"Just a minute," she whispers.

"Just a minute," I repeat.

Chapter 58

Natalie

Squeezing my eyes shut, I slap at my phone on the nightstand, the alarm piercing through my brain.

When I finally hit it, I drop my face back down on the pillow.

I'm never drinking again.

My head pops back up, and I squint at the time on my phone.

"Shit," I hiss and force myself to sit up.

I have to be on my way to the airport in an hour.

I squint harder.

Forty minutes.

Extra shit.

Luke is still snoring behind me, so at least my snoozing alarm didn't wake him up.

Hurrying, I roll out of bed and scurry across the large bedroom to the attached bath.

My suitcase is still open on the bathroom floor from when I dropped it off earlier and changed shirts, so I lock the door behind me and move straight to the shower.

As the water heats up, I strip off the pajamas I put on halfway through the night when I woke up, sprawled across Luke, needing to pee.

With my head pounding, I go through the motions, starting with taking a few painkillers and chugging a bottle of water.

The shower is too fast to enjoy, and I make a mental note to come back and really appreciate this suite with Luke sometime.

Feeling slightly better, I dry off and check the clock.

Twenty minutes.

I'm heading straight from the airport to a meeting, so as much as I don't want to, I put on my full routine of makeup and take the time to dry my hair.

Not wanting to straighten or curl the wave, I smooth some product over my tresses and twist it up into a bun.

Dressed in black pants and a navy silk shirt, I step out of the bathroom and scoop up my discarded clothes from last night, along with my slushie cup.

I bring it all back into the bathroom, so I can pack them into my suitcase, when I hear my jeans crinkle.

"What..."

Dropping the rest, I stick my hand in the pocket of my jeans.

The folded piece of paper sparks a blurry memory of leaving the dance party last night, but I can't remember what it was for.

So I unfold it.

And my mouth drops.

Chapter 59

Luke

"Luke! Oh my god, Luke, wake up!" Natalie's voice finally breaks through my dream.

"Huh?" I lift my head, then groan. "Oh fuck." I drop my head back down, feeling like I was hit by a truck.

"Luke, you need to wake up."

Hearing the stress in her voice, I pry my eyes open. "What time is it?"

"Seven."

I reach for her with a groan. "It's too early, Green Eyes."

She's standing next to the bed, and my fingers brush silk before being slapped away.

I smile even as my head throbs.

"Player, you need to focus." Natalie pokes her finger into my bare side.

Not remembering closing them, I open my eyes. "What's wrong?"

She's staring down at me, looking so pretty.

"Do you remember that paper we signed before leaving the party last night?" she asks me.

"Yeah, the photo disclosure." I reach for her again. "You look so pretty."

Her lips twist like she's trying not to smile. "This is serious, Luke."

"So am I." I roll onto my back. "Come here and I'll show you just how much I mean it."

"Luke." She holds up the paper, and I can see the creases where it had been folded. "This isn't a disclosure. It's a marriage certificate."

"Who's marriage certificate?" I try to read it, but it's not angled toward me.

Natalie puffs out her cheeks. "Ours. This is *our* marriage certificate."

I blink at her.

And I think about what she just said.

Then I think about last night.

The invitation only.

The sea of couples. *All couples.*

I think about the DJ telling us to say *I love you* and our promises to not be hos anymore.

And I think about the way we were told to kiss.

"Did you hear me?" Natalie shakes the paper.

I swing my feet over the edge of the bed and sit up. "I heard you, Wife."

I grip her hips and pull her in a step so she's standing between my knees.

"Luke, we can't be married." Her stern tone falters when I slide my hand under the hem of her shirt and run my thumb across the warm skin just above the band of her pants, where I know that pretty tattoo is.

"I'll admit, it wasn't part of my plan for last night, but if the paper says we are." I lift the bottom of her shirt so I can press a kiss to the soft skin of her hip.

159

A palm connects with my forehead and pushes. "Luke, I'm gonna miss my flight if I don't leave right now."

I grumble but drop my hold of her.

I want to tell her to stay, but I know she's leaving for a meeting, and I won't fuck up her work.

She hesitates, then leans down and presses her lips to mine.

It's quick.

And adorable.

I grin up at her as she backs away. "What about the Mr. and Mrs. thing?"

"I'll figure it out." She grabs the handle of her suitcase. "But you should get down to your room before you fall asleep again."

My grin turns into a frown. She's right, but I don't want to get up.

Natalie starts toward the living room area but glances over her shoulder at me.

I watch her eyes travel the length of my naked torso. "Bye, Mr. Muscles."

My grin returns. "Bye, Mrs. Anders."

She shakes her head, but I don't miss the way she bites down on her lip.

I shouldn't love teasing her so much.

And certainly not over the fact that we're apparently married.

But it's just second nature. And she's always so entertaining to fluster.

The hotel door clicks shut, marking Natalie's exit, and I drop onto my back and stare up at the ceiling.

How the hell did we let that happen?

And why am I not freaking out?

When my eyes start to shut, I force myself to get up.

With nothing left in Natalie's monstrous room but my

clothes from last night, I put them on and pick up my slushie cup.

I pat my pockets, double-checking for my wallet, and find something else I'd forgotten about.

I slide my hand into my front pocket and pull out the little white party bag.

And when I pull the drawstring open, it's my turn to shake my head.

Two bright pink rings. I take the bigger one out and test the size.

The soft silicone material slides easily onto my ring finger, fitting surprisingly well.

I like it.

It's crazy.

The wedding. The rings. The girl I met about a month ago.

It's completely unhinged.

Something my mom will want to smack me for doing.

But... I don't think I'll mind being married to Natalie Wagner.

Chapter 60

Natalie

On the way to the airport, I smooth the marriage certificate across my lap.

I want to keep it.

I want to just stay married to Luke Anders, a man of strength and humor. A man who makes me smile as much as he makes me swoon.

A man I could love.

A man I might already be falling for.

But I can't do that.

I can't do that to him.

And I don't want to marry someone who doesn't love me. Even if I think that maybe they could.

Not to mention if the board finds out about this. It will just be one more reason for them not to trust me to lead. Even if all the other reasons are bogus, I don't need to hand them ammo.

And if my dad finds out I accidentally got married to a famous hockey player because I was drunk in public, that might be enough to make him second-guess giving me control of the company. And I've worked too hard, for too long, to just let my future go.

So, I can't stay married to Luke.

And no one can ever know it happened.

Chapter 61

The Newlywed Text Messages

Luke: Let me know when you land, Wifey.

Princess: Landed.

Luke: Landed... what?

Princess: Landed in LAX.

Luke: You know that's not what I meant.

Princess: Landed, Lukey.

Luke: Woman, you are not behaving.

Princess: You didn't marry me because I behave, Hubby.

Luke: There's my girl.

Princess: Byeeeeeee.

Luke: Have a good meeting. I'll let you know when I'm back in Minnesota.

Luke: Landed.

Princess: Back at LAX. Will tell you when I get to Chicago.

Luke: Have a safe flight.

Princess: Landed. Going to sleep the second I get home.

Luke: Did you drive?

Luke: If you're too tired, take an Uber and get your car tomorrow.

Luke: Or call me, and I can keep you awake on your drive home.

Luke: Call me on your drive home.

Princess: Omg, Mom, give me a moment to collect my luggage.

Luke: Morning, Green Eyes.

Luke: I didn't forget about that little detail you mentioned when we were leaving that party. And by party, I mean our wedding ceremony. And by detail, I mean the fact that you said you were moving up here this week.

Princess: I mean this with all my heart.

Princess: Go back to bed.

Luke: Can't. Already at the gym.

Princess: Bless you and your muscles. But my squishy ass is still in bed.

Luke: Mmm… that ass.

Luke: You could come watch me.

Princess: Watch you... at the gym?

Luke: Yeah. See how the muscles are made.

Princess: Can I bring a coffee with me?

Luke: Don't see why not?

Princess: Are there other hot guys working out there?

Luke: Now why would you need to know that?

Princess: I like to be well informed.

Luke: Just for that, I'm leaving my shirt on while you watch me.

Princess: Don't want to make the other guys jealous over you being the hottest. I get it.

Luke: Aww, Princess. You know how to spoil a man.

Princess: As tempting as this all sounds, I'll need photos of the benches so I can see if they look comfortable enough to lie on.

Luke: I'll have a lounge chair brought in.

Princess: I don't think they'll like that.

Luke: I bet I could get Beth to write me a note saying I needed it, then the owner would have to let me.

Princess: Who the fuck is Beth?

Luke: Just some girl.

Luke: She helps me out sometimes. Real good with her hands.

Princess: Maybe I don't have to bother with divorce papers. I can just ask Beth and her hands to help me murder you.

Luke: *sends selfie of huge grin and sweaty hair*

Luke: This is how happy your jealousy makes me.

Princess: It's good to die happy, I suppose.

Luke: I just laughed so loud I made some guy drop a dumbbell.

Luke: Beth is the physical therapist here.

Luke: Pretty sure she's sworn an oath or something to do no harm.

Luke: And she's married.

Luke: Princess, I promise you, I'm only teasing about her hands. If her husband ever heard me say that, he'd rip me to pieces.

Luke: I mean that literally.

Luke: *sends pic of a gigantic man doing pull-ups with weights hanging off his waist*

Luke: See? Terrifying.

Luke: Come to think of it, you should probably come here with me all the time as my bodyguard. He doesn't always like my jokes. You'll be my buffer.

Luke: Princess, you there? You didn't go back to sleep, did you?

Princess: I can't fall back asleep. Some guy keeps texting me.

Princess: And I'm debating if I forgive you.

Luke: *sends selfie with lower lip sticking out in a pout*

Princess: I believe you said something about taking your shirt off?

Luke: That's only for in person. I don't want to make the ogre jealous of my muscle definition.

Princess: I want you to know I'm rolling my eyes.

Princess: Hey, so I've talked to a lawyer in Minneapolis, and she's writing up a divorce contract for us. Since we don't have any shared assets and won't contest anything, then it should just be a matter of signatures.

Princess: Sorry, that sounded really... I don't know. Not great. Sorry.

Luke: Don't apologize, Green Eyes. Thanks for taking the lead on this. I know neither of us meant to get married.

Luke: That's a sentence I never thought I'd use.

Luke: But I hope you know that getting a divorce doesn't mean we're breaking up.

Princess: Hmm, I don't know if I can date my ex-husband. Seems kinda weird.

Luke: You can and you will.

Princess: So bossy.

Luke: Damn right. Now tell me when you're moving.

Princess: Tomorrow.

Luke: Tomorrow? Seriously?

Princess: Seriously.

Luke: Morning, Almost ex-wife Girlfriend. Are you on the road already?

Chapter 62

Natalie

Almost ex-wife Girlfriend.

I shake my head and send a quick reply, telling him I'm just about to start driving, then I put my phone in the cupholder.

It feels so weird to be divorcing this man. We get along so well, and there's a small, quiet part of me I've been trying to ignore that believes he might be *the one*.

And if he is *the one*, won't it be weird to divorce him and then marry him all over again in a few years?

But I guess it's weirder to stay married just with the hope that it will turn into a forever kind of love.

So I shift into drive, my vehicle filled with my clothes and necessities, the rest of my possessions headed to storage, and I start the drive from Illinois to Minnesota.

Chapter 63

Luke

I PUT my car in park and look up at the building in front of me.

This can't be right.

I look back down at the text message Natalie sent me, double-checking the address.

It's the same address I'm parked in front of.

Climbing out of my car, I shake my head.

I knew Natalie had a fancy title at some corporation. I could see that the clothes she wore were expensive. I've known about all the business trips she's been on since we met all those weeks ago. But I never put it together. I never looked it up. Never asked.

My fingers flex around the edge of my car door before I swing it shut and start across the parking lot.

I try not to grimace as my insides give an uncomfortable twist.

Today doesn't feel like it's going to be a good day.

It should be good because I'm about to see Natalie again.

The woman I haven't been able to get off my mind.

The woman I want to have closer.

The woman who just moved into my state.

Except I'm not just here to see her. I'm meeting Natalie at her office. To sign divorce papers I have no interest in signing.

And apparently, Natalie's office is inside the brand-new training facility for Minnesota's professional football team.

What the fuck?

Seriously. What in the actual fuck?

Does Wag Corp own the Biters?

My tennis shoes are quiet as I step onto the sidewalk leading to the front doors, and that's when my phone blows up with messages.

Chapter 64

Natalie

My steps are nearly silent as I pace behind my desk.

Luke will be here soon.

It's the first time I've seen him since Vegas, and even though it's only been a few days, it still feels... big.

I stop and turn to pace the other way.

It's fine.

You're fine.

He's fine.

Getting a divorce is the right and normal thing to do in this situation. Plus, he was the one to say he still wants to date. And he still seems happy about me moving here.

I take a deep breath.

It will all work out fine.

I glance at the clock on my wall.

Luke should be here.

I'm tempted to go check my phone, but I left it on Do Not Disturb in anticipation of this awkward interaction.

Not just the divorce. The... office.

I ignore the Biters jersey framed on the wall.

I probably should have told Luke about my dad buying the team. But the *accidental marriage* thing kind of took over my brain this weekend, and I didn't find the time to tell him.

It's not a big deal though.

Our relationship has nothing to do with Wag Corp.

It's all fine.

"Natalie!" My dad's angry voice slices through my thoughts.

I turn in time to see him striding through my open office door.

"Dad—"

He cuts me off. "What the hell is this?"

"What—"

He holds up his phone, the screen facing me, and my blood crystallizes into ice.

"Where?" I whisper, the rest of the question stuck in my throat.

Even from several feet away, I can recognize what's in the video he's showing me.

Because it's me.

Me, on my dad's phone, in what must be video surveillance from the elevator Luke and I took up to my hotel room.

The camera angle is from the opposite corner.

It's a side view.

It's clearly Luke.

And it's clearly me.

And even though we're fully clothed, it's... Well, it's graphic.

My leg is lifted and hooked around Luke's thigh as he holds me open, grinding into me.

My hands are all over him.

His hands are all over me.

And it doesn't take a doctorate in assumptions to know we're moments away from having sex.

"In public?" Dad hisses, and I don't know if I've heard him this mad before. "Have you lost your mind? The board is already breathing down my neck over nepotism, and you go and do something like this?"

"Dad—" I glance from his face back to the phone he's still holding out. The camera shot changes from the elevator to us stumbling down the hallway. I avert my gaze. "We weren't *in public.* Those should never have been shared."

Dad finally lowers the phone. "You know better. Or I thought you did." He shakes his head. "Maybe you're not ready."

Panic cracks through my frozen state. "No, Dad, it's not like that."

"Really? You're going to go with *it's not what it looks like?* Because it looks like you're hooking up. *In public.*" He emphasizes those two words. "With a professional athlete." He throws his hands up. "At least it's some hockey player and not one of the Biters."

I wince, knowing the professional athlete connection makes this worse.

"They're calling it The Hockey Player and the Heiress." He shakes his phone again. "It's playing on ESPN."

Oh god.

"Please." I try to make him listen to me even as I feel myself spiraling. "Dad, it wasn't just some hookup."

Movement fills the doorway behind my dad.

My gaze darts over to a pair of familiar dark eyes as Luke steps into my office.

And I know what I have to do.

I can only hope Luke will understand.

"We got married," I blurt out. "I'm sorry for not telling

175

you. And for the videos. But it isn't some sensational one-night stand caught on tape. It's a couple on their wedding night."

"You're married?" Dad's head jerks back like I hit him, and I feel even worse than I did a second ago.

I nod, refusing to look over his shoulder. Not willing to watch Luke's expression as I keep going. "We love each other, and we wanted to get married without making a spectacle of our relationship."

Dad huffs. "I'd say you made a spectacle."

"I'm sorry. You're right. We should have been more careful." Even if it's bullshit that one of the employees of the resort leaked the footage, we still should have waited to maul each other until we got inside the room.

His shoulders drop. "Why wouldn't you tell me? I didn't even know you were seeing someone."

A large dose of guilt mixes in with all the other heavy feelings twisting through my ribs.

"I didn't want you to tell me no." My voice cracks as I say it, but we both know it's true.

I love my dad. He's a good parent. He's given me a wonderful life, and we've always been close. But we're a prominent family. And as much as I value his opinion, there's a chance he would have tried to tell me I couldn't date Luke with the whole pro-athlete connection. And even though I want to make my dad proud, I'd never break up with someone just because he didn't like the optics. And Dad would never have given his blessing for a Vegas wedding.

His mouth goes flat, and he nods once. "Alright."

He starts to turn like he's going to leave without saying more, then he spots Luke.

My dad has always seemed larger than life to me, even now, but seeing him standing across from Luke, I realize that he's not the biggest man I know. And something about that makes me sad.

"You the one who married my daughter?" Dad practically growls.

I hold my breath, unsure of how Luke is going to respond to my dad's judgment and anger.

But Luke just nods. "Yes, sir."

They stare at each other for a moment before Dad looks back at me. "This why you didn't buy a place? You're going to live with him?"

Oh fucking hell.

I glance at Luke, but, for once, his face doesn't give anything away.

"I am," I lie.

I'm not moving in with Luke. I was never planning to move in with Luke. But he was part of the reason I didn't buy a house. Because a side of me was hoping that maybe, in the future, we *would* live together. And even though I didn't expect that to happen soon, I figured I'd find a rental once I got here and go from there.

But now I'm going to have to pretend that I'm living with Luke and not in a hotel. And honestly, I don't know how I'm going to pull that off.

Dad's jaw works, and Luke's silence doesn't make me feel any better about the success of this lie. But it's probably better than him saying anything right now.

"This isn't the end of this conversation." Dad shakes his head one last time. "I'm disappointed in you, Natalie."

I try not to flinch.

That sentence.

I've worked my whole life to avoid hearing that sentence.

My hummingbird cowers behind her wings, and I resist the urge to press a hand to my chest.

Dad turns away without saying more, and Luke sidesteps out of the way as my dad storms out of my office.

I force myself to meet Luke's eyes as we wait for my dad to get farther down the hall.

When a door slams somewhere down the hallway, Luke walks toward my desk.

"So," he says in too casual a tone. "I thought we were getting a divorce without telling anyone."

"I know, I know." I twist my fingers together as Luke comes to a stop across from me. "I'm sorry. I know it's a mess, but I can't let him cut me out of the business."

Luke dips his chin. "The money is too good. Got it."

"What?" I lower my brows. "No, it's not like that."

"Isn't it, *Princess*?"

The way he says it feels like barbed wire around my throat.

He says it like it's a curse word.

Like I'm nothing but a spoiled child.

Even the hummingbird in my chest recoils farther behind her wings at his tone.

"It's not about money." I put as much force into my voice as I can.

"Really? Because as soon as your dad threatened to cut you off, it was suddenly important that we married for love."

"It's the business," I try to explain. "I'm supposed to take over for him, but the people—" I untwine my fingers to gesture with my hands. "If the public views me as irresponsible, the board will put pressure on my dad to pick someone else as his successor."

Luke nods. "So I'm a political ploy."

"You're not..."

Not to me.

You're not a political ploy to me.

My head is spinning, my thoughts tangled, and I can't

figure out the right way to explain this. Not when Luke is looking at me with the same *disappointment* as my father.

"Why should I go along with this?" Luke slides his hands into his pockets. "What's stopping me from walking down the hall and telling your dad everything?"

That barbed wire tightens.

He can't.

Luke can't do that.

If he tells my dad it was all an accident...

He just can't.

"Well?" He lifts his brows and takes a step back like he's going to do exactly what he threatened.

I swallow, dreading what's coming next. But knowing I need to stop him before he makes this all so much worse.

"It would be bad for you too," I say quietly. "The accidental marriage. The video. You're the golden boy. Your team wouldn't like it."

The words taste like bile on my tongue, but we both know it's true.

He's even more of a public figure than I am.

More well known. More recognizable.

Luke scoffs. "Jackson's the golden boy. I'm just the fool."

"Luke..." My mouth is so dry I can hardly say his name.

"Don't." He pulls a small cloth bag out of his pocket. "I wore this here as a joke." He tosses the bag onto my desk, and for the first time, I notice the bright pink band on his ring finger. "Guess I'm leaving it on *as* the joke."

"Please—"

I don't finish the sentence.

I don't know what to say.

Please listen to me.

Please try to understand.

Please just give me a fucking moment to process what's happening.

But it doesn't matter because Luke is already striding out of my office.

Feeling like I might be sick, I slowly lower myself into my chair.

Breathe.

I take a slow inhale and try to exhale just as slowly.

Everyone is mad at me.

I have so few people I'm close to, and right now, they're both mad at me.

Disappointed.

Angry.

I swallow.

It will pass.

I want to think Dad will forgive me, but I don't even know which part I need him to forgive me for first. For not telling him I was dating someone, for getting married without inviting him, for lying to his face.

And Luke...

I drag the small bag across the desk toward me.

Luke just needs a moment to cool down.

Once he's calmed down, I can explain everything.

I can tell him how much good I can do running Wag Corp. How it's not about the money or the power. How I'm not doing this to be greedy.

I open the bag and tip it upside down over my palm.

A silicone ring, like the one Luke was wearing, falls out.

I vaguely remember Luke getting this after the party while I was signing what turned out to be our wedding certificate.

If only we'd looked in the bag at the moment or read the contract, this all could have been avoided. We could have scratched out our signatures and walked away. And the scare would have sobered us up enough that we probably wouldn't have been pawing at each other in the elevator.

If we'd just taken one second, today could have been avoided.

I stare at the folder on my desk, the one holding the unsigned divorce papers, and I slide the ring onto my finger.

One day.

I'll give Luke one day to be mad, but then he'll come around.

He has to.

Chapter 65

Luke

THE MIX of embarrassment and betrayal makes my skin hurt.

Your team wouldn't like it.

How did I not see it?

The calculation.

The coolness.

My finger trembles as I press the button to call the elevator.

I thought I knew her.

Thought I was falling for Natalie Wagner.

But I was just a pawn.

The doors slide open, and I step in.

I don't think she orchestrated the group wedding. There's no way. And I can't think of a single reason for her to be behind the release of those fucking surveillance videos.

Those fucking videos that eighteen people sent me as I was walking into this fucking building.

This Biters building.

I clench my fists.

How could I be so damn stupid?

As the elevator doors close, my phone rings.

When I see the screen, I somehow feel even worse.

This isn't going to be fun.

I answer the call. "Hey, Mom."

"Lucas Marie Anders."

"Mom," I groan. Why did I have to be an only child of a single parent in a family that insists on passing down middle names?

"Don't Mom *me*. I'm the one who just had to see you humping some rich girl on the TV?"

Humping?

"Mom—"

"Your aunt damn near gave me a heart attack with the way she screamed when she saw it on the news. *The news*, Lucas."

The news? That's not good.

"Look, I know—"

"And you were drunk." She gasps like she didn't catch me drunk when I was seventeen.

The elevator doors open on the ground floor, and I step out. "Mom—"

"And then they showed the clip of you winking at her from the penalty box," she whispers, like that's even worse than the rest.

"What's wrong with winking?" I ask, but she ignores me.

"Is this how you act after your games? You go out, get drunk, and publicly canoodle with Sleet Sluts?"

"Mom!" If I didn't feel so close to puking, I might laugh at hearing her say *slut*. "That's the name of one fan club; it's not what we call... the girls." I cringe as I say it.

"No?" Mom's tone is full of exasperation. "Well, what should I call this girl?"

Either I'm in, or I'm out. And as much as my chest hurts right now, I know what I'm going to do.

I take a breath. "You can call that particular girl my wife."

There's a second of silence before I hear the phone clatter out of her grasp.

Chapter 66

Natalie

MY HANDS ARE STILL TREMBLING from the confrontation, but I know what I have to do.

I sit down behind my desk and pick up my phone.

It only takes me a few minutes to get the head of public relations on the line.

"What can I do for you, Miss Wagner?"

I tap my fingers on the desktop, eyes on the pink band circling my ring finger. "We need to put out a statement."

"What is the statement about?" she asks, but I'm sure she's been alerted to the video by now.

"About the videos. And letting everyone know it was a private, heated moment between myself and my husband, Luke Anders, on our wedding night." I pause for a moment while she gasps. "You can add an apology or whatever your department deems necessary. But I'd like the world to know that it was a private moment between a married couple. Which we all know is much less scandalous."

"Okay, um, we can do that. When would you like it out?"

"Within an hour," I answer.

If those videos are blowing up, we need to address it immediately. I can only hope Luke goes along the story. Because there's no avoiding it now.

Chapter 67

The Unreturned Text Messages

Princess: I'm sorry for how everything went down yesterday. I know it was bad. Can we please talk?

Princess: I understand why you're mad. I would be too. But we need to talk about it.

Princess: Please answer the phone.

Princess: Luke, we can't just avoid this.

Princess: It's been a week. If you want to just do the divorce, we can, but you need to answer me.

Princess: I'm trying to be understanding, but you need to talk to me. Let me explain. I won't do it over text.

Princess: So you can talk about our "whirlwind romance" in a postgame interview, but you can't answer my texts?

Princess: You know how to get a hold of me.

Chapter 68

Natalie

I set my phone down on the nightstand and turn off the light.

I know what I did wasn't right, but if Luke would just take his head out of his ass for five minutes, I could explain it to him.

I deserve better than this.

Pulling the hotel blanket up to my chin, I ignore the way my eyes fill.

I've cried enough.

I won't cry any more over this disaster of a marriage.

Chapter 69

Luke

I toss my phone to the other end of the couch and watch it bounce off the cushion and land on Jackson's floor.

You know how to get a hold of me.

"I think that's enough for the night." Coach stands and stretches his back.

We've been watching game tapes, but really, it's just been him and Jackson watching and discussing. I haven't heard a word.

It's been over a week since the shit show in Natalie's office.

Natalie Wagner of *Wag* Corp. A woman whose individual worth is estimated at over one hundred million dollars.

Just thinking about her makes me angry.

The whole fucking situation makes me angry.

And what makes me the angriest is that I don't even know who I'm angriest at.

Her for not spelling out who exactly she was? Or me for never even thinking about looking her up?

Her for practically blackmailing me into playing along? Or me for feeling so damn hurt about it?

Her for being mature and reaching out to me like this can be fixed with a simple conversation? Or me for not wanting to face her when all I really want to do is see her?

We had some away games in the days after I stormed out of Natalie's office, but since we got back, I've been crashing at Jackson's.

Natalie doesn't have my address, or at least I haven't given it to her, but I'm sure someone with her means could find it. And I couldn't take the chance of her showing up, so I've been hiding out here.

Like a fucking coward.

Which makes me even angrier.

I snag my phone off the floor as Jackson and I get up and follow Coach toward the door.

My steps are heavier than they need to be, but I can't help it.

I'm not an angry dude. I don't like feeling this way.

Coach gives Katelyn, Jackson's wife, a hug goodbye before turning back to us. "I'll see you boys at practice tomorrow."

"Night, Coach," Jackson tells the older man.

"Night," Coach replies before moving his attention to me. "You've been playing well."

I dip my chin. "Thanks."

"But..." I knew there was a fucking but. "You're gonna get burned out playing on emotion. Fix the shit between you and your heiress."

"My—" Did he seriously just use the name from the title of that video?

"Sorry to burst your bubble, Luke." Coach pats my shoulder. "But I know the story. And that you've been avoiding her."

"Great," I deadpan.

Coach smiles, not put out by my attitude. "You're a smart

kid. I trust you'll find a way to make it work. But quit putting it off."

Then he turns and leaves.

Jackson shuts the door behind him, then faces me. "He's right, you know. You've been avoiding this long enough."

My mouth flattens into a line. "It's barely been a week." *It's been over a week.* "And he wouldn't *know* anything if he wasn't sleeping with your mom, hearing her repeat everything you say during their pillow talk."

Katelyn snickers.

Jackson pulls his shoulders back. "Have fun sleeping at home tonight."

"Seriously?"

"Yeah, man. If you stay any longer, I'm gonna have to tell my mom, and then she'll have to tell Coach."

"You're right. We can't have that!" I throw my hands up and stomp away from my best friend to collect my things from the guest room.

I knew bringing his mom up was a mistake, but I couldn't help myself. Jackson's mama started dating Coach after Jackson and Katelyn got married. We're all used to it by now, but throwing it in Jackson's face that way wasn't the best decision. But clearly I don't make good decisions when I'm upset.

According to the world, Natalie and I are madly in love. The unlikely but wildly popular pairing of the business mogul's daughter and the professional hockey player.

And Natalie is right. I did talk about our relationship in a postgame interview. Because I was asked, and there really wasn't a choice but to go along with the story. Because she was right in the office too. Coach wouldn't bench me for a drunken, accidental wedding, but my sponsors might have cut their contracts with me.

It wouldn't be the end of the world if they did. I've been

smart with my money. I could retire after this season and be fine. But I don't really want to end my career like that. I want the sponsor money, and I want to end my career on my own terms.

And doesn't that just make me the biggest fucking hypocrite in the world?

I stuff my scattered clothes into my duffel bag and zip it up.

I'll go home and gather my thoughts.

Then I'll figure out what to say to Natalie.

Chapter 70

Natalie

"Nat!"

I pause, hearing my dad's voice call out from his office.

I haven't exactly been avoiding him since we work in the same building, one hall away from each other, but I also haven't gone out of my way to see him since *that day*.

But to be fair, he's been doing the same.

And if he assumes that I leave right at five because I'm in a hurry to get home to my husband, well, that's his assumption to make.

Which is the exact assumption I want people to make.

But in reality, I'm going back to my hotel to work on my laptop from bed.

It's a fine hotel, nothing fancy, nothing like the room I had in Vegas, but it's one of those extended-stay places with a separate bedroom, a mini kitchen with a table, a desk, and a couch-TV area. So my four suitcases and I are quite comfortable.

"Nat!" Dad calls again, and I turn, lunch in hand, back toward his door.

When I step into Dad's office, I pull up short, not expecting the giant man standing in front of his desk.

"Uh, hi." I'm sure my eyes are wide. This guy is huge. Definitely a football player.

"Hi." He smiles warmly and holds out his hand.

I shift the cafeteria salad and bottle of cherry sparkling water into my left hand, then take his offered one with my right.

"Natalie Wagner." I introduce myself.

His smile doesn't waver. "Harrison Danvers."

"Linebacker, right?"

Harrison is six foot something and wider than two of me, with short light brown hair and smile lines next to his eyes. But friendly or not, I cannot imagine being tackled by this guy.

Harrison nods. "Right."

He lets go of my hand and takes a step back, thankfully not saying anything about my recent change in marital status.

"Harrison here is a big supporter of Marie's House, so he's going to join us at the Mazzanti fundraiser in a couple weeks," Dad explains.

"Oh, that's great." Some of my tension over being in the same room with my dad starts to melt away. If he can act normal, then so can I. "I've heard rumors of them opening a second location."

Harrison nods. "I've heard the same rumors. And really happy to hear y'all are involved with their fundraising."

I relax a little further. "So are we. The Mazzantis are good folks."

"Yes, yes." Dad claps his hands together. "Well, Harrison, I didn't mean to keep you so long. But glad you two got a chance to meet. And we'll be cheering you on tomorrow night."

The big man nods to my dad. "Appreciate that. Hope we can pull a win for you."

"Wouldn't mind if you did," Dad jokes.

Harrison dips his chin to me. "It was nice to meet you, Natalie."

"You too." I smile.

Since it would be weird to sprint down the hall ahead of him, I step out of the way and let Harrison leave Dad's office.

I wait a moment before moving my gaze to meet Dad's. "He seems nice."

Dad's smile is a little more hesitant than it was a moment ago. "He is." He gestures to the round table in the corner of his large office. "Want to eat that in here? I was just gonna order something to be brought up."

I only chew on my lip for a second before nodding.

While Dad calls down to the cafeteria, I pull out a chair and take the lid off my salad. The food here is remarkably good, but I shouldn't be surprised since they feed hungry football players along with the staff.

"So." Dad sits opposite me. "Want to join me in the owner's box for Sunday's game?"

"Yeah, I'd like that," I answer honestly.

The Biters played an away game last week, so this will be the first time we get to see them play in person since Dad bought the team. And no matter how uncomfortable things might be between us right now, I don't want to miss that.

"Your, uh, husband"—he clears his throat—"can join us."

Oh right.

That detail.

"I'll ask him." My voice is a little higher than usual. "I think he might have a team thing though."

I made that up, but since he won't answer my calls or texts, there's a chance that it's true. Schrödinger's schedule. Or something like that.

My left thumb automatically rubs at the underside of the pink band circling my ring finger.

I hate that I kind of love the cheap silicone ring.

I hate that I have to wear it for show.

I hate that if Luke were talking to me, I'd still want this ring and not one with diamonds.

"Good, good." Dad taps his fingers on the table, then lets out a large sigh. "I'm sorry."

"Dad, you don't—"

"No." He cuts me off. "You look stressed and exhausted, and you shouldn't look that way as a newlywed."

I try for a smile. "Just busy."

He shakes his head. "I know what your busy face looks like. This is different. And I'm sorry for my role in it."

"Please don't apologize." I don't like how he handled everything, but I can't exactly blame him for his reaction.

And since I'm still lying to him, it doesn't feel right for him to apologize.

I slump in my chair. "I wasn't expecting that stupid video. I should've known better, and I'm sorry for the attention it's brought the company."

Dad makes a disagreeing sound. "No. I was being unreasonable. You were in an elevator alone, not on the strip. And really, instead of being mad, I should've been grateful it took you thirty-two years to make it into the tabloids."

I snort. "I'd prefer never being in the tabloids. Or on ESPN. Or on the freaking news."

Dad laughs. "People love celebrity shit."

I make a face. "I'm not a celebrity."

He smirks at me. "You're rich. It's the same thing."

I make another more disgusted face.

"And," he keeps going, "you married a well-known professional athlete. People are gonna care."

I want to tell him the truth.

I want to tell him everything.

But as I open my mouth to do just that, one of the building staff knocks on the doorframe and enters with my dad's lunch.

Watching Dad unbox his sandwich, I decide to stay quiet. At least for today.

Telling him will only make him want to get involved, and this is my problem to fix.

Chapter 71

Luke

SOMEONE WALKS past me on the sidewalk, wearing a red and yellow Biters hat, and I have to fight the urge to glower at them.

It's like everywhere I turn, I'm hit with reminders of Natalie.

Even in my own building, I couldn't get away from it. My neighbors cheered every time something happened in the game. Maybe I've just never noticed it before, but it was too much. So I decided to walk the mile to my favorite coffee shop.

Ash and Meghan don't live far from here, which is how I found out about this specific location of BeanBag Coffee. But I'm not particularly good company at the moment, so I'm not going to bother to see if they're around.

I just want to sit in the relative silence of a rustic coffee shop in downtown Minneapolis, sip a black coffee that I could have easily made at home, and have no TV or evidence of a football game in sight.

The sound of a rainstick fills the air as I push open the front door of BeanBag, and I'm greeted with the rich scent of in-house roasted beans.

About half the tables are full, and I start to relax as I cross over to the counter.

Then I see Benny.

Benny has been a barista here forever. And I'm pretty sure he became the manager over the summer.

Benny is great. He's funny and friendly and knows how to make any sort of drink you ask for.

He's also had hipster vibes since the first day I met him. Always wearing tight jeans and snug button-down flannels. And for the past year or so, he's been rocking suspenders.

Always.

Except today.

I stop across from where he's standing at the register.

"What. The fuck. Are you wearing?" I sound way angrier than I have any right to, but I can't help it.

Benny, on the other side of the counter, looks down at himself. "Um, a football jersey."

"A football jersey," I repeat. Then I bend over until my forehead hits the counter.

"Uh... Luke?" There's a light nudge against my shoulder. "You okay?"

I shake my head back and forth, my forehead probably leaving a smudge on the light wood countertop. "No, Benny. I'm not okay." I force myself to straighten back to my full height. "This"—I press my finger to the counter—"is supposed to be a safe space."

Benny's eyes widen in shock, like I just said that the floor was made of poop.

I keep going. "This is supposed to be a place where I can come and relax. But you." I lift my finger to point at him. "You are wearing a fucking football jersey."

It's not just a football jersey. It's a Biters jersey.

"Look, man, I'll wear a Sleet jersey on your game days if you want," Benny says reasonably.

I groan. "That's not it."

"What is it, then?" Benny holds his arms out at his sides.

"It's the team!" I don't mean to raise my voice.

"What's wrong with the Biters?" Benny's voice goes up to match mine.

"Nothing!" I reach up and grip my hair.

Benny looks around, probably for help. "I don't understand what's happening!"

Hands still in my hair, I tip my head back and groan at the ceiling.

I'm losing my mind.

This is what losing your mind feels like.

"Our boy is upset that his wife is at that game, but he isn't," a woman says. "I'd say make him a decaf or a triple shot. Just don't tell him what you choose."

Slowly, I turn my head to see a woman with curly red hair piled into a bun on the top of her head and a smirk aimed my way.

"Meghan." I greet her.

My eyes slide to the other person sitting at her table, but it's not her husband, Ash. It's a woman I don't recognize whose hair is buzzed short and who is also wearing a Biters jersey.

"Luke." Meghan lifts her mug in a mock toast.

I turn back to Benny, pull a twenty out of my wallet, and set it on the counter. "Her plan sounds good."

Benny keeps his lips pressed together as he gives me a thumbs-up.

Meghan has a laptop in front of her, so I'm not sure if she's with a client, but I still approach her table.

If she was trying to have a professional event-planning meeting, she wouldn't have shouted at me from across the shop.

"Can I join you?" I don't bother mustering up a smile. I think it's obvious to everyone in the city that I'm not having a great day.

Meghan nods. "Take a seat. Luke, this is Kerissa." She gestures to the woman sitting across from the chair I pulled out.

"Hi, Kerissa." I drop into the chair, and I don't miss the way I'm nearly eye level with the stranger.

"Hey." Kerissa smiles. "Benny talks about you guys all the time. It's nice to meet you."

My brows go up. "Benny?"

"Yup." Kerissa pushes her chair back. "Sorry to ditch, but I gotta go let our cats out."

Our cats.

"No worries. See you later," Meghan says, and I lift my hand in a wave.

And then, like a toddler seeing something new for the first time, I stare, wide eyed, as Kerissa walks around the back of the counter and grips Benny by the face before pressing her lips forcefully against his.

His arms go around her waist, and when they shift, he disappears from sight altogether.

Benny isn't short, but his lady friend is pushing six feet.

Meghan chuckles beside me. "That was a bit much."

"I know," I agree. "Who kisses like that in public?"

"I was talking about you."

I turn toward her. "Me?"

Meghan lifts her coffee. "You and your meltdown over Benny's choice of clothing."

I slump in my chair.

We both look over at the couple. And I pretend not to notice when the Kerissa girl slaps Benny's ass as he starts to walk our way.

When he reaches our table, the tips of his ears are bright red. "She's great, isn't she?"

"Uh-huh," I say as Meghan gives a much more enthusiastic "Very."

We all look over to watch the tall woman. At the door, she turns and blows a kiss to Benny, then she steps outside.

"You guys have cats?" I ask.

Benny beams. "Yeah, we found a pair of abandoned kittens on our second date and rescued them. We tried trading off who got them, but after a few weeks, we decided to just"—he lifts a shoulder—"live together."

"You moved in together after a few weeks?" I ask with my brows raised.

Benny sets my drink down on the table, then moves his hands to his hips. "And you randomly got married but apparently hate the sight of the football team your in-laws own. So which one of us is making worse decisions?"

"Day-yum!" Meghan laughs as Benny backs away.

He has a point, but I still narrow my eyes at him.

"I'll take it all back if you can hook me up with a pair of Biters tickets," Benny says, still backing up. "Kerissa is a huge fan."

I keep my eyes narrowed as he spins around and hurries behind the counter.

My attention moves down to the drink before me.

I pry the lid off, the pale brown color nothing like the plain black coffee I usually drink.

Bending forward, I sniff it and crinkle my nose. "What the fuck is that smell?"

Meghan pulls the cup closer to her and sniffs. "That's pumpkin spice."

I pull a face. "Fucking why?"

"No reason necessary." Meghan sets the cup in front of me. "You're a PSL girl now."

Carefully, I lift the full cup and take a sip, expecting to hate it.

I take a second sip.

And a third.

And then I stare at the wall across from me.

"Welcome to the spicy side of life." Meghan holds her arms out.

"This is really fucking good." I take another sip.

"Well, duh. Millions of people don't flock to them because they're gross."

"Touché." I settle back in my chair, accepting that I'm going to consume this whole drink in the next five minutes, decaf or triple shot be damned.

"Can I ask you something?" Meg breaks the silence after a moment.

"Go ahead," I exhale.

"Do you like her?"

"Kerissa?"

Meghan kicks my shoe under the table. "Your wife, dum-dum."

"It's not that simple," I answer.

"It never is," she counters. "Now tell me, do you like her?"

I think about Natalie.

Think about the first time I saw her lying on that weight bench.

Think about the first time she made me laugh.

About the way her lashes glistened as we floated in the ocean together.

And the way we can't keep our hands off each other when we're near.

And I sigh. Because yeah, I like my wife.

Like I do every night when I'm lying in bed, I scroll through all the major sports sites.

Sports are my life, so it's what I do.

I'm ready to see stuff about the Biters, but I'm not ready to see Natalie's pretty face on my feed.

I click on the link to read the article.

It's short. Just a mention of the new owner, the company he runs, the daughter set to take over for him, and the recent addition of a son-in-law.

My chest aches as I zoom in on the picture.

It's taken from inside the stadium, the camera aimed up at the box where she and her dad are standing and clapping.

The smile on her face looks forced, and that ache inside me turns into a burn.

What excuse did she make for me not being there?

What does she tell her dad when she sees him at work?

Where is she sleeping at night?

That last one hurts.

I don't know why. She's not destitute. She can afford any hotel.

Then another thought hits me.

She can afford any home.

What if she decides to buy something now?

Her dad made that comment about her moving in with me, and that's why she didn't buy something. But you don't have money like that and throw it away renting when you could be investing.

I set my phone down on my chest and just breathe.

I should've been there with her tonight.

I hated what she said to me that day in her office. Hated the way she twisted it to her benefit. But now I get it. I understand she was right.

After that damn tape leaked, her plan was the best way to handle it.

And I'm fucking it all up.

I'm fucking up her strategy, and I'm fucking up my chance to be with her.

I take another breath.

Tomorrow, we fly to Canada for our game on Tuesday, but then we're back in town for a game Thursday. I'll call her after that game.

Then I feel like a coward because I know I'll text instead of calling. But then we can set up a time to talk next weekend. We can figure out a way to make this work.

Chapter 72

Natalie

I SHAKE hands with the owner of the Minnesota Sleet. "Nice to meet you. I'm Natalie."

"Of course, of course!" The man who looks like Santa clasps my hand between both of his. "I was so thrilled when I heard you married one of our own."

My smile slips a bit before I'm able to catch it. "He's a special guy."

Oh. My. God. A special guy?

Is Luke my grandson?

Santa doesn't seem to see anything wrong with my statement because he nods. "He really is. We're lucky to have him. This season is gonna be something exceptional." He finally drops my hands.

"Oh yeah?" Dad chimes in. "I haven't had time to follow them much."

The other man beams. "We have a great group of guys. A number of them have been playing together for years, so they just instinctually know where to go, how to find the openings. Really mature lineups."

As my dad replies, I look out onto the ice below, wondering where Luke is right now.

I feel like a total fraud, even as I'm dressed for the occasion, wearing an oversized Anders jersey.

Since I knew we were going to be watching from the owner's box, I classed it up with a bright white turtleneck underneath and a pair of dark-wash jeans with ankle boots.

At least I look the part of a player's wife, even if I don't feel it.

I tap my fingers against my thigh, wondering if Luke will find out I'm up here.

They usually show shots of the expensive box seats during breaks, so he'll probably figure it out.

And he probably won't be happy about it.

A hand lands on my shoulder. "Sorry, Dear. I wasn't thinking," Santa tells me. "My crew up here can get you downstairs so you can say hi to your husband before the game. Maybe see some of the underbelly of the arena."

"Oh, um, okay." I answer the only way I can. Because *Oh god, please, no* would raise some questions.

My dad gestures for me to go ahead, so, against every wish inside my body, I walk out of the suite and follow one of the arena employees to a private elevator.

We ride down in silence, and when the doors open, I put a hand up to stop the employee from following me. "I know the way."

They nod and stay put when I step out.

I know I'm being rude, and what I said was a complete lie, but I'd rather be lost down here by myself than escorted to the husband who can't be bothered to acknowledge my existence.

As I walk through the empty concrete hallway, a little of that pain I've been working to bury for the past several days starts to push back up.

I just want this nightmare to be over.

I don't want to keep lying to people.

A single tear breaks through my defenses, and I wipe it away as the hallway intersects with a wider, busier one.

I should just find a place to sit for a few minutes, then I can go back upstairs and pretend to enjoy myself.

There's another turn ahead of me. I'll round the corner and lean against the wall there, act like I'm waiting for someone.

The noise level increases as movement echoes through the hall. And that should've been my warning.

As soon as I turn the corner, I know I made a mistake.

Hockey players.

I almost walk right into the moving mass of Sleet players, decked out in all their gear, larger than life walking on their skates.

I jump back.

I literally jump back around the corner and backpedal as fast as I can.

Straight into a body.

We both go down.

My elbow bangs against the wall, but I manage to land on my butt. While it sends a jolting sting up my tailbone, it prevents me from cracking a joint on the unforgiving floor.

But the sound of pain from the man who went down with me says his fate is different.

"I'm so sorry," I say as I shift to look at whoever I crashed into.

And then I pause, because I'm staring into a giant, grinning yeti face.

It's Blizz, the Sleet mascot.

It's Blizz.

I knocked over Blizz, and he's gripping his ankle with both hands.

This isn't good.

"Oh no," I whisper as he groans. "Oh fuck."

"I'm so sorry," I say again. "Are you okay?"

"Yeah." I can hear the wince in his voice. "Just gotta walk it off."

"Alright. Okay." I use the wall to get to my feet, then I hold out my hands to help him up.

Big furry paws grip my hands, and the man gingerly gets to his feet.

Then he crumples against the wall, lifting one foot off the ground.

"I can't—Fuck." Still leaning against the wall, he yanks his head off, revealing the face of a pained man in his twenties. "I think it's sprained."

"I'm sorry," I squeak, my fingertips pressing against my cheeks.

"What do I do?" His eyes are wide.

"I don't know."

We're both starting to panic.

"It's only my second game." He glances around like he's worried someone will see him.

"I'm sorry!"

"They'll fire me if I don't go out there." He shifts his weight and winces again.

I want to tell him I can talk to the owner, but I don't actually want to do that.

"Can we call someone?" I worry my hands together. "There has to be someone."

He shakes his head. "It's too late. The game—"

He doesn't have to finish the sentence. Because we both hear it.

The thundering music.

We look at each other in horror.

There are only minutes left before the announcer introduces the starting lineup.

Then the game starts.

"Can you skate?" the man asks me.

"Me? Kinda." My breath starts coming in faster pants.

"Kinda will work," he replies as he grips my shoulder. "Help me over there." He gestures to a door across the hall.

"Works for what?" I ask with dread in my voice.

We hobble together the handful of feet, and he pushes the door open, revealing a large storage closet.

The music changes.

He hops through the doorway. "We have two minutes."

The door shuts behind me. "Two minutes for what?"

"Before you need to be on the ice." He reaches behind his back and starts to pull down a zipper. "You're Blizz tonight."

My brain blanks for a long second.

You're Blizz tonight.

I start to shake my head. "No. I can't."

"You have to. Or I'm gonna lose my job." The yeti suit pools around his ankles, and he sits on a crate. "Help me with these laces."

I drop into a crouch to help him remove his skates even as I keep shaking my head. "Seriously, I can't do this. I'm sorry, but I can't."

I could still run upstairs and talk to the owner, but it's not like I have any actual sway around here. And a whole lot of people will notice Blizz is missing. And an angry crowd is never a good thing.

We get the skates off, and he kicks the suit the rest of the way down his legs.

He holds my wide-eyed stare. "You said you can skate."

"Not well!" I screech.

"You'll be fine." He throws the suit at me. "Hurry up."

My heart is pounding in my chest as I shove off my shoes and start to pull the suit on.

We both see the problem at the same time.

My hips.

The suit catches at the widest part of my hips.

I tug, but it's stuck.

The man clears his throat. "I'm not saying this to be a pervert, but you gotta take your pants off."

My eyes snap up to his. "You can't—"

The music changes again.

"One minute! Just hurry!" He waves his hands.

"Cover your eyes!"

We're both shouting, but he slaps his hands over his eyeballs.

I drop the suit and shimmy out of my jeans.

When I get them off, I kick them across the closet and yank the suit back up. It's still tight around the hips and ass, but I get it up.

"Okay," I breathe.

He opens his eyes and holds one of the skates steady for me.

I jam my foot into it as I pull off my bulky jersey and turtleneck, positive I'll die of heat stroke if I leave it on, meaning I'm left in nothing but my underwear and my bra.

This is why you always wear a comfort tank top under your shirt.

The man works on my laces, and I pull the zipper up as far as I can reach.

Thirty seconds later, the slightly too-large skates are tied tightly onto my feet, I'm zipped the rest of the way up, and the Blizz head is securely on my head.

The man opens the closet door and points to the left.

"There will be someone dressed in all black, and they'll tell you when to go out. When they do, you just gotta carry the Sleet flag to center ice. Then stand there and wave it around while they introduce the players. When the anthem starts, rest the bottom of the flagpole on the ice and stand still. Then when it's done, come back here."

"I'm gonna throw up," I tell him.

He snorts. "You're gonna be fine. Now hurry!"

Holding my arms out at my sides, I shuffle-run down the hall in the direction he pointed.

My balance is questionable, and I can already tell wearing the wrong size skates is going to be a problem. But when I reach the turn, I find myself in a wide opening right at the end of the ice rink.

"There you are!" A woman in black rushes to me, a giant Minnesota Sleet flag in hand.

"S—" I swallow and deepen my voice. "Sorry."

She shoves the flag into my hand, then crouches down.

I just look at her until she slaps my leg. "Lift your foot."

I teeter as I do what she says, but she's quick to take off the blade guards.

Oh, right.

A second later, she gestures for me to go through the open section of the rink wall. And onto the ice.

"Fuck me so much," I whisper.

I haven't ice-skated in a dozen years.

I close my eyes and say a quick prayer to the goddess of humiliation.

Please let me get through tonight without ripping the ass of this suit open.

Of all the days to wear a thong.

Someone hisses at me to go, so I go.

Chapter 73

Luke

FROM THE TUNNEL, I watch as the mascot takes to the ice a few beats later than usual.

I'm ready to play.

Ready to take out my pent-up feelings on Chicago. Like if I can beat their team, I can conquer my issues with the woman who hails from there.

I jump up and down.

The announcer is doing his ramp-up, getting ready to call us onto the ice.

Blizz is moving a little slowly across the ice. None of the usual flash. And the Sleet flag that should be waving above his head is pointed straight out in front of him, like a joust.

It's funny to watch, but the problem with that is—

I watch it happen before I can even think it.

The flag sags lower, so it's dragging on the ice, and, as predicted, Blizz's skate catches the edge of the material.

I wince as he face-plants onto the ice, and the arena lets out a collective "ooh" in sympathy.

As Blizz struggles to get back onto his skates, I catch my eyes moving lower.

Blizz's ass is really filling out that suit tonight.

I avert my eyes.

I did not just think that.

Chapter 74

Natalie

I WANT TO DIE.

With a giant spotlight centered on me, I use the flagpole like a walking cane and get back to my feet.

The crowd cheers.

I want to disappear. I want my whole person to vanish into nothingness, leaving nothing but a puddle of this goddamn Blizz suit behind.

With my arms trembling from exertion and rioting nerves, I lift the flag high above my head and wave it back and forth in big movements.

The crowd gets louder.

Torn between laughing and fucking sobbing, I carefully skate the rest of the way to center ice.

I have no idea which way I'm supposed to face, so I turn to face where I think the home bench is. The visibility is better than I expected in this bobblehead, but it's still far from great.

My arms start to really shake.

Why is waving a flag so hard?

Finally, the spotlight leaves me, and I lower the flag.

If I'm going to make it off this goddam ice without falling again, I need a break.

The announcer's voice bounces through my skull as the opposing team enters the rink, and that's when I realize we're playing Chicago.

Just perfect.

I prop the end of the pole against my hip and straighten my arms so the flag is jutting up and out. Then I sway, the flapping fabric following the movements.

It's the best I got right now. And if anyone is focused on me at this point, that's their problem.

Chapter 75

Luke

On our cue, we race onto the ice as a team.

I shoulder Zach as I skate next to him, and he shoulders me back.

We've already warmed up, but these laps around our half of the ice are for the crowd. And to get the rest of the jitters out.

I've wondered all day if Natalie would be here tonight. Or if she just has to lie to her dad again and tell him she's going.

Tonight. I will message her tonight.

The announcer starts to call out the starting lineup, so I listen for my name.

When he calls it, I jump into a short sprint and slide to a stop beside Jackson near center ice.

I try not to look. Try to keep my gaze forward. But my eyes drop on their own, focusing on Blizz's thick ass. But it's only because he's swaying back and forth, practically shaking it for the crowd. It's the motion that drew my attention.

I blink and jerk my eyes away from the yeti's rump and focus on getting my head back in the game.

Chapter 76

Natalie

THERE'S no one to give me a cue, but as soon as the national anthem ends, I turn and start toward the exit behind the goalie net—the way I came in.

And, of course, I crash into someone.

Before I can lose my balance, gloved hands grip my shoulders. "Whoa, dude."

I tense at the sound of Luke's voice, my eyes automatically moving to his face.

My body freezes, worried that he might be able to see through the mesh parts of the Blizz face, but then the flag flutters down into the space between us, draping over the top of Luke's head.

I channel my man voice again and mutter a quick "Thanks."

Luke lifts a hand to push the flag out of the way, but I push off with one skate, and with skill I could have used five minutes ago, I glide around behind him.

Focusing on every single inch of ice ahead of me, I hold the flag as high above my head as I can manage, just to ensure I don't trip over it.

Chapter 77

Luke

I TURN MY HEAD, watching Blizz skate away as I move toward the bench.

Just as the mascot reaches the edge of the ice, the flag—raised way higher than necessary—catches on the net that stretches above the glass to catch stray pucks.

The top of the flagpole jerks in his hands, throws him off balance, and once again, Blizz goes down. Ass in the air.

Chapter 78

Natalie

CRAWLING the few feet so I'm completely off the ice before I try to stand up, I decide that I'll just be buried in this fucking suit. That way, no one will ever need to know it was me tonight. I can just be a missing person. They'll do a documentary about it. Luke will probably be questioned since it's always the husband who disappears the wife, but since he's the reason I'm even at this godforsaken arena, he deserves it. I hope the media sets up outside his house, hounding him at the grocery store. And I hope no one ever dates him again and he ends up becoming an old cat lady.

When I'm on my feet, I take the skate guards from the woman in black and stumble away without putting them on.

I make my way to the closet as quickly as I can and check over my shoulder before I pull the door open.

The real Blizz is standing just inside, using a rack of cleaning supplies to keep himself upright on one foot, and I can tell he's trying not to smile. The bastard clearly snuck out of the closet to watch.

"Not a fucking word," I snap as I drop onto the crate he'd been sitting on earlier.

He mimes zipping his lips.

I groan and drop my giant head forward into my paws. "I can't do a whole game like this."

The man starts to chuckle but tries to cover it by clearing his throat.

I shift my face into one hand and hold out the other. "Can you hand me my phone?"

The man, whose name I don't even want to know at this point, digs out my little purse from the pile of clothes I left on the floor.

I need to text my dad and tell him I'm going to watch the game from down here before he sends someone to look for me.

And for once, what I'm telling isn't a lie.

I'll just be watching it even closer than he thinks.

"Good news," the guy says as he sets my purse in my hand. "You get to switch to tennis shoes for the next part."

I lift my head. "What's the next part?"

He tries not to smile. "The T-shirt cannon."

Chapter 79

Luke

WE'RE up three to one and in the locker room before the start of the final period.

"Thanks for the assist." Jackson grins at me before taking another drink of water.

"My pleasure," I reply, taking my own swig of water.

On the TV screens in the entryway to the locker room, I caught a glimpse of the little kid game they always have during one of the intermissions between periods. Nothing was special about it. Same old chaos. Except Blizz was once again slipping all over the ice.

"Have you noticed..." I start asking Jackson but trail off.

"Noticed what?"

"Ice seems extra fast tonight," I finish instead of saying *have you noticed the way Blizz is filling out that suit tonight?*

I take another drink of my water and avoid making eye contact with my friend.

I'm positive he hasn't noticed.

And I know I shouldn't be thinking of yeti ass when I have a wife somewhere in the state that I need to make up with.

Chapter 80

Natalie

My knees and elbows are sore from how many times I've fallen, and I'm pretty sure the woman who has been giving me my cues is fully aware I'm not the person who is supposed to be in the suit. But she's not saying anything, and neither am I. When this is all over, I'm planning to take this experience to my grave, take a bath in Tylenol, and never leave my hotel again.

There are only a few minutes left in the game. I just need to survive that, then I can enact my pain-relieving plan.

Trying to get comfortable in skates that have surely rubbed my feet raw, I prop the bottom of the flagpole on the ground and lean on it.

I'm a few feet back from the glass, right behind the net, with the Sleet goalie right in front of me.

If we win, I have to go back out onto the ice, waving this motherfucking flag.

If we lose, I get to hurry back to my closet.

And as much as I want to shove this polyester rag down Luke's throat for being a hockey player and ultimately being responsible for me being here, I still don't want them to lose.

Chapter 81

Luke

THERE ARE LESS than two minutes left, and Chicago scored a few plays ago, so we're only up by one.

I don't want to lose.

And I don't want to go into overtime to settle a tie.

I want to finish this game so I can go home and call Natalie.

I shouldn't have waited.

I should have called her the day I pulled my head out of my ass.

I should have jocked up and gone to her office. Begged her forgiveness. Asked her to explain everything she's told me she wants to explain.

But I waited. And that's going to be the last dumb decision in a long list of dumb decisions.

My mind focuses back on the game as Zach takes a shot on goal.

It gets deflected.

I'm moving for the rebound, but a Chicago player cuts through an opening, snagging the puck.

He breaks free and races down the ice toward Ash. Heading toward a one-on-one.

I shift and sprint after him.

The crowd is screaming.

The noise is deafening.

But my focus is zeroed in on the Chicago player.

I'm not staying for fucking overtime.

I have a wife to see.

Chicago is flying.

My teammates are behind me.

But they're behind me.

And they aren't as fast as I am.

Ash is getting low in the goal, preparing for the shot.

Chicago shifts to an arcing approach, planning to take the shot from an angle.

But his plan is cocky.

And I'm not gonna let him take a shot at all.

Pushing everything I have into my legs, I go a little faster.

And it's all I need.

Chicago is locked on the goal, not seeing me beside him.

My stick connects with the puck.

I knock it forward and away from the net, clearing the puck and trusting my teammates to handle it.

But Chicago and I were speeding down the ice at intersecting angles, and neither of us took any care to slow down.

I'm slightly in front when we collide, and Chicago uses his momentum to push me past the edge of the net toward the boards.

But I'm not looking to fuck my shoulder up again so soon. So, at the last second, I'm able to twist. And since this Chicago dickhead is holding my jersey—against the rules—he follows my twist. Straight into the fucking boards.

The already loud crowd gets even louder at the same time the ref blows the whistle.

I don't mean to look up, but movement on the other side of the glass catches my attention.

Not just movement.

Blizz.

He lifts a hand into the air, cheering for my hit and causing a few of the people nearby to snap their heads in his direction.

I have no idea what he shouted, but clearly, it wasn't expected.

As I start to laugh, Blizz starts to tip.

His arm up in celebration apparently throws him off kilter.

His other hand is holding the flag, and he uses it like a walking stick, lifting it and jabbing it at the ground ahead of him for balance. But he's already tipping, so instead of helping him, his big Blizz face hits the top of the pole, knocking his head sideways.

Before the entire Blizz head can pop off, he lets go of the pole and grips his face with both furry hands.

And that's the last thing I see, Blizz holding his head on as he falls below the level of the glass and out of sight.

Chapter 82

Natalie

I swear I can hear Luke's laughter. But that's impossible.

Or maybe I actually died last week in some accident I can't remember, and this is all just some sort of purgatory.

Clutching my yeti head in place, I roll onto my back.

I have no idea how to secure this fucking headpiece, so I keep a hand on it as I struggle up to my feet.

I fully intend to steal and burn this suit when I'm done, but I gotta say, whatever the material is made out of, it's held up.

The woman in black comes over and helps me up just as the final buzzer goes off, announcing the end of the game and the Sleet win.

She leans in so I can hear her. "Just skate out to center ice with the flag again, then once all the players are off the ice, come back here. We'll need you to stand in for some photos, but it shouldn't take too long."

Her tone is kind, and I could hug her for it.

I didn't miss the way everyone looked at me when I shouted after Luke crunched that guy to the glass.

I was so in the moment, forgetting how mad I am at him, that I didn't change my voice.

So yeah, pretty sure everyone heard my girly scream.

The woman pats me on the back.

"Thanks," I say so just she can hear me.

She shakes her head. "Thank me by getting through the rest of the night without falling again. You've taken years off my life already."

I can't help my laugh. "Girl, same."

I look both ways, then yank open the closet door and dart inside.

My feet are killing me, and I just want to transport myself three days into the future when my body won't hurt so much anymore.

I stand in the closet, and it takes me a second to realize that the real Blizz is nowhere to be seen.

"Great."

I eye my pile of clothes, then the door handle and the lack of a lock.

Standing for photos took longer than I expected, so the hallways are mostly empty. But that might actually increase the chances of someone coming into this closet to retrieve or return a cleaning item. And the last thing I need after surviving tonight is someone walking in on me half naked in a stolen Blizz suit.

Gathering my things, I check my phone before wrapping my pile of clothes and shoes in my jeans, creating an easy-to-carry bundle.

Thankfully my dad texted back at the beginning of the game, telling me to have fun and that if I don't come back up, he'll assume I'm riding home with Luke.

Something finally going my way. Thank you, Dad.

That just leaves changing back into my street clothes and ordering an Uber.

With my bundle against my chest, I sneak out of the closet. I just need to find a bathroom or at least a room with a lock.

I reach an intersection, and hearing voices in one direction, I turn in the other.

There's an open door ahead on the right.

Hoping it's something I can use, I quicken my pace.

But just as I start to turn into the doorway, someone steps out.

With my hands full and my body just fucking over it, I go down.

Again.

Chapter 83

Luke

BLIZZ BOUNCES OFF MY CHEST, and before I can grab his shoulders, he falls backward.

My mouth opens to apologize, but then Blizz hits the ground, and his head pops off.

And then I can't say anything because it isn't a *him*.

It's a Princess.

Long dark hair spills around her shoulders as big, beautiful green eyes blink up at me.

Green eyes that I've missed like hell.

Green eyes that are filling with tears.

"Aw, Princess." I rush to step over her, one foot on either side of her hips. "Please don't cry."

I hook my hands under Natalie's arms and pull her to her feet.

She grips my biceps to balance herself.

A tear tracks down her cheek, then another.

I brush them away, keeping one hand on her shoulder. "Are you okay?"

"I fell down a lot," she whispers.

I nod instead of smiling. "I saw."

Natalie sniffs and bites her lip.

She's taller like this, wearing skates. But she's still so small compared to me. Short and soft, and my urge to protect is always strongest when I'm with her.

And tonight, she was so close to me. But I watched her fall over and over. Without ever catching her. Without ever knowing.

The urge to smile leaves me, and all I want to do is keep her safe.

"I'm sorry." I brush my thumb over her cheek. "For all of it. I'm so sorry."

"I'm—"

I shake my head and move my hands so they're cupping her cheeks. "I'm an idiot. I should have just listened." Another tear trails down her cheek, and it pierces through my chest. "I've been here pacing, trying to decide whether I should call you or try and find where you're staying." I catch a tear with my thumb and brush it away. "No, please stop crying. I'm sorry. I promise I'll listen. You were right."

She presses her lips together and sniffs again. Those bright eyes are full of so much emotion.

Then she opens her mouth and says the last thing I'd expect her to say.

"I missed you, Luke."

I missed you.

Heavy air fills my lungs. "I fucking missed you too, Princess."

She clutches at my forearms and stretches up as I lean down. And for the first time in weeks, I kiss my wife.

Chapter 84

Natalie

I know we have to talk.

I know nothing has changed.

But in this very moment, I don't care.

It's been a long, horrible day, and I want to feel good.

It feels like it's been forever since I've felt good.

Luke slides his hands down the sides of my neck as he plunges his tongue into my mouth.

And I let him in. I open wider.

It shouldn't feel so right.

He shouldn't feel so right.

Not after these last couple of weeks.

But still.

"Luke." I cling to his arms with my oversized paws. Needing the balance. Needing it to come from him.

"My pretty girl." Luke's lips never leave mine. "My fearless wife."

When he starts to walk backward through the doorway, I pull my mouth away from his.

"My clothes." I point to the floor and the bundle I dropped.

Luke lets go of me just long enough to pick up the pile, and I look past him to see we're at the entrance to the locker room.

Luke steps back in front of me. "Hang on."

He wraps his arms around my waist, and I reach my arms up around his neck. And when he lifts me, I hang on.

I bend my knees, keeping my skates off the ground, as his mouth finds mine again.

Something rolls across the floor, and I open my eyes long enough to see the Blizz head—that Luke must've kicked—bounce across the locker room floor.

Luke walks us farther into the locker room, and the door thuds shut behind me.

"I can't believe it was you in this suit all night." He kisses me. "My naughty Little Royal." His lips smile against mine. "Always getting in trouble."

"It's you." I kiss him again. "It's only with you."

Luke lowers me, my body dragging against his. His hardness presses into me.

My skates connect with the floor, and I hardly notice how uncomfortable they are. My mind is too focused on the rest of my body. Too engrossed in the man before me.

Luke drops my clothes to the floor. Then his gaze follows the fabric before snapping back up to mine.

"Are those your pants?"

I nod.

"What are you wearing under this?" He grips the fuzzy white fur covering my arm.

A small laugh bubbles up my throat. "Not much."

Luke groans and grips the fabric at my side with his other hand, then pulls me tightly against him.

"I'm so fucking glad it's you in this suit. You have no idea." He leans down and presses his mouth against the side of my neck, murmuring something about losing his mind.

"I'm glad it was you I ran into," I admit.

He lifts his head. "Me too."

Luke slides a hand down my back until he's cupping my ass.

"God, you feel good." He squeezes. "Tell me you'll come home with me. Tell me you'll let me apologize."

I pull on the back of his neck. "I will."

He moves the hand not on my ass to palm my breast.

I moan, pressing my lips to his again.

His mouth is so warm.

More familiar than it should be.

But it's not enough.

His hand flexes again over the thick material, and he makes a frustrated sound.

"Gotta get you out of this fucking suit," he growls.

"Please."

Luke spins me around so I'm facing the lockers. Though they're really more like individual seats with cubbies above and below.

The bench seat is padded, and dividers stick out like little walls between each spot, creating a private space for each player if they were sitting.

The name *Anders* is painted on the back wall underneath the upper shelf.

The tips of my skates are against the toe guard at the bottom of the bench, and I brace my palms on the dividers, holding myself upright so Luke can unzip me.

But instead of unzipping me, he grabs my butt again, with both hands this time.

"Fuck, Princess, I love your ass."

"Focus, Luke," I say with a half laugh, half moan.

He groans as he grips me, his fingers pressing through the fabric into my soft cheeks.

Finally, he lets go and moves his hands up to the zipper at the back of my neck.

I can feel him pulling it down, can feel the cool air as it hits my overheated skin, but the suit isn't loosening at the collar.

"Luke."

His fingers drag over my bare skin, following the zipper, until they catch on the band of my thong. "Fuck." He stretches the word out. "You were out there, in front of thousands, wearing nothing but a bra and this skimpy ass pair of panties under this?"

I nod. "It wouldn't fit over my clothes."

Luke grips the back of my thong and tugs, pulling the fabric snug over my pussy.

"Luke," I gasp.

"Yeah, Green Eyes?"

Every time he uses one of his pet names for me, my brain glitches.

"The neck," I pant. "You gotta undo it."

"Hmm?"

I tip my head forward, making my hair slide out of the way, showing whatever clasp is at the top.

Luke drags his hands up my bare back until I can feel a slight tug around the collar of the suit.

There's another tug, and Luke's hot breath is on the back of my neck as he leans closer and presses his hard length against my ass.

The collar doesn't loosen.

My mittened hands curl around the edges of the dividers gripping it tighter.

Luke groans and presses his whole body against my back, letting go of the clasp and sliding his left hand down my left arm until his hand is over my furry white paw.

His left hand. Adorned with a bright pink silicone ring.

"I couldn't take it off," he whispers. "Tell me you're wearing yours too."

Luke's other hand spans across my stomach, holding me in place as he grinds into me.

"I am," I whisper back. "I didn't want to wear it. I'm still mad at you."

He nuzzles against my hair. "You should be. I've been a stupid dick. *I'm sorry* isn't enough."

"I'm sorry too." I mean it. "I could have handled everything differently. I have so much to tell you."

He presses his lips against my ear. "Tell me later. Let me get inside you now."

Electricity dances up my spine at his words, and I don't care how bad of an idea it is.

"Get me out of this damn suit and you can have me," I pant.

The hand on my stomach flexes, and he holds me tighter. "I don't have a condom, but I haven't been with anyone but you since the season started and we had our physicals."

More heat flares in my belly.

We should've had this conversation in Vegas since we didn't use protection then either. But...

"It's, um, been a while since—" I start.

"Don't bother finishing that sentence, Princess, unless you plan to give me a name and a free pass to beat the shit out of the last man who touched what's mine."

Touched what's mine.

I sway.

I literally sway on my skates.

"Luke."

The hand over mine drags back up my arm.

I look back at him over my shoulder. "I'm on birth control."

His jaw clenches, and I feel his hips jerk.

Luke tears his eyes from mine and goes back to working on

the clasp.

It still doesn't loosen.

"What the fuck is this made of?" Luke pulls on the material. "Is there a secret to getting it unclipped?"

I almost tell him I don't know, that the original Blizz was the one to help me with the collar and secure the head. But it seems like it might be a bad idea to tell him about that right now. Especially since he knows I'm practically naked under here.

So, instead, I tell him to hurry.

"I'm trying," he grunts.

I tilt my hips, pressing my ass into him.

Now that we've started, I need to finish. I need him to fulfill his promise and get inside me.

I'm confident we'll work everything else out between us. We aren't there yet, but the fact that he was so eager to apologize tells me we can do it. We can talk it out. But right now, I don't need talking.

Right now, I need his hands on me.

"Luke. Please."

This pull between us hasn't dimmed at all in our time apart; it's grown brighter. And I'm about to burn up.

His hands leave the collar and grip my hips so he can rock against me. "Say that again, Princess. Say please again."

I lean forward, bending my arms and keeping my hands braced on the dividers. I arch my back, still clothed but presenting myself to him.

"Please, Luke," I beg. "I need you."

His hands drop away.

I hear the sounds of a belt being undone and a zipper being yanked down. And then his hands are back on my yeti suit.

Except he's not gripping the collar.

Fingers brush against the top of my ass as Luke grips the

material on either side of the zipper, and then he pulls.

The suit splits with a loud tearing sound.

Air rushes in between my legs.

Luke tore the fabric the exact way I was afraid it would tear every time I fell down. Split right down the ass. Revealing everything.

"Fucking hell."

A hand tugs at my underwear, pulling it to the side and exposing me.

Fingers trail down my cheek until they reach my center.

"So fucking wet." Luke groans as he drags his fingertips through my slickness.

My body is trembling.

He's touching me where I need him. But I need *him*.

Then his fingers slide away, and something blunt bumps into my entrance.

I tense, then relax, and he pushes just the smallest bit inside me.

I drop my head forward and close my eyes in anticipation.

But he doesn't move.

He just keeps that first inch inside me.

Stretching me.

I try to push back, but the hand holding my underwear splays across my ass, preventing me from deepening our connection.

"Luke," I whine.

His hand lifts and slaps back down.

I clench. Squeezing the head of his cock in my entrance.

His groan is so low it gives me shivers.

"You know how to ask," he grits out.

I focus on breathing and gathering the letters of the word he wants. "Please."

It's the magic word.

My new favorite word.

Because the second I say it, Luke starts to push forward.

We've hardly even touched, and I'm moments from imploding.

His dick is so hard, so thick...

With one unexpected thrust, he sinks himself in to the hilt.

Together, we make low noises of pleasure.

"Christ." He pulls his hips back, then snaps forward. "Fuck." He does it again.

I think I say his name, but I'm struggling to breathe.

I'm so full.

Luke slides his right hand around my hip, inside my suit.

His fingertips brush against my clit, and I can feel the buildup already.

He leans against my back, moving his left hand so it's braced right above mine on the divider wall.

Luke keeps moving.

Keeps thrusting in and out.

Keeps holding me steady with his fingers on my clit and his palm pressed into my softness right above my pussy. Like he can feel himself inside me.

Luke tilts his hips and hits even deeper.

I cry out.

"These fucking skates." His shoes bump into the outside of my ice skates. Trapping me further. "Make you the perfect height for this." He drags his cock out, then pushes it back in. "Gonna buy you so many pairs."

I press back into him.

His body heat is making me too hot, but I can't move away.

I don't even try.

His fingers start to rub circles, and I'm so close.

"What the fuck?" A voice booms from somewhere in the locker room, and we freeze.

Chapter 85

Luke

I whip my head over to find Jackson standing in the entrance to the locker room, looking furious.

"Are you fucking Blizz?" He's practically shouting.

From his angle, he can't see Natalie's head bowed into the locker, just the furry-covered body in front of mine.

I crowd farther over her back, making sure Jackson can't see any inch of her bare skin.

"Get the fuck out!" I snap back at Jackson, too aware that I'm seconds away from blowing my load, friend watching or not.

"No." He points a finger at me. "Pull out of Blizz, right fucking now."

Jesus Christ.

"Jackson." I grit my teeth and clench my stomach. "Get out."

"You're married!" he booms. "And I'm not friends with fucking cheaters!"

Oh my god.

I need him to leave.

"It's me," Natalie squeaks.

Jackson's eyes go wide as his gaze leaves mine to look at the body in front of me. But when he realizes what he's doing, he jerks his eyes up to the ceiling.

"Uh…" He places his hands on his hips, keeping his eyes averted. "Natalie?"

"Yep!" She sorta giggles after she says it, and it makes her pussy spasm around my cock.

I groan and drop my forehead to her back. "Jackson, get the fuck out before you witness something neither of us will recover from."

Natalie laughs again.

I groan again.

And Jackson makes a sound that can only be described as uncomfortable before I hear his retreating footsteps.

Natalie lets out a louder laugh. "I can't believe—"

I pinch her clit, and her words cut off in a yelp.

"I can't believe you almost made me come in front of my friend." I stay draped over her as I start to thrust again. "And if you laugh every single time I fuck you, I'm gonna get a complex."

She starts to snicker, but it turns into a groan when I roll my fingers against her bundle of nerves.

"Time to come, my dirty little Hummingbird." I keep moving my hips. "Come all over my dick before someone else catches us."

Her heat tightens around me, and I push in as far as I can go.

With one last brush of my fingers, she goes over the edge.

I don't let up, pressing circles around her clit as her body convulses.

Then she cries my name, and it's the push I need.

My balls tighten, and I pull my fingers away from her pussy so I can hug her to me as I fill her with my release.

I come so hard each pulse of my cock feels like a tiny heart attack.

Slumping against her, I inhale her scent. That sweet, floral hint her hair always has.

This time, I hear the door when it creaks open.

"You mind hurrying up?" Jackson's annoyed voice calls from the doorway.

"You mind not listening?" I shout back.

"You mind thanking me for telling the cleaning crew to come back in fifteen minutes?"

Okay, he has a point.

"Thank you!" I call back as I start to unwrap myself from around Natalie.

Leaning back, but still lodged inside her, I take in Natalie.

Hair a mess. White paws clinging to the wood panels. Spine exposed. Yeti butt torn open. Thong ruined.

As I stare, I slip free from her body and watch our combined mess ruin the Blizz suit even more.

My sensitive dick twitches.

"I think I have a new fetish."

Natalie clenches her thighs together.

A shudder of pleasure rolls through me at the sight. "Okay, *I know* I have a new fetish."

"Luke," Natalie whines.

"Right." I take a wobbly step back.

I think for a moment. "Hold on a second."

"Not exactly going anywhere," Natalie snarks. And I grin as I rush across the locker room, tucking my dick back into my pants as I go.

A few seconds later, I'm back with a pair of scissors.

They're for cutting stick tape, but they should also work on a yeti suit.

"Okay, hold still."

Even as I say it, Natalie turns her head to look back.

I pull the scissors back. "Princess, these are sharp. I won't cut you, but you need to stand still."

She turns her head forward.

I make sure her hair is out of the way, then I cut through the collar of the suit, around the clasp that won't come undone.

As soon as the neck is free, I help Natalie shimmy the fur down her arms.

When she slips her hand out of the material, something swells inside my chest. Not able to help myself, I reach out and touch her wedding band with my fingertips.

She gives me a shy smile as she turns to face me. But when I bend down to kiss her, she holds me off with her other hand. "We're in a hurry, remember?"

"Oh, right."

"Can you untie my skates please?" There's a wince in her voice. "They're killing me."

"Shit, sorry." I crouch down in front of her. "Sit down while I do this."

"I can't," she whispers. "I'll make a mess."

I try not to smile, but I fail. "We've already made a mess, and this suit is coming home with us. So, sit down."

She rolls her eyes but gathers up the material, tucking it underneath her. Then she plops down onto the seat in my locker.

Blizz from the waist down, topless with her big tits spilling out of her bra from the waist up... God, she looks fucking perfect.

"Luke!" she snaps.

"Yep, right, I'm on it. As soon as we're out of here, I need the story," I say as I quickly untie both her skates.

When I see the way she gingerly places her feet on the ground, I instantly feel like a piece of shit.

"Fuck, I'm so sorry, Princess. I shouldn't have made you stand in those."

I'm still looking at her feet, hoping they're okay under her thin gray socks, when she tugs on my hair.

I bring my eyes up to meet hers.

"Hey." Her voice is soft. "I have no regrets." She smiles, then uses my shoulders to help herself stand. "Now, please tell me there's a bathroom in here."

Chapter 86

Natalie

"I don't think you can just keep that," I tell Luke as he bundles the torn Blizz suit under his arm.

He places his palm on my back. "I'm pretty sure no one is going to want to use it anymore. Unless they don't mind their ass hanging out of it."

I snort and shake my head.

I'll figure out a way to replace it, at least.

Dressed in my own clothes again, we head toward the door.

I've pulled my hair up and am walking as normally as possible, considering how tired and sore my body is. But if we run into anyone, I'm sure I look just as deliciously fucked as I feel.

Thankfully the hallway is empty when Luke opens the door, and I don't have to face the man who walked in and saw us... like that.

Jackson seemed really chill when I met him in Vegas, but I'm not sure how chill he'll be toward me after tonight. I feel like that might have been as traumatizing for him as it was for me.

248

I move to step past Luke into the hall, but he grips my upper arm, stopping me.

"What?" I look both ways down the hall but still don't see anyone.

"When did you buy this?" His voice is soft.

It takes me a moment to realize what he's talking about.

The jersey.

The *Anders* jersey.

I lift a shoulder. "Yesterday."

His fingers flex around my upper arm.

Before he can say more, a door closes somewhere in the building, and Luke urges me forward.

We're both silent as we walk through the nearly empty arena. And I'm glad for it. The buzz of release is starting to dull, and I'm all too aware of all the things we still need to say to each other.

When we reach the player parking ramp, I let out a breath of relief. At least we avoided any more embarrassment.

Then I notice the vehicle idling several spots away and the man standing next to it.

Someone reaches out the driver's window and sets something in Jackson's hand.

I freeze.

Please, concrete gods, let the floor swallow me before he notices us.

"That Katelyn in there?" Luke calls out, standing casually like he doesn't have the yeti head and suit tucked under his arm as Jackson turns our way.

I've never wanted to murder someone more.

Jackson holds up the item. "She brought me my spare set of keys. I left mine in my locker..." Jackson lets the sentence hang, and I start to edge my way behind Luke.

"Let's go," I whisper-hiss.

Luke doesn't budge.

Jackson leans toward the open car window, then turns back to face us. "Katelyn wants to invite Natalie to their girls' brunch on Sunday."

"Aw, that's nice of her," Luke replies.

No, it's not nice.

There is no way that Jackson isn't going to tell his wife about what he walked in on in that locker room. I can literally never face that woman.

"It's at our place at eleven," Jackson tells us.

I'd rather eat gravel.

I poke at Luke's back.

I've completely hidden myself from the other couple, but I hope he can read my energy.

"I'll drop her off," Luke calls back. Like a fucking traitor. "I can pick you up at the same time if you wanna go to Puck Off for food."

I jab two fingers into Luke's lower back, but he doesn't even flinch.

"You're paying," Jackson replies.

I peek around Luke's side, and Jackson has turned back to his wife.

"For the love of god." I start to shove at Luke. "Get me into your car before I have to meet his wife looking like this."

Luke huffs a laugh but takes my hand and leads me toward some sleek-looking SUV.

The fates finally smile down on me, and I get into the vehicle, seat belt buckled and door shut, before Jackson's wife drives past us to exit the lot.

Another car passes as Luke climbs into the driver's seat, and I assume it's Jackson.

Luke tosses the Blizz suit into the back seat, then starts the engine, but as he reaches for the shifter, he pauses.

"What?" I ask, wanting him to hurry before anything else happens.

He turns toward me, his expression suddenly serious. "Will you come stay at my place tonight?"

I roll my lips, then nod.

I don't know if it's the right call. We still have *everything* to sort out. But even with my lingering anger, I want to be near him. And it'll give us time to talk.

His brows raise as he nods back. "Yeah?"

"Yeah," I breathe. "But can we swing by my hotel for some stuff first?"

"Of course." He starts to back out of the space. "Just tell me where to go."

Chapter 87

Luke

Pulling out of the parking ramp, I turn the way Natalie directs me.

"So..." I drag the word out. "Care to explain why you were Blizz tonight?"

Natalie groans. "Not really."

"Sorry," I chuckle. "I shouldn't have worded it as a question. I *need* to know."

Natalie backhands me in the stomach. "Quit laughing!"

I don't block the hit; I'm too busy wiping tears from my eyes as we wait at a red light.

"I'm sorry," I laugh. "I just..."

I didn't know about the dude she hit in the face with a T-shirt out of the T-shirt cannon. Or, more specifically, the beer cup she hit that he was in the process of drinking from.

"It was awful." She tries to sound serious, but when I glance over at her, she's smiling.

"Did he at least catch the shirt?" I take my foot off the brake when the light changes.

"Yeah. Probably soaked in beer though."

"Well, there you go. He got a free shirt and a great story." I chuckle again. "I'm sorry I missed it."

She huffs. "I'm sure it was recorded by somebody."

I sit up straighter. "I'm gonna have to search for that."

Natalie points out the windshield. "Turn up there."

Following her directions, we pull into the parking lot of a hotel not too far from her office at the Biters training facility.

The hotel is fine. It's just not the type of place I'd expect her to stay in, though I don't know why I have that assumption.

"I can just run up," she tells me.

I shift into park. "I'll come with you."

She doesn't bother arguing, and we get out of the SUV together.

We meet at the back bumper and head across the blacktop.

The lobby doors automatically slide open as we approach, and I frown.

I know it's a normal feature of a hotel, but I don't like that she's staying in such an unsecured building.

We walk through, and there isn't even a visible employee behind the desk.

It's getting late, but it's not *that late*. I'm sure the employee is sitting in some back room watching TV, but there should be someone watching who's coming and going.

I don't like this.

We get on the elevator, and I wrinkle my nose. It smells like the dance party we got married during, which is fine for a dance party, but not for a hotel elevator.

I really don't like this.

253

The cab stops on the third floor, and I follow Natalie out.

She walks us to her room, and her door is at the farthest point from any of the fire exits.

"Nope," I say as she unlocks her room.

"No what?" Natalie looks back at me as she enters the room.

"No, you aren't staying here." I follow her into the room. "Pack it all up."

She stops and turns to face me. "What are you going on about?"

"Princess." I step up to her so we're chest to chest. "I'm going on about the fact that this place isn't safe. You're coming home with me. We can argue about it later."

Her mouth drops open, then she closes it with a scowl.

Not waiting for her agreement, I cross the living room and lift one of the suitcases lining the wall. It feels empty, so I drop it onto the couch.

"Luke, I can't just move in with you."

I turn to face her. "Why not?"

She blinks at me. "Because."

"Because why?" I cross my arms.

"Because." She starts to cross her arms, then makes a face like it hurts and drops her arms back to her side.

I frown, knowing she must've banged her elbows a few times when she fell. "Come on, the quicker we go, the quicker we can get you off your feet. You know, an ice bath would be good for all those aches."

She dips her chin down and looks up at me like I just said the most absurd thing in the world. "If you think, for a single second, that I will willingly step into an ice bath, you're even more disturbed than I thought."

"Stop." I lift a shoulder and lean into it. "You're gonna make me blush."

Natalie rolls her eyes at me.

I reach for the next suitcase, this one much heavier, and roll it toward the center of the room. "Now tell me your *because*."

Natalie huffs. "I can't just move in with you *because* of lots of reasons. One being the fact that you've been ignoring me for two weeks, Luke."

The humor evaporates off me. "I'm sorry." I step closer to her, wanting to touch her but keeping my hands at my sides. "I was feeling... used. And my stupid ego couldn't move aside long enough to listen to reason. Anyone's reason. And that was shitty of me."

She bites her lip. "I... I'm sorry too. Sorry for roping you into this." She gestures between us. "This marriage. It wasn't fair of me to say... what I said to you in my office. Your reputation could've held up to the hit. It might have even been a boost for you. But I was thinking selfishly because my situation is different. Society is always harsher to women in these sorts of situations. And if the board—the Wag Corp board—heard the real version of the story, they'd do everything they could to convince my dad that I wasn't cut out for CEO."

Natalie looks so upset, and I hate it because, honestly, I'm not even mad at her anymore. I get it without her even explaining it. I don't want to run a giant corporation, but clearly, she does. And I know she's worked hard for it.

I think about the stuff her dad said. About him being disappointed.

"I heard some of what your dad said that day in the office," I tell her. "That wasn't fair. And I should have stood up for you."

She gives me a half smile. "Thanks, but that wouldn't have helped. My dad is normally really chill. But his company is his second child, so he's protective of it." Her expression changes to exasperation. "Which is why I'm the one who should run it when he retires. I can actually implement the plans I've had for years—" Natalie shakes her head. "Never mind. That's not important now."

"It is important. And I'd like to learn more about those plans," I say truthfully. "Maybe you can fill me in on some business lingo so when I have to meet your dad again, I don't sound like a total dumbass."

Natalie sighs. "I feel bad you two met the way you did. But I guess your girlfriend's dad is supposed to be scary."

She snaps her mouth shut, and I swear her cheeks pinken.

I reach up to brush my thumb over her cheek. "Are you blushing, Green Eyes?"

She swats my hand away. "No."

"You can be my girlfriend and my wife at the same time." I grip her sides and haul her against me.

Her hands land on my chest. "How does that work?"

"Girlfriend on your knees, wife in my bed."

"Luke." She gapes at me.

I hum and hold her tighter. "But if we get going again now, we aren't checking out before tomorrow." I drop my hold of her and step back. "And that just won't do."

"Certainly not," Natalie grumbles, making me smile.

I cross the suite and look around the bedroom, spotting two more suitcases. "Do you have a specific way you like to pack?"

"I'll just grab an overnight bag."

I groan as I turn around to face her. "Natalie. The world believes our whirlwind wedding story. Your dad believes it. Most of my teammates believe it. I promise I'm done being a dickhead. You said sorry about the whole blackmail thing you pulled." I watch the edge of her mouth twitch, and I know I have her. "And now that it's all over, I can admit I got a little hot with you snapping at me."

"Oh my god, Luke."

"And even though I'm starting to think that your bank

account could mop the floor with mine, I won't even charge you rent."

She shakes her head again. "Your salary history is public record, Mr. Muscles. So long as you haven't blown it all on the ponies, I think you're probably doing fine."

I smirk. "You looked me up?"

She lifts a brow. "You didn't?"

I tap my temple with my finger. "Ego, remember?"

"I remember," Natalie sighs.

"Had I looked you up, I probably could've easily figured out that your family bought the Biters. Then I wouldn't have been so taken aback when I showed up at your office." I blow out a breath. "Not that any of that should make a difference, but I think I was already off-kilter when I walked up there. A little intimidated, if I'm honest."

Natalie pulls a face. "Sorry I didn't tell you."

"Water under the bridge. And it's on me for not doing a single Google search about my wife."

She huffs. "Okay, so what's the plan? I move in. We keep up the ruse. But for how long?"

My gut reaction is to say forever.

The plan in my mind is that she moves into my place, then stays there forever.

Natalie keeps going. "We can't file for divorce now. Not until we want everyone to know about it, since there's always the risk of someone leaking it. And if we file for divorce but keep seeing each other, it will cause speculation, which only leads to issues."

"That's true," I say, because she's not wrong.

It's crazy to not want a divorce, but this is the same way I felt walking into her office that day—before it all fell apart.

I like Natalie.

We work well together.

We fuck good together.

She makes me laugh.

I make her blush.

What more do I need?

I nod once. "I know living together after just meeting is a bit… unconventional. But we're both busy. You seem to be traveling half the time for work, and I have the rest of the season that will have me flying all over, so we really won't be there together that much." I lift a shoulder. "And I'm not gonna complain about having you in my bed on the nights we are home together."

She's looking at me like she's considering what I'm saying.

I plow ahead. "If we can't get a divorce without causing a stir, then I say we don't do it at all."

Her brows raise. "You want to just stay married?"

"I think we should just forget about that part." My tone is casual.

"Forget about that part." She repeats it in a tone that tells me she thinks I'm losing it.

I hold up my hand. "We'll still be married. We'll wear the rings, show up to events together. But really, we're dating. So let's keep dating. We can do all the dating things. People will just see them as married things, and if it doesn't work, we can get a divorce when we break up."

It hurts my chest to say that last part out loud, but I'm trying to be reasonable. And I feel like this is the right direction to take with Natalie.

Chapter 88

Natalie

WHEN WE BREAK UP.

As the one who was pushing for a divorce, that sentence hurts a lot more than it should.

Luke keeps a smile on his face. "I'm not saying we will or when it would hypothetically happen. But I'm saying, why publicly end a relationship we're both still interested in having?"

I purse my lips, feeling slightly better.

It's a fair point.

"So... we just live together?" I circle back to the immediate situation.

"Why not?" He shrugs. "With our schedules, we'd hardly see each other if you got your own place. And it would be hard to pull off fake living together when your dad eventually insists on coming over and it's either at my place with none of your stuff or your place with none of my stuff."

Every single thing about this is ridiculous. But I guess, at this point, we can only control what we can control.

I let out a breath. "Okay."

Luke lifts his brows. "Okay?"

"Yeah, okay. I'll move in with you." My heart starts to race. *I'm moving in with Luke.* "But if you turn out to be someone who wakes up early and instantly wants to have a conversation, this divorce is gonna happen sooner rather than later."

It didn't take us long to pack up my stuff and load it into the back of Luke's vehicle.

I told him about the furniture and other things I have in storage, and he said we could go through his condo and decide what to swap.

And that was that.

Then, for the entire ride over here, Luke's been listening to my plans for investing in tidal energy, my outline for making Wag Corp carbon neutral, and my ideas for scholarships for STEM programs with the hopes of educating our future employees.

It's a lot. It's very big picture, long term. And it's why I was so adamant that everyone believe we're in a real, planned marriage.

I know I won't be able to single-handedly save the planet. But I believe I can do a better job trying than anyone else.

It's my passion, and as I went on and on, Luke didn't just listen, he asked questions. Responded with his own thoughts. Reacted the way I'd always dreamed a partner would.

And now, as Luke slows in front of a beautiful brick building that's going to be my home for the foreseeable future, I wonder if maybe this will turn out to be the best thing that ever happened to me.

Chapter 89

Luke

WHEELING TWO SUITCASES EACH, we walk down the hall to my condo on the fourth floor, and I try to remember what state I left my place in. It's usually pretty clean, but my bedroom and closet... not so much.

The building itself is pretty cool. It used to be a school, way back when, but they tore out the inside and remodeled the building into large industrial-style condos.

"You good?" I ask Natalie, hating that she's hauling suitcases too. But when I suggested she wait in the car while I ran up the first set, she refused, insisting that it would be easier and quicker this way.

But when I look over my shoulder, I can see she's falling behind.

And I can see her tilting her head back to look at the black metal ceiling as she walks.

"Hey, Green Eyes." I try for her attention again.

Natalie drops her chin so she's back to looking forward. "Huh?"

I smile. "We're almost there."

"Don't worry about me." As she says it, her toe catches on the floor, and she stumbles.

I let go of my luggage handles, but she catches herself with a laugh before I get to her.

"Christ, Woman," I grumble, taking the suitcases from her hands.

"What?"

I shake my head, putting the pairs of luggage back to back and pushing all four at once. "If you fall one more time, I'm going to have permanent heart damage."

She snorts. "If I fall one more time, I'm just going to stay there."

"Well, let's get you inside so you can fall into bed. You can unpack tomorrow."

Natalie makes a noise of agreement as I reach the door.

I unlock it and shove the luggage through, letting them roll a few feet on the concrete floor, then I hold the door open. And Natalie steps into my home.

Chapter 90

Natalie

I BLINK.

Then I blink again. Because Luke's condo is nothing short of stunning.

It's all blacks and woodgrains, with exposed ductwork and raw brick on the outer walls.

The feel is dark and a little edgy but also extremely cozy.

I can imagine curling up on the giant couch with a storm raging outside the black-framed windows and the Edison bulb chandeliers on low.

Iron and raw-wood shelves are built into the walls, covered with well-cared-for potted plants. And the shelves turn into a well-stocked bar situated in the space between the living area and the airy kitchen.

The whole place almost has a speakeasy feel to it. And I love it.

"Do you—"

"I love it." I cut Luke off, saying exactly what I'm thinking.

"Yeah?"

Hope tints his voice, so I turn to face him. "Luke, it's beautiful. Like..." I shake my head. "Like really beautiful."

His smile is slow. "Thanks, Princess. I'm glad you like it."

My feet throb, reminding me I need to get off them.

I toe my shoes off. "I hope you know I'm going to dig through all the cupboards tomorrow."

Luke grins at me. "I'd expect nothing less." He sees my wince when I set my bare foot on the ground and takes my hand. He leads me past the kitchen and down a hallway, leaving my luggage behind. "You can wear some of my clothes to bed."

"I... Okay." I accept because I don't want to dig through my suitcases right now.

He loosens his grip and slides his hand up my arm to my back.

When we step into his room, I have to bite my lip to keep my smile in check.

"I know it's a little messy." Luke reaches up with his other hand to rub at the back of his neck.

The room is just as stunning as the rest of the condo.

Tall ceilings painted black. Bulbs hanging down on thick cords. Built-in shelving. And clothes.

Clothes strewn across the floor.

A hoodie on the unmade bed, blending in with the black bedding.

And an overstuffed leather armchair in the corner piled high with discarded clothes.

Luke looks down at me.

I look up at him.

"So... no closets in this place?" I ask, finally letting my smile break through.

The edge of his mouth pulls up. "I just really hate laundry."

"And yet, you surround yourself with so much of it."

He snorts. "I know. It's an illness."

Luke steps away from me, stopping before the armchair and digging through the pile.

He turns back to me with a T-shirt and a pair of boxer briefs. "These are clean."

"If you say so." I take his offered clothing, then head into the attached bath.

Chapter 91

Luke

THE BATHROOM DOOR CLICKS OPEN, and I lift my gaze.

And then I just stare.

Because she looks so good. So freaking good, standing there in my clothes.

The boxer briefs are stretched tight over her thick hips, and I want to lift the hem of the long shirt to see the rest of them.

"Nice outfit." Natalie's voice is sleepy.

It takes me a second to realize she's talking about mine, and when I glance down, I smirk.

"Matching jammies aren't just for the holidays." I'm also in a Sleet T-shirt and wearing black boxers, identical to the pair I gave her.

She chuckles, but it turns into a yawn.

"Come here." I stand up from the edge of the bed and flip the covers back.

While she was getting ready for bed, I rushed around the room, shoving my dirty clothes into the hamper in the corner and pulling the blankets into place on the bed.

I know she's tired because she doesn't put up any sort of

fight, just crawls obediently into bed and flops down on her back.

I sit back on the edge of the mattress next to her. "Tell me where it hurts."

Her eyes are closed. "Everywhere."

She looks so cute.

"I'm happy to slather every inch of you, but this will work better if you give me some specifics."

Natalie opens one eye. "Slather what?"

I hold up my little jar of salve. "Trust me, this will help."

She lifts her arms. "My elbows and wrists hurt."

I unscrew the jar and scoop out a little of the thick substance.

Using the tip of my finger, I rub some around her elbow, making sure to be gentle, seeing the start of a bruise on the back of her arm. Then I move to her wrist before repeating the process on the other arm.

"Knees?" I ask, scooting down the bed.

Natalie nods. "Those are the worst. And my feet." She lets out a deep breath when I start to apply the salve to her knees. "What about you?"

"What about me?" I scoop out a little more.

"How's your shoulder?"

It takes me a second to remember that I hurt it during that Vegas game. "It's good as new."

Her little huff is adorable. "Sure it is, Mr. Muscles."

I grin at her use of that nickname.

And I grin even more when I start to massage the salve onto her foot, and she falls asleep.

Chapter 92

Natalie

"Do I HAVE TO?" I hate myself a little for how whiney I sound. But I'm stressing out.

I have no idea what to expect, and since I have to leave town tomorrow for work, I really just want to stay here and rot on the couch with Luke. Like we did yesterday.

"Sorry." My unapologetic husband lies. "All the wives are doing it."

I narrow my eyes at him, then hold my arms out. "Well, do I at least look okay?"

Luke straightens from pulling on his shoes and walks to me. "Natalie, you look beautiful. Perfect for a brunch at home with the girls." He sets his hands on my cheeks. "Or maybe you're super overdressed. I have no idea."

I stare at him. "How do you not get punched more?"

He barks out a laugh, then kisses me on the lips and steps back.

I grip the edges of my knitted cardigan.

Why don't invites come with a dress code?

It's a cool, almost-winter day outside, so I dressed for a

brunch out. But I know we're eating in. So, for the eightieth time, I wonder if I should change into something more casual or if the silk cami, sweater, and black slacks are appropriate.

I could put on a hoodie and jeans. But what if I show up and all the other women are in nice outfits? Wouldn't it be worse to be underdressed than overdressed?

Plus, I already matched my nails to my cami—both the same ice-pink color.

Luke looked at me like I was losing it when he found me lining up all my nail polish bottles on top of the outfit I'd laid over his bed. I'm not sure what surprised him more. That I paint my own nails or that I was doing it to match my outfit. But when he tried to rearrange the order I had them in, I slapped his hand away, and he left me alone.

It was a real marriage moment for us.

Making a sound in the back of my throat, I accept I just need to wear what I'm wearing.

I shuffle over to the bench next to the front door, drop down, and stare at my selection of shoes.

What shoes does someone wear to brunch with the girls?

The Sunday brunch that Luke agreed to on my behalf, in the parking garage of the arena, after his friend walked in on us having yeti sex in the locker room.

I've done my best to put that whole *Blizz sex incident* on Thursday out of my mind since it happened, distracting myself with moving into Luke's place.

Okay, well, not the sex part, just the getting caught part. No offense to Jackson Wilder, fan favorite of the Minnesota Sleet, but I would love to never see that man again in my lifetime. Maybe even two lifetimes.

Sighing, I drag my black ballet flats toward me.

Luke helped me unpack, but I only left a handful of my shoes out; the rest are in the guest room closet.

He already had it set up as an office but claims he never uses it, so I took it over for the days I work from home. And there's a second full bathroom in the condo as well, but it has nothing on the main suite, so I'm sharing that one with Luke.

If I were going to live here for real, there are a few art pieces I would get out of storage, but that seems a bit like over-stepping, no matter what Luke says. And the place really is gorgeous as it is.

With a final sigh, I tuck my phone into my purse and grab the bottle of champagne I took from Luke's pantry, then follow him out the door.

The drive from Luke's, or rather *our,* place in Minneapolis to Jackson's place in St. Paul is just long enough for my anxiety levels to really spike.

Halfway through the drive, a warm palm settles on my bouncing thigh. "What are you so nervous about, Princess?"

"I'm not nervous." My voice comes out squeaky.

Luke squeezes my leg. "You didn't even try to sound convincing. Now tell me."

"What am I nervous about?" I repeat his question and lift my hand to count off the reasons. "One, you're taking me to the home of the man who literally walked in on us fucking. And there's no way he didn't tell his wife about that."

Luke makes an amused sound. "Oh, he definitely told Katelyn."

I shoot a glare at Luke. "Two, his wife will either find it funny, think I'm trashy, or she'll be pissed about it, thinking that her husband saw parts of me he shouldn't."

The hand on my thigh flexes. "The only parts of you that Jackson saw were covered in fur. I made sure of it. Or else I'd be taking Jackson to an active construction site today to bury him in concrete rather than buy him a French dip."

That's...

I focus back out the windshield.

That shouldn't be hot.

"Two." I refocus and tick off my second finger. "This is the same apartment you told me you were hiding in while you were mad at me, so I'm betting they've heard some not-so-nice things about me."

"First," Luke grunts. "I wasn't hiding. I was sulking. There's a difference. And second, they literally always sided with you, even when I was having my liveliest of pity parties."

Luke slides his hand farther up my thigh.

I push it back toward my knee.

"Third." I let my shoulders slump. "I... I don't really have girlfriends." I glance at Luke, and at the same time, he glances at me, and I know I can admit this truth to him. "I don't really have that many *friends* at all." His thumb rubs small circles over my jeans. "I work too much. I travel too much. I have work acquaintances who are friendly. I have specific people I tend to gravitate toward during happy hours or work dinners, but none of them are my *friends*. We wouldn't meet up for brunch on the weekend."

Luke lifts his hand to grab mine.

He entwines our fingers and settles our hands back on my lap. "I'm your friend, Little Royal."

Something thick drapes over my shoulders, and that spot between my eyes feels tight.

"And I'm great at gossiping," Luke adds, squeezing my fingers.

I bite down on my lip.

"Thanks, Player," I whisper.

"And if you want to complain about me, I'm okay listening to that too."

His words should be silly, but they aren't. Because I think he knows I'm telling the truth.

These past two weeks, when he was with Jackson, I was in that hotel room. Alone. Without a soul to confide in.

Luke pulls to a stop at the curb in front of a fancy building, puts the vehicle into park, then turns in his seat to face me.

"I'm sorry." He squeezes my hand in his. "I'm really fucking sorry I didn't just listen. If..." Luke glances past me to the building and shakes his head. "It was annoying having those two telling me their opinions every time I saw them, but I don't know what I would've done if I couldn't talk to anyone about it. And I feel like an even bigger piece of shit knowing you had to deal with it by yourself."

"Luke," I sigh.

"No." He stops me. "I know we spent half the weekend talking about how we both wish we'd handled it differently, but let me apologize this one last time."

I roll my lips together and nod once.

"I'm sorry, Natalie. You're not alone anymore. I might be an idiot sometimes, but I'll always be your friend. Okay?"

I nod once, needing to keep my composure.

The corner of Luke's mouth pulls up. "Now you're going to go in there, and you're going to have a good time. And when I pick you up in a few hours, you're going to climb into that seat with a whole set of new friends."

I take a breath.

Then a second.

"Thank you," I say quietly, wishing there was a better phrase for how much his words mean to me.

The other side of his mouth tips up. "That's what friends are for." *This man.* "Now hurry up and give me a kiss before Jackson taps on your window."

Chapter 93

Luke

As I HOPED, my words startle Natalie, snapping her out of her heavy thoughts.

Her eyes widen as she jerks her head around to look out the passenger window.

He's not there—yet.

"Luke!" She breaks her hold of my hand and shoves at my chest.

"What?" I laugh.

"I don't want to see him!" She scrambles to unbuckle herself, then leans forward and grabs the bottle between her feet.

"I know he's hideous but—"

She shoves at my chest again with her free hand, but this time I catch it.

I rotate her hand, then lean down and press a kiss over the pulse point in her wrist.

"You're the worst," she says without heat.

"Go have a nice brunch." I let her go. "Top floor, closest door to the left when you get off the elevator."

The way she looks at me warms every bit of my insides.

It's appreciation. And fondness.

Natalie opens the door, and I try my best to hold in a laugh when she lets out a little yelp, seeing Jackson standing on the sidewalk.

He opens his mouth, but Natalie speaks first, letting out a high-pitched "Hi!" before rushing past him toward the building.

Chapter 94

Natalie

CHEEKS RED from embarrassment over seeing Jackson again, I push through the doors and enter the building.

The lobby is pristine, with high ceilings and a manned front desk.

It's very high end and the sort of place I expected Luke to live in.

The man behind the desk smiles at me. "Mrs. Anders?"

I swallow and nod. "That's me."

"Mr. Wilder told me to expect you." He tips his head toward the elevator bank. "Have a nice brunch."

Trying not to feel awkward about the personal greeting, I thank him and move into the large alcove.

Out of sight from the front desk guy, I take an extra moment to breathe before hitting the button for the elevator.

Luke wouldn't be sending me in here if he didn't think I'd get along with these women.

It's just brunch.

I remind myself again as I press the button to summon the elevator.

My attention turns back out the glass front doors to the sidewalk.

Luke's SUV is gone, but another car is in its place. The blue sedan is parked as the driver and passenger make out.

Having recently been caught in a compromising condition —twice, if we want to include that damn video—I should probably look away.

Just as I convince myself to stop, they also stop, and the woman climbs out of the car.

And heads toward the building.

I avert my eyes, but just as the elevator dings its arrival, I hear the front doors open.

I hear a female say, "Hey, Henry. How's your morning?"

"Going just fine," the doorman replies. He might say more, but his voice doesn't carry as I step into the elevator.

I can hear the woman's footsteps, and as much as I don't want to, I place my hand against the edge of the door, holding it open.

A pretty brunette, in an outfit similar to mine, smiles as she steps onto the elevator with me. "Thanks," she exhales.

"No problem." I take my hand away from the door, and they slide closed. "What floor?"

"The—" She glances at the buttons. "The same one as you, apparently."

My smile back to her feels awkward, and I drop my eyes to study the floor.

The woman makes a humming sound in her throat. "All Sundays should start with champagne."

My smile is more natural this time. "They really should. Probably Mondays too."

She chuckles, and I relax a tiny bit more.

I can do small talk with strangers. And I need to remember that's what this brunch is: small talk with strangers.

The ride is blissfully quick, and when the doors slide open, I step out.

I smile at the stranger again and plan to tell her to have a nice day, but she's turning the same way I am.

I wish I'd waited for her to get off first because now I have to slow for my destination and wait for her to pass and...

She's slowing too.

We look at each other, then her eyes widen. "Oh my god, it's you!"

My own eyes widen. "Me?"

She nods. "You're the heir—" She cuts herself off, and I feel my face blush. She was going to say heiress. As in The Hockey Player and the Heiress video.

"I'm Natalie," I squeak, holding out my free hand. "Luke's wife."

She takes my hand. "Steph. Jackson's sister."

I swear my heart stops for a moment.

No one told me Jackson had a sister. Or that she'd be here.

He wouldn't tell her about the Blizz thing, would he?

"Oh my god, please don't look so scared." Steph laughs. "Promise I'm a last-minute add-on, but it's just me."

"Just you?"

"Well, just me and then the other three. But I just mean that they're always here, so Luke probably told you about them. I make it when I can. And I'm glad I did, Miss Champagne." She grins as she knocks on the door. "For real, though, these ladies are the best. You have nothing to worry about."

I have nothing to worry about.

The door swings open before us, and a woman about my height, with hair a little lighter than Steph's, beams at me.

"Hi!" She holds her hand out. "I'm Katelyn."

Katelyn.

As in Jackson Wilder's wife.

"Hello." My voice almost sounds even. "I'm Natalie."

Katelyn smiles as she presses her lips together, and I know she's thinking about it.

She's thinking about *it*, and she's trying not to laugh.

Steph keeps me from having to address *the it* when she throws her arms around Katelyn in an exaggerated hug. "Sister, it's been too long."

Katelyn laughs and hugs her back. "Maybe if you weren't so busy working all the time, I'd see you more."

Ending the embrace, they step into the apartment, gesturing for me to follow.

As we walk through the entryway and toward the kitchen, I try to make conversation.

"Are you married to one of the hockey players too?" I ask Steph while I take in the large, contemporary, open living space.

"No." She shakes her head. "Just a sister to one."

"Oh, um..." *Ask normal questions.* "What does your husband do? Or boyfriend... Sorry, I shouldn't assume who he is."

We've reached the kitchen now, and the scent of warm cinnamon makes my mouth water.

"I don't have a boyfriend," Steph says quickly.

"No, no, what are *you* talking about?" Katelyn narrows her eyes at me.

"I just meant the guy..." I trail off.

"Did Meghan make her coffee cake today?" Steph asks loudly, trying to change the topic but making herself sound guilty.

I look back and forth between Steph and Katelyn, biting my lip.

Two more women approach from the far side of the large

island, and I suddenly feel like I said something I shouldn't have.

"Whoa, whoa, whoa." A beautiful woman with long red hair, in black leggings and a tie-dye hoodie, steps up to our little group. "Hi, I'm Meghan." She greets me with a wide smile, then turns to face Steph. "Do you have a secret boyfriend?"

Secret boyfriend?

"What? No." Steph's voice is as high as mine was when I saw Jackson.

Okay, I really shouldn't have said anything.

The redhead, Meghan, turns back to me. "Sorry, I know I'm being rude, but do you know something that would lead you to believe she is seeing someone?"

"I—"

Steph groans and tips her head back. "Would you please not interrogate the new girl? We want her to like us."

I'm back to biting my lip.

Nothing says good first impression like outing Jackson's sister for being in a relationship.

When the parallel hits me, that this is quite literally what happened to me and Luke with that damn video, I feel even worse.

"I'm sorry," I blurt out. "I must be mistaken."

Steph groans some more. "No, it's fine. I'm assuming you saw us in the car." She sighs. "And that's on me for being sloppy."

"What car?" A blond in a bright blue long-sleeved wrap dress steps up, completing the circle. She lifts a hand to wave at me. "Hi."

I lift a hand back. "Hello."

"What was happening in the car?" Meghan moves her gaze between me and Steph.

"Kissing," Steph says, like it's the most boring thing in the world. "I was kissing my... man, in the car, outside the building."

"I didn't mean to watch." My eyes widen. "Look." I correct myself. "I wasn't watching. Not like..."

The blond woman snickers. Then she holds her hand over her mouth. "Sorry. Sorry."

At my side, Katelyn bumps me with her elbow. "Giggles over there is Izzy. She's a financial adviser who works mainly with athletes. And she's married to Zach Hunt."

My brows go up.

Zach was the one in the penalty box with Luke in Vegas, and thinking of him married to this brainy, curvy blond makes me smile.

"You know I'm married to Jackson, and I work from home as a copy editor for a publisher that mostly does romance," Katelyn tells me, and I make a note to ask her more about her job later.

Then Katelyn points to Meghan, who is still trying to get Steph to tell her more about the man in the car. "Megs has her own event-planning business. So if you have a corporate thing or something you need help with, she's your girl. And she's married to Ash LeBlanc, the goalie."

Ash is the one Luke is no longer allowed to make bets with.

Meghan, overhearing, rolls her eyes. "Fair warning, our husbands become morons when they're together."

A laugh jumps out of me, and I slam my mouth shut.

"Is the food ready?" Steph reaches for the bottle in my hand, and I let her take it. "We brought champagne."

I smile at Steph's use of the word *we*.

Meghan side-eyes Steph. "We're not done with this conversation."

Steph lifts her chin. "When I've hidden this relationship as long as you hid yours with Ash, then you can talk shit to me."

Katelyn snorts out a laugh. "She has you there."

Chapter 95

Sugar

WHILE WE ALL load up our plates with fresh sourdough, soft scrambled eggs, cream cheese, and smoked salmon, Katelyn keeps up conversation with Natalie, asking how she likes Minnesota.

We all know the basics of what happened. Because of our gossiping husbands. But I still have so many questions.

I won't ask them though. Not yet. Because I'm familiar with the look in Natalie's eyes. It's a look I carried for a long time.

It's the look of someone who doesn't have close friends.

And it's hard to make new ones. The idea can be terrifying, and trying to infiltrate an established friend group can seem impossible. But I did it. And she seems like she'll fit in just fine.

Plus, I brought a little welcome gift for Natalie. Just something small, but maybe it will help her feel more welcome.

Katelyn already has the carafes of coffee and juice on the table, and Meghan snags champagne glasses out of the cupboard while Steph pops the top of the bottle and pours.

We take the drinks and our plates to the table, and once everyone is seated, I lift my glass.

"To new friends." I smile.

Natalie is seated across from me, and I hope I'm not trying too hard. I don't want to weird her out. But she seems to be relaxing. Even if it's just a little bit.

As everyone starts to dig in, I reach under my chair and pull the gift out of my purse. I hold it in my lap so it's hidden by the table.

"Okay, so I know this might be..." I shift in my seat. "Silly. But I just wanted to give you something to welcome you to Minnesota."

Natalie sits up straighter, her brows rising on her pretty face. "You got me a gift?"

I nod.

Then I hand her the stuffed Sleet mascot.

A fuzzy little Blizz.

Natalie's eyes widen.

And Katelyn dissolves into laughter.

I look between them. "What?"

Chapter 96

Natalie

MY FACE literally bursts into flames as I take the Blizz stuffie from Izzy's hands.

Okay, not literally, but it might as well, because the way Katelyn is laughing means she knows.

Like *she knows*.

"I'm sorry," Katelyn says. But she's still laughing, so it's kind of hard to understand her.

"What's so funny?" Izzy furrows her brow.

I instantly feel bad for our reactions to her gift. She clearly didn't buy this as a joke but as a nice gesture.

I clear my throat. "Thanks, uh, thank you. This is really nice."

"You're welcome." Izzy is still looking at Katelyn, who is slowly composing herself. "What am I missing?"

I look at Katelyn, but she's wiping tears off her cheeks and not making eye contact with me.

Then I glance at Meghan and Steph, who are both watching us like they also have no idea what's going on.

"I don't get what's so funny," Steph says. "He's so cute and furry."

Katelyn loses it again.

And... I start to laugh.

Because, *oh my god, she knows.*

I lift Blizz and press my face into his belly as I try not to choke on my own laughter.

It's all just so ridiculous.

I shake my head at myself, even as I ready to lower the yeti.

You make friends by sharing, right?

Chapter 97

Banshee

I BLINK.

Then I blink again.

Because did this corporate big shot just say what I think she said?

"You were doing it with the Blizz suit on?" Izzy squeaks out the question I was thinking.

Only I wouldn't have used the phrase *doing it*.

Natalie—the girl with the expensive clothes and dark hair pulled back into a perfect ponytail—nods. Confirming she had sex with Luke in the locker room while stuck in the motherfucking Blizz costume.

Steph is trying so hard not to laugh, and I'm afraid she might throw up.

I scoot my chair a few inches away from her.

"Jackson feels terrible, by the way," Katelyn says to Natalie. "And he wants you to know he didn't see anything, you know, that he shouldn't have. He really thought it was the Blizz dude in the costume."

"Wait, did Jackson walk in on you?" Steph grips the table like she might tip over.

Natalie hugs the little Blizz to her chest, probably for support. "He did. And he was *mad*."

"Like Kiss Cam mad?" Izzy asks.

Natalie gives a little frown. "I don't know what that means."

Katelyn waves the question off. "He was mad because he thought Luke was cheating on you."

Natalie chuckles. "Yeah, that was apparent. Especially when he shouted at Luke to *pull out of Blizz*."

That one gets me, and I lose my battle against laughter as Steph almost falls out of her chair.

Izzy is blushing, but I see the gleam in her eye. She's as intrigued as the rest of us.

"Question." I hold up my hand.

"Yes, Meghan?" Katelyn calls on me.

"You said you were stuck in the suit," I ask, and Natalie slides the yeti higher over her mouth like she's going to hide behind it. "Did you put it on just for sex?"

"Meghan," Izzy whisper-hisses.

"What?" I hiss back.

"It's a fair question." Natalie lets out a big breath. "I did not."

"Then why...?" I let my question linger.

Natalie glances around the table before her green eyes move back to me. "I was Blizz the whole time. Like, the whole game."

Chapter 98

Natalie

MEGHAN BLINKS AT ME.

They all blink at me.

Then Izzy gasps. "You fell so much!"

And like a switch was flipped, I see them all remember. Because, of course, they would have been there.

Two hours, one bottle of bubbly, three rounds of coffee, and an endless serving of coffee cake later, I think I can say this has been one of the best afternoons of my life.

The entire story came out.

How I sprained that guy's ankle. How I want to burn that godforsaken flag when the season is over. How Luke and I made up, and everything that happened before that—in Vegas, in my office. I told them my reasoning and my plans for the future.

I told them everything.

And it was... wonderful.

They all understood.

They got where I was coming from. They supported my decisions. They cursed out Luke when I needed them to. And they *awwed* when I told them about falling asleep while he rubbed my feet.

Katelyn sighs. "I'm so glad you're working things out. I don't know if Luke has ever had a serious girlfriend, but he's been talking about wanting one for the past, like, year."

I make a face. "Is that a nice way of saying he slept around a lot?"

Katelyn shakes her head. "He really didn't. Not that I know of. I just know his family is always in his ear, telling him to be careful of women who want him for his money."

"That trust fund should shut them up." Izzy snorts, then bolts straight up in her chair. "Oh my god, I'm so sorry. That was super rude."

I laugh. "It's not rude. My finances are pretty much public knowledge."

"Is it rude to ask how much it's for?" Steph asks.

"Stephanie!" Izzy does her loud whisper again.

"What? I'm not asking her for money." Steph lifts her hands. "She said it was public knowledge. Either I google it later, or I just ask her now."

I shrug. "The trust is for one hundred million."

I don't mention that I haven't needed to touch the trust, that I have enough funds elsewhere and my salary more than covers my living expenses.

Steph lets out a happy laugh. "Yeah, I'd say that should shut Luke's family up."

Meghan drums her fingers on the table. "I have one last question."

"Okay."

She narrows her eyes at me. "What does he call you?"

"Um, what?"

Meghan gestures to Izzy and Katelyn. "All these hockey players seem to give out nicknames. What's yours?"

I think of the very first time we met and can't stop my smile. "He calls me Princess."

While the other girls make happy sounds, Meghan throws up her hands. "Ash is such a dick!"

Not understanding why this is funny, I look around the table.

"Don't ask." Meghan answers my unasked question as she rises from the table. "Okay, who wants to bring some coffee cake home?"

I roll my lips together, not wanting to seem greedy, but when she tips her head my way, I nod. "Yes, please."

Chapter 99

Kitten

THE FRONT DOOR closes behind Steph, and we all stop talking.

"We're following her, right?" Meghan asks.

"Uh, duh," I reply, setting down the pan I was rinsing off.
We were in the middle of putting food away when Steph *suddenly had to leave.*

None of us said anything to stop her, but it's obvious her secret boyfriend is picking her up. And we wouldn't be friends if we weren't nosy. So we're gonna find out.

Natalie looks at her phone. "Luke messaged me a few minutes ago saying they're on their way back."

"Perfect." Izzy hands her a container of coffee cake. "We're not spying; we're just walking Natalie down."

"Uh-huh, sure. Let's call it that." Meghan wipes off her hands, and we all start toward the front door.

I press my ear to the door, waiting to hear the ding of the elevator.

Natalie has a guilty look on her face, but before I can tell her not to worry, Izzy beats me to it.

"I know this seems crazy, but this is what we do." Izzy places her hand on Natalie's arm. "What's the point of friends if they aren't all up in your business?"

"She's right. This isn't an invasion of privacy. If anything, she's in the wrong for hiding it from us. Steph should know better," I tell her. Then I hold up my hand. "I hear the elevator."

I wait another few seconds before opening the door as quietly as possible.

When I stick my head out into the hall, I see the elevator doors slide closed.

I swing the door all the way open. "Let's go."

Meghan rushes out first and runs to the elevator bank to press the call button.

"Want me to carry something?" I ask Natalie.

She has the Blizz stuffie under her arm, the container of food in one hand, and her purse in the other.

"I'm good." She squeezes the yeti tighter.

The chime alerts us to the elevator opening, and Meghan ushers everyone on board.

I end up in the back corner, behind Izzy and Natalie.

There's something so similar about the two of them. Maybe it's the upbringing. Being close with their dads. Working in high-stress careers. But I can see the way Izzy is taking Natalie under her wing, and it's adorable.

"I know a guy who owns a solar company," Izzy tells Natalie. "He's a retired football player, lives here in the cities. I can introduce you if you want."

Natalie is nodding before Izzy finishes. "That'd be great. Local connections are good to have."

As the elevator starts to slow, everyone goes silent.

Meghan holds a finger to her lips, then leans out to see if she can see Steph.

"Hurry!" she suddenly shouts, then sprints out of the elevator.

This is probably a really bad introduction to our friend group, but I put a hand on both Natalie's and Izzy's backs and urge them out.

It's so ridiculous. Izzy is in her wedge heels. Natalie with her hands full. And I'm urging us all to run across the nice, slightly stuck-up lobby of my building.

Meghan reaches the doors, then stops.

Her mouth drops open.

"What?" I rush past the other two, fully invested in catching Steph.

"Oh my god," Meghan gasps. Then she starts to laugh.

I reach the doors and shove them open. All four of us spill out on the sidewalk just in time to see Steph climbing into a car. One that I recognize.

"Alex?" I screech.

Steph freezes, but she doesn't look back. And a second later, she dives the rest of the way into the passenger seat.

One of my unlaced tennis shoes flies off my foot as I try to run to catch up. But the man with hair the same color as mine steps on the gas the second Steph shuts her door.

Standing there, in the middle of the sidewalk, with one shoe on, I gape.

"Hey, Kitten, what's going on?" My husband's deep voice surprises me.

I spin around to find Jackson standing behind me with a smile on his face.

I shake my head. "Oh, ya know. Just your sister hiding a relationship from us."

His smile drops. "What? With who?"

I point in the direction the car just took off in. "My brother."

Jackson narrows his eyes. "If he doesn't marry her, I'm going to kill him."

Chapter 100

Natalie

I LOOK around for my husband, but I don't see him.

I drop my eyes to my phone and use my thumb to tap the screen, but there aren't any new texts from Luke.

I look back at the cars on the street. If Jackson is back, Luke has to be here, but I don't—

A heavy arm drapes across my shoulders.

"Looking for someone?" Luke's voice sends warmth down my spine.

I tip my head back to look at him as I lean into his side. "Yeah, maybe you've seen him. He's tall, handsome, covered in tattoos."

Luke hums. "I keep telling you, Wife. Ash is taken."

"Why are you talking about me?" A deep voice rumbles from behind us.

Luke brings me with him as he turns to face his friend. "Just saying how ugly you are."

A laugh pops out of me, and I press my lips together when Luke drops his narrowed gaze on me.

I only have eyes for Luke. My libido is apparently broken

for any man who isn't mine, but even a dead person could appreciate how handsome Ash LeBlanc is.

"Sure you were," Ash replies in that low voice of his before he dips his head in my direction. "Nice to see you again, Natalie. Sorry for your misfortune of marrying this dumbass."

Luke kicks out at Ash's leg, but the goalie jumps away before any contact is made.

"Like I said, morons." Meghan steps up next to her husband, reaching up and pinching one of his nipples.

The big man yelps and puts her in a headlock. "I told you, that one isn't healed yet."

I widen my eyes at Luke, but he just shakes his head, reaches down, and takes the container of food out of my hand with his free one. "If they're sending you home with some of Meghan's baking, then it must've gone well." His voice is quiet, just for me.

I smile up at him. "It did."

"So you had a good time?" he asks, making sure.

And that question... that reiteration... it changes something.

The hummingbird in my ribcage flaps over to my heart, rips off a little corner with her beak, and tucks it under her wing, saving it for him.

I have to swallow before I can answer. "Such a good time."

He lifts the hand on my shoulder and brushes his thumb across my cheek. "I'm glad."

Needing to break the tension building inside my chest, I use my now free hand to pull Blizz out from his spot tucked under my arm. "Izzy brought me a gift."

Luke looks at the gift. Then looks again.

As if summoned, Izzy and her husband, Zach, appear before us, with Jackson and Katelyn next to them. The whole group stands on the sidewalk in front of Jackson and Katelyn's building.

Luke looks at Jackson. "You told Zach?"

He sounds a little mad, clearly having gotten the wrong impression. Which is dense of him since I just said how good of a time I had.

"No, Luke—" I try to interrupt.

"Told me what?" Zach asks before he smiles at me. "Hey, Natalie."

"Hi." I sort of grimace the greeting even though I don't mean to.

"I didn't tell him anything." Jackson cuts in, and I can tell he's making a point not to make eye contact with me. Which I appreciate.

"What the hell are you guys talking about?" Ash chimes in, with Meghan tucked into his side.

"The locker room," Luke says, while I poke him in the side and say, "Nothing."

Luke reaches his arm farther around my neck so he can grab Blizz out of my grip and hold it up. "If you guys want to harass me over the *Blizz bang*, that's fine. But leave Natalie out of it."

"Luke!" I snap.

But I'm once again drowned out because now all the girls are snickering.

I try not to look at Jackson, but I can't help it as I glance his way, and I notice that his cheeks are getting pink. Though probably not as pink as mine.

Zach's eyes are wide. "I'm sorry, but the *Blizz bang*? What the fuck are you talking about?"

Luke looks from Zach to Jackson. "You didn't tell him?"

Jackson shakes his head, and instead of looking embarrassed, he just looks like he's trying not to laugh.

Ash isn't as successful, barking out a loud noise that makes me jump.

"Meghan!" Izzy hisses because Ash is leaning down with his ear near Meghan's mouth.

Meghan cringes but shrugs. "Sorry, I tell him everything."

"I would like it if someone would tell me everything." Zach glares around the group.

Jackson reaches out and claps Zach on the shoulder. "I'll tell you when you're older."

Zach shoves his hand away. "I'm telling Dad to bench you next game."

"I'm telling Dad," Jackson repeats back to Zach in a mocking voice.

"Who's his dad?" I ask no one.

Izzy, having heard me, lifts her hand. "My dad. I'm the coach's daughter."

I lift my brows. Bet that's a story.

"Wait." Ash cuts back into the conversation. "Did you keep the suit?"

"What fucking suit?" Zach looks at him, then jerks his gaze back to Luke. "Hold up."

"Bye!" Luke says loudly as he turns us away from the group.

While we move away, I start to chuckle. And after two breaths, it turns into bigger laughter.

Blizz bang.

"Something funny, Princess?" Luke asks as he guides me to his vehicle, parked just around the corner.

"Nothing at all." I smile up at him.

He meets my gaze. "Want to head home, or do you need to stop anywhere?"

Home.

"Take me home," I tell him. "And take me to bed."

Chapter 101

Luke

I WANT to bottle the happiness in her eyes.

I want to keep it on my bedside. There to touch whenever I need to feel better.

So I do as my wife says.

I take her home.

And when we get home, I strip her bare.

And I take her to bed.

Chapter 102

The Travel Text Messages

Princess: Did you seriously eat all the coffee cake?

Luke: You were gone!

Princess: I was gone for one night. You ate the whole thing.

Luke: It was a long night. The bed is lonely without you.

Princess: Sucking up won't get you out of this one, Player.

Luke: Fine, I'll let you spank me when I get home Wednesday.

Princess: You'd like that too much. And I won't be here Wednesday. I have to fly to Quebec that morning.

Luke: Fuck. I forgot.

Luke: That sucks.

Luke: You can still spank me though.

Luke: How was your meeting?

Princess: Productive. French.

Luke: Hold up. You speak French?

Princess: Pas bien.

Luke: What did you call me?

Princess: My French is barely passable.

Luke: I'll be the judge of that.

Princess: How could you possibly do that?

Luke: It's the language of love, right?

Princess: So some say.

Luke: That's all I need to know, Green Eyes.

Princess: Bye, Luke.

Princess: Good luck at your game tonight.

Luke: Thanks, Wife. You going to watch?

Princess: Blizz and I have our spots ready on the couch.

Luke: Blizz the stuffed animal or the suit?

Princess: Are you honestly asking me if I draped the empty Blizz suit on the couch and put his head on the back cushion, so it's like he's watching too?

Luke: Well, when you word it like that... Yeah.

Princess: You are unwell.

Luke: I can't believe I'm missing you by six hours.

Princess: I know. This is stupid.

Luke: When I'm offseason, I'm coming with you to the cool places you go.

Princess: I'm in Nebraska.

Luke: I know. They invented the Reuben.

Princess: Hold, please.

Princess: Okay, I just looked that up. Why do you know that?

Luke: Why don't you know that?

Princess: I can't believe you kept your cup!

Luke: What cup?

Princess: The slushie cup from Vegas.

Luke: Oh, you mean my half of our wedding glasses? Of course I kept it.

Luke: Don't tell me you threw yours away.

Princess: There were times I thought about it. But I didn't.

Luke: Good.

Princess: Are these my sunglasses?

Luke: The white ones?

Princess: Yeah.

Luke: You really are snooping through every cupboard.

Princess: I thought I lost these in Mexico.

Luke: Funny, I found them in Mexico.

Luke: You still want me to meet you at the thing tomorrow night?

Princess: If you don't mind. My dad is for sure going to be there, and we can't put off seeing him forever. Public event might be better than a private dinner.

Luke: Agreed. What's the dress code?

Princess: Black and white. I'm wearing white.

Luke: Classy.

Luke: I might be just a little late, but I'll find you.

Princess: Thank you. I owe you for this one.

Luke: Let me take a pic of you in the suit and we're even.

Chapter 103

Natalie

WEALTH AND CELEBRITY tend to go hand in hand, so even though I'm the furthest thing from a celebrity, and I dislike being in the spotlight, I take a deep breath to prepare myself for it anyway.

I wish Luke was here.

I look out my car window at the section of red carpet rolled out in front of the Mazzanti Enterprises building. Along the building, behind the carpet, are giant free-standing banners with the Mazzanti logo, the name of the charity organization that will be speaking tonight, and then the emblem for Marie's House, making sure all the photos shared from tonight have the proper branding.

Marie's House is the main recipient of tonight's donations, and hopefully the sum will allow them to start work on a second location.

For the first one, they remodeled an old hotel into no-cost transitional housing for women and families. It was the love project of Marie Mazzanti, mother of *the* Vincent Mazzanti, the man who currently runs Mazzanti Enterprises and was formally known as Mr. Sin before his now wife, Sasha, ran his PR campaign and transitioned him to an upstanding businessman.

I've met Vincent and Sasha a few times over the years, typically at events like this, where a table costs five figures. But for a family once rumored to be in the mafia, they do a lot of good. And I'm looking forward to being more involved in their future projects.

So, with that, thinking of the greater good, I straighten my shoulders and tell my driver I'm ready.

I could have driven myself, but I plan to partake in the bar tonight, and it's easier to get through this part being dropped off.

While the driver circles the car to open my door, I smooth my hands down my embellished skirt.

As I told Luke, the theme for tonight is black and white, and I chose later because I've been waiting for a reason to wear this dress.

The scoop neckline covers my cleavage, and the long sleeves are conservative, but the bright white material is covered in thousands of tiny crystals, and the way it clings to my body is anything but conservative. Not to mention the only thing breaking up the glittering fabric is the slit that runs halfway up my thigh.

I finished the look with white silk pumps and white enamel jewelry.

It's almost bridal but more *winter royalty* than anything else.

And if I'm honest, I'm excited to hear Luke call me a Princess while wearing it.

The driver opens my door, and I climb out of the back seat.

Chapter 104

Luke

My Uber driver turns in his seat to look at me. "You sure this is the right place?"

I let out a laugh, not offended. "Pretty sure."

I may be dressed up in a black suit, black loafers, and black button-down shirt—with the top two buttons open—but I'm in the back of a fucking Honda, and I'm pretty sure that's a Maserati SUV waiting in the line of cars that are idling in front of the massive Mazzanti building.

We watch the driver get out of the expensive-as-fuck SUV and walk around to the back.

"You want me to get out and open your door?" My driver lifts a brow.

I smooth my hands down my pants and shake my head, then straighten my green silk pocket square.

"Nah, man. I..."

The Maserati driver is at the rear passenger door and mostly blocked by the vehicle, but when he steps back, a head of dark glossy hair peeks above the roof. Big curls shine under the bright lights set up around the red carpet.

I hold my breath as the woman steps away from the car toward the person directing people down the carpet.

She steps into view.

Something big—and important—settles in my chest. Because it's her.

It's my fucking wife.

And she doesn't just look like a princess.

She looks like a fucking queen.

Chapter 105

Natalie

WHEN I'M WAVED FORWARD, I take my place on the carpet and smile. Trying to place my hands just right. Trying to turn my body in the most flattering way. Trying to look calm and comfortable.

Then the flashes intensify, and I see the cameras shift.

The people around me murmur. And I hear someone say, "It's him."

I blink against the brightness and turn my head.

Dots of light dance in my vision, but there's no mistaking what I'm seeing.

Luke.

My hockey player.

My husband.

Jogging up the sidewalk. Cutting in front of the other people waiting in line behind me.

I can feel the shift inside me as the smile on my mouth changes into something real.

Luke slows as he reaches me. "Hey, Green Eyes."

My gaze darts down to his pocket square. The only spot of

color between us, aside from our pink rings. And I want to press my palm over my beating heart.

He just doesn't miss.

"I thought you were going to be late." I keep my tone as casual as I'm able.

Luke smirks. "I thought so too. Then I remembered how much I like the drama of making an entrance."

I tip my head toward the photographers. "I think they approve."

Luke reaches his tattooed hand up and cups the back of my neck. "How do you feel about making even more of a scene?"

I part my lips to ask him...

But I don't get the question out. Because Luke drops his mouth to mine.

My eyes close on their own.

My hands reach for him on their own.

And that damn bird inside my chest starts tearing more bits off my heart, pressing them against my ribs, like she can push them from my body and straight into his.

I squeeze my eyes tighter.

I grip his lapels harder.

And I pretend he's kissing me like this because he's falling for me, like I'm falling for him. And not because he's making a show for the cameras.

Chapter 106

Luke

SOMEONE WHISTLES, and I force myself to break the kiss.

I didn't mean to get so carried away.

I told Natalie it was just for the cameras.

But that was a lie. It was for me.

I flex my hand around the back of her neck, and she blinks her eyes open.

They look glassy in the bright flashes.

I almost think I see sadness, but then she blinks, and it's replaced with heat.

"That was quite the scene." Natalie lets go of my suit coat and flattens her hands on my chest, smoothing down the material.

"Luke!" one of the photographers calls out.

I swallow the urge to ignore him, and, letting go of Natalie, I present her my arm.

She takes it, tucking her hand into the crook of my elbow, and we turn to face the cameras.

She's the big shot here, and I'm just the arm candy.

I'm perfectly okay with that because, at the end of the night, she's going home with me.

Chapter 107

Natalie

I DIG my fingers into Luke's arm, but he doesn't complain as we wade through the rest of the photographers, the journalists in the lobby, and the throng of people stopping to greet us when we make it into the ballroom a few floors up.

"Talk about marrying Mrs. Popular," Luke whispers as we move away from the last couple to flag us down.

"I don't know that I've ever seen those two so excited before," I whisper back. "I bet they're secretly hockey fans but were too shy to admit it."

Luke looks down at me. "Why would anyone be shy about liking hockey?"

I shrug. "Rich people are weird." He snorts, and I narrow my eyes at him. "What?"

He holds up his free hand. "Nothing. I have absolutely nothing to say to that."

I squeeze his arm. "That's what I thought."

Luke turns us toward the bar set up at the back of the room. "Drink?"

"Yes, please."

As we walk, Luke looks around. "Warn me if your dad is approaching."

"I will." I don't even tease him since I'm also a bit nervous about sitting through a dinner together with my dad. "I don't think he's here yet."

I feel Luke relax next to me.

"Damn, they really go top tier here, don't they?" Luke's eyes bounce over the liquor options.

He probably has more money than half the people here, but he's taking the time to actually appreciate the details around us. And it only makes me like him more.

When it's our turn, Luke politely asks for a glass of chardonnay for me and a Perro Rabioso Whiskey on the rocks for him.

Luke lifts his drink. "I wonder if this guy is here tonight."

"The person who makes the whiskey?"

"It's owned by a guy who used to play for the Biters."

I eye his glass. "Huh." I should probably have known that. "Speaking of..." I look around the room but don't spot the man in question. "There's another football player here my dad introduced me to the other week, and I'd like to say hi."

Luke makes an unimpressed sound.

I nudge him in the side. "Play nice."

He makes another sound as he takes a sip of his whiskey. "So, how does this go?"

I dropped my hold of Luke's arm when I ordered our drinks, but as we start to stroll around the outside of the room, he twines his fingers with mine.

It's sweet.

Intimate.

I take a big swallow of wine as I remind myself about expectations.

"Well, there are silent auction items we can look at. Then we'll find our table and eat dinner, and then someone, possibly Vincent, will get up for a speech. There will be a show of people donating money, and then we can go home."

Luke gives my hand a squeeze. "You have one of those giant checks hidden inside your dress?"

A laugh pops out of me. "Um, no. Wag Corp already made our donation, and it was through a wire transfer."

"Sounds fancy." Luke hums as we reach the auction tables. "I know I've thought it a thousand times already, but I don't think I said it out loud."

I look up at him. "Thought what?"

"How fucking beautiful you look tonight."

There's no humor in his tone. Just honesty.

"Thank you," I whisper. "You look rather amazing yourself."

I mean it. The black on black, with his neck tattoo on display and the...

My eyes move to that damn green pocket square.

"I'm passable," he says. "You are way beyond that, Princess. And if you don't want me to ruin this dress when we get home, you're gonna need to—"

A throat clears behind Luke.

"Daughter." My dad's voice cuts in.

Luke widens his eyes, and I press my lips together, my mouth starting to pull into a smile.

With his back still to my dad, Luke squeezes my fingers as he mouths *Oh my god*, and I have to try not to laugh at his expression.

"Hi, Dad." I greet him brightly as I step around Luke.

Luke continues to hold my hand tightly as he turns to face my father.

"Hi, uh, hello, sir." Luke stumbles over his words, making it even harder to keep my composure.

I know I shouldn't find this funny. I don't want Luke to feel uncomfortable around my dad. But... it is funny.

"Luke." Dad dips his chin.

Neither man attempts to shake the other's hand, but I let go of Luke's so I can give my dad a hug.

He accepts it, of course, and some of the tension lessens around us as I let go.

"You look wonderful tonight, Natalie." Dad smiles down at me.

"Thanks." I twist side to side, making my skirt dance. "You don't look too shabby yourself."

Dad sighs and places a hand on his tux-covered stomach. "The tailor has been sneaking into my closet and making everything smaller again."

I snort. "I'll be sure to chastise Mr. Thompson the next time I see him."

Dad narrows his eyes at me. "Pest."

Luke makes a choking sound.

"Something funny?" I ask my husband.

He shakes his head. "Nope."

"No need to lie, son." Dad claps him on the shoulder, apparently over the awkwardness. "It's no secret my daughter is a stubborn woman."

Luke grins, also moving past the weirdness. "I have no idea what you're talking about."

"Smart man." Dad nods. "Alright, I'm gonna hit the bar. I'll find you at our table."

"'Kay." I smile, then turn back to Luke. "Well, that broke the ice."

Luke groans. "I swear, I keep looking worse and worse in

front of him. The next thing will be your dad walking in on us having sex."

"Like what Jackson did?" I lift a brow.

He grimaces. "Yeah, I guess we already ticked that box."

I reach for Luke's hand. "I'd love to leave that as a one-time-only experience."

He closes his fingers around mine. "Deal."

Together, we take our time looking at the auction items, and I put in a few bids on random items. But it's mostly just to bump up the prices since I don't care that much about winning.

"Did you want another drink before we sit?" I ask Luke.

He shakes his head. "You?"

"There's wine on the table, so I'm set. But I think your whiskey is just at the bar."

"Then let's find our table. I need to stop after one anyway."

My mouth pulls down. "I forgot you're leaving again tomorrow."

Luke's hand flexes around mine. "Just for two nights. Then I have a surprise planned."

I side-eye him as I lead him toward our table. "Hopefully a good surprise."

He just smirks.

"Natalie!" A brunette woman holds her hands out toward me as she comes around the table. "So glad you could make it."

"Hi, Sasha." I greet her, accepting her hug. "Wouldn't dream of missing it."

Sasha Mazzanti pulls back, beaming at me. "I can't tell you how excited I was when you emailed to say you were moving here. And please let me apologize again for that asshole employee in Vegas. As soon as we realized it was our resort that leaked those videos, Vincent fired him. And blacklisted him from any other hospitality job in the state."

I let out a slightly awkward chuckle. "I appreciate that, but it's all water under the bridge now."

"Well, I insist we do coffee soon to catch up. Then you can tell me just how choppy that water was." She steps back just as her husband stops at her side.

I smile at Sasha, then take her husband's offered hand. "Vincent, nice to see you."

I've met the tall, dark-haired, dark-eyed man several times. He's been nothing but kind. But I don't think I'd ever dare try to hug him.

"It's an honor to have you join us." He smiles at me before turning his gaze to the equally tall man beside me. "And I see you brought your husband."

"I did." I look up at Luke. "This is Luke Anders. Luke, this is Vincent and Sasha Mazzanti."

Because I know him, I can see the tiny shift in his features, putting together who we're talking to. The couple who owns this whole building. Owns several massive buildings here and across the country. Wag Corp has money. But Mazzanti Enterprises *has money*.

"My cousin and his kid talk about you all the time," Vincent says to Luke. "Noah still hasn't shut up about the time you showed him some workouts."

"Noah," Luke repeats. "Wait, Angelo is your cousin?"

"True fact, pipsqueak." A deep voice cuts in from the other side of Luke.

We both turn, and an involuntary sound of surprise leaves me.

The man is massive. Like legitimately massive.

Luke is over six feet tall, but this guy probably has half a foot on him. And he's wide. Built like a wall.

"Jesus," I mutter.

Luke glares at me over his shoulder. "He's not that big."

The giant barks out a laugh and reaches his hand past Luke toward me. "Angelo Rossi. Nice to meet you."

I let my hand get swallowed by his as I shake it. "Natalie Wagner."

Angelo lifts his brows. "Wag Corp Wagner?"

I nod. "One and the same."

"I worked with your security guys last year setting up some new protocols. Good company." He tips his big head toward Luke. "You find this guy on the street and decide to bring him inside?"

"Ha, ha." Luke fake laughs and shoves at the giant. "That's enough."

Angelo, who is apparently Vincent's cousin, lets go of my hand and steps back.

"How do you two know each other?" I ask.

"The gym." Luke pulls his shoulders back. "Can't you tell we go to the same place?"

I bite my lip and nod. "You're basically twins."

Angelo laughs again. "I like this one. You should keep her."

Luke grins and holds up his hand, showing off his pink silicone ring. "Already married her."

"So the rumors are true? Well, congrats, man." Angelo slaps Luke on the back, causing Luke to stumble forward a step. "Nothing beats marrying out of your league. And I say that from experience."

Sasha says something to Angelo, asking where his wife is tonight and pulling attention away from us.

I reach up and gently rub my palm across Luke's back. "You okay?"

Luke rolls out his shoulders. "Nothing a good chiropractor can't fix."

"Such a baby." Angelo snorts, apparently still listening.

The music in the room changes, and Sasha gestures for us all to sit.

We're all seated together at the same table, which shouldn't come as a surprise, considering the size of the donation my dad decided to give this year. But it's a pleasant surprise since I really do like Sasha, and I'd love to get to talk to her more.

Dad shows up just as we're sitting and does his round of greetings.

Nametags are in front of each spot, and the empty chair next to me has his name in front of it. But he sits in the only other empty chair, next to Vincent, across the round table from Luke and me.

"Dad, that's not your spot."

He looks down, seeing the paper marker, but instead of moving, he just holds it out to me. "Switch 'em for me, will ya?"

I roll my eyes but hand him his name and take the other one from him.

"John Clark." I read the tag. "Another cousin?"

Sasha snorts. "That's my brother."

"Does he work with you too?"

She shakes her head. "He's an FBI agent."

"Oh, wow." I don't know if that's a weird way to react to that, but I've never met anyone in the FBI before.

Movement catches my attention, and I see a man striding toward our table. He's tall and built, like all the men at this table—well, not quite like Angelo. And his hair color matches Sasha's, so I'm guessing this is her brother.

He's almost to our table when another man intercepts him, stopping him to talk in his ear.

The new man has dark hair buzzed short and more tattoos than Luke, his going from his neck to his fingertips. And damn, he's handsome too.

A hand settles on the back of my neck, and Luke leans into

my side. "If you keep staring at other men, I'm going to start to get jealous."

Sure, these other men are all good looking, but they aren't Luke. And they don't have Luke's energy. That aura that calms me.

I lean back in Luke's hold. "What other men?"

He presses his lips to my temple. "Good answer."

Chapter 108

Luke

NATALIE LEANS into my side as we walk toward the exit. We're not the first to leave, but we're not the last.

Tonight was... surprising.

And it shouldn't have been. I just didn't want to have to share Natalie after not seeing her for so long. And I didn't think I'd enjoy the company at an event like this.

Of course, that was before I realized my occasional workout buddy would be here. I knew the big ogre worked for Mazzanti, but I didn't realize he was part of the actual family.

But the biggest surprise of the night was Natalie's dad.

After a couple of drinks, he started asking me about my career, congratulating me on my stats, having clearly looked me up after finding out I married his daughter.

It was a lot of fun, actually. And I'm looking forward to seeing him again, preferably in a situation when I can also cut loose, and we can share a bottle of whiskey.

I make a mental note to buy him some for Christmas.

"The driver is here," Natalie tells me as she slips her phone back into a hidden pocket in her skirt.

My arm is draped across her shoulder, and I use my thumb to trace a pattern around the crystals sewn into the fabric of her dress. "You sure you don't want me to call my Uber? Joey was pretty cool."

Natalie shakes her head as she smiles up at me. "I'm really glad you came tonight."

"Me too, Little Royal."

I slide my hand over until it's between her shoulder blades and guide her through the doors until we're back on the sidewalk in front of the building.

The Maserati she arrived in is parked directly in front of us, and as we approach, the driver starts to get out. But I wave him off and reach for the rear door.

If anyone is opening doors for Natalie tonight, it's me.

Her dress isn't so long that it drags on the ground, but I still help her with the skirt as she climbs into the back seat. As she settles, the slit in the material, the one that's been taunting me all night, flashes more of her soft, tempting thigh.

Since the first second I saw her tonight, I've been on the edge of embarrassing myself. Too close to tenting my suit pants. And now... Now there's nothing stopping me.

I clear my throat. "You ready, Princess?"

Her gaze darts up to mine, probably hearing the heat in my voice. But then her eyes move to where my hand is resting on the door.

Natalie presses her thighs together, giving extra space between her and the door, then nods.

I shut the door carefully, then stride around the back of the vehicle. And as I do that, I remove my suit coat.

Chapter 109

Natalie

I KEEP my thighs clenched together while I wait for Luke to round the back of the car.

I don't think I've ever enjoyed an event as much as I did tonight.

Luke might be an obstinate jock half the time, but he's easy to be around. He makes everything... fun.

But the look in his eyes a second ago has me thinking about a different sort of fun.

A less civilized sort of fun.

The door across from me opens, and I swallow.

Luke has taken off his jacket, leaving him in just his button-down. The top buttons are still undone, and the urge I've had to lick his neck since I first saw him hasn't decreased. But now he's rolled his sleeves up too.

I don't know why that's so hot. But I'd be willing to fund the research to find out.

One long, muscular leg stretches into the back seat, then the rest of him follows.

Luke doesn't waste time shutting the door and buckling his seat belt, and suddenly the SUV feels like a tiny sports car.

The air between us is heavy and thick with need. And I hear it in his voice when Luke tells the driver we're ready.

I keep my eyes forward, not sure how to handle myself, but then Luke drapes his suit jacket over my lap.

"Since you're cold."

His words are quiet, barely audible over the soft classical music the driver has playing.

I turn my head to look at Luke as we pull away from the curb, away from the bright lights at the front of the building.

We're still downtown, and there are headlights in every direction, but the darkness that settles in the interior of the vehicle feels profound.

Luke sets his hand on the small section of the seat between us.

And my heart starts to beat faster.

Because I never said I was cold.

I'm the opposite. I'm on fire.

Chapter 110

Luke

I INCH my hand a little closer to her hip.

Natalie looks down at it. Then up at me.

And underneath the material of my jacket, she spreads her legs.

Chapter 111

Natalie

Dampness floods my core.

This is crazy.

I shouldn't be encouraging this.

But then Luke slips his hand under the jacket over my lap, and his warm palm settles on bare skin.

Sitting, the slit in my dress rises to a near indecent level.

A perfect level.

I work to keep my breathing even and turn my gaze forward, acting as though nothing is happening.

This isn't a limo.

There is no divider between us and the driver.

There are barely a few feet.

But Luke apparently doesn't care.

He slides his hand across the top of my thigh. And he doesn't stop.

He keeps pushing his hand farther under my skirt. Between my thighs, until the edge of his hand presses against my soaked panties.

I bite my lip to keep from making a sound.

Gripping my inner thigh, he gives a little tug, and I spread my thighs even farther. As far as I can without having to adjust my skirt.

But it's enough.

From the corner of my eye, I can see Luke lean just the smallest bit my way, his body facing forward just like mine. But then he's cupping me. There.

His whole big hand is shoved between my legs, and he's gripping my pussy like it belongs to him.

My eyes close.

And then his fingers apply pressure.

His fingers are low. At my entrance.

He pushes against the thin material of my panties and rubs.

And I know he can feel it. I know he can feel how wet I am.

Chapter 112

Luke

I'm gonna have a fucking wet spot on the front of my pants before we get home because Natalie's little princess slit is fucking soaked. And it's affecting me. Badly.

I wiggle my fingers as I slide my hand up just a bit, wedging the damp material of her panties between her puffy lips.

She squirms.

And then I find it. That little bud of nerves. Needy and ready.

I press my fingers against it.

Her body clenches.

I press my fingers against it harder.

And then I start to rub circles.

Little circles around her clit.

Natalie's far hand grips the door. Her other hand is balled into a fist and pressed against her stomach.

She's trying to stay in control.

Trying to resist.

But I'm not going to let her.

Chapter 113

Natalie

HOLY SHIT.

Holy shit. Holy shit. Holy shit.

Luke isn't stopping.

He just keeps going.

Keeps rubbing.

Every turn we make, every time the driver brakes, Luke applies more pressure.

The friction of having the layer of fabric between my throbbing clit and his fingertips is more intense than I know what to do with.

And he's not stopping.

"It's better if you take the next turn," Luke says in a casual voice to the driver.

I don't know if he's serious or trying to cover up the sounds of me panting. But I don't care. I can't stop myself.

The driver says something back, and Luke replies, but he keeps working his fingers.

Never stopping.

I want him inside me.

I want him to touch my breasts. Kiss me.
I want to feel him everywhere.
I don't want to come like this.
But I'm going to.
We're two blocks away from home, and I'm going to.

Chapter 114

Luke

My cock is rock hard inside my pants.

But I don't stop rubbing Natalie's clit. Because we're almost home. But she's even closer.

I know she is.

I press harder.

Circle my fingers once more.

Hear the tiny hitch in her breath.

And then she breaks.

Her mouth drops open on a silent cry, and both her hands slap down to grip my wrist.

But she doesn't try to pull my hand away. She just holds on to me. Her body trembling. Her pussy convulsing around nothing.

A jolt of release seeps from my cock.

God, she's fucking perfect.

"We've arrived," the driver announces as he pulls to a stop in front of my building.

I clear my throat. "Thank you." I slide my hand away from Natalie's core. "Stay put, Princess. I'll get your door."

Natalie nods but doesn't say anything as I unbuckle my seat belt and exit the SUV.

While I once again circle the back of the vehicle, I adjust my dick so my arousal isn't completely obvious.

Natalie has undone her buckle, and as soon as I open the door, she starts to climb out.

She keeps the jacket over her lap, covering the slit in her skirt, and I take her free hand.

Before shutting the door, I reach through and drop a pair of hundreds onto the front passenger seat. I don't know if Natalie already tipped the driver, but that was the best car ride of my life.

Chapter 115

Natalie

LUKE KEEPS his hand on my back as we walk into his building.

He keeps his hand on my back as we take the elevator up.

His hand on my back slides up to the base of my neck when we reach the door to the condo.

And when we step through, he shifts his hold to the tab on my zipper and starts to drag it down before the front door even slams shut.

"Luke." I'm saying his name as I help him shove the dress off my arms and down my hips.

"Princess," he groans as he grips my ass.

Then the words are lost, and all that's left are sounds.

He unclips my bra as I undo the rest of his buttons.

I toss my bra to the side as he rips the shirt off his body.

We kick our shoes off together, and he undoes his belt.

He pushes his pants and boxer briefs off.

I shove my panties off and sink to my knees.

Luke grips my hair, murmuring something about *just for a second.*

And I close my lips around the end of his cock.

Luke is hot. And so hard.

He groans.

He pushes his hips forward.

He pulls my face closer.

My body tightens.

My throat constricts.

My core clenches.

Luke drags me off him.

Then he pulls me back down his cock.

Sinking into my throat.

His groan is louder this time. And even though I just came minutes ago, I'm ready all over again.

I wrap my fingers around the base of his dick.

I dig my other fingers into the back of his thigh.

And then he's pulling my head back again.

His dick slips from my mouth, and he hauls me up to my feet.

Luke's mouth slams into mine, and we stumble down the hallway.

My hands never stop touching him.

His never stop touching me.

And when the back of my knees hit the bed, Luke lets go of me.

I fall and he follows.

My legs spread.

And then he's there. Between them. Pushing inside me.

I'm so primed.

So wet.

So ready to take him.

Luke shoves his hips forward.

He's as deep as he can go.

I press my heels into his lower back.

He leans his weight onto his elbows.

I cling to his back.

He presses his open mouth against my temple.

I cry out when he hits that perfect spot.

He doesn't stop moving.

And when I reach between us.

When I mimic his movements from the car.

When I rub my clit.

He moans. And the rumble of it sends me to the cliff.

And when he tells me to let go.

When Luke begs for his Princess to come all over his cock, I do exactly as he asks.

And he follows me over the edge.

Chapter 116

Natalie

"You ready for the board meeting this week? Natalie?"

I jerk my head up at my dad's voice. "Huh? Oh, yeah. I have my reports ready."

He tilts his head. "You okay?"

I nod.

But it's a lie.

I'm not okay.

Yesterday morning, Luke woke me by softly pressing a kiss on my forehead.

It was the sweetest, most tender thing anyone has ever done to me, and I couldn't handle it.

He was just saying goodbye, letting me know he was leaving, but my hummingbird wanted so badly to chase after him as he walked out of the room. Either to beg him to stay or beg him to take us with him.

But he never asked us to come.

He's never asked if I'd like to attend one of his away games.

And I missed the last home game he had, the one after the whole Blizz thing, because I was out of town.

The Blizz thing...

I'm so glad Dad didn't ask any questions about what happened to me that night.

"If you're not feeling well, you can go home." Dad leans his elbows on the table in his office, where we're sharing our lunch hour.

I stab my fork into a potato wedge. "I'm fine. Just feeling sad."

I didn't really mean to admit that. But it's true. And it's nice to be truthful with Dad again.

Dad hums his understanding before asking, "Luke's out of town again?"

I nod.

Luke is out of town again.

And I'm sad I have to wait another whole night before he comes home.

And I'm sad that tomorrow night is going to be some sort of romantic date—I just know it.

And it all makes me sad because it's going to make me fall even more in love with Luke Anders.

And I'm not supposed to fall in love with him.

We're only living together until we break up.

He never wanted to marry me.

He's my husband by accident.

He's everything I want in a partner, even if I didn't know it.

But loving him if he doesn't love me...?

I don't think I can act my way through that.

I don't think I can pretend that wouldn't shatter my heart.

Chapter 117

Luke

I DON'T KNOW why I'm nervous.

Every time I'm with Natalie, we have a great time. Sure, this might be our first actual date. Or maybe our accidental wedding was our first date? Either way, we've been out together. We did that event together a few nights ago. Hell, we fucking live together. Which is good since I hardly get to see her. I can't imagine what my head would be like if she hadn't agreed to move in.

I should really start asking her to come to my away games. She can't fly with us, but it wouldn't be a burden on either of us to buy her a few plane tickets.

Next game.

My wife is coming with me to my next game.

I slow as I turn my vehicle onto our street.

And then I smile.

Because there she is.

Standing on the sidewalk, under the glow of the streetlights with soft fluffy snowflakes floating down around her, is Natalie.

In a perfect world, my flight home wouldn't have been

delayed, and I would have been home when she was done with work. But since that didn't happen, I told her to be ready for me to pick her up.

I told her to dress comfortably and casually and that we'd be outside for a little while.

She followed my directions—wearing a pair of jeans tucked into furry ankle boots and a puffy baby-pink winter jacket.

I want to get out and open the door for her properly, but she's already reaching for the handle before my SUV is even stopped.

I grin at her as she pulls the door open.

Her hair is pulled up into a ponytail, and her cheeks are flushed.

"Hey, Beautiful."

Her smile is shy, and the temptation to call the whole night off is real. But I want to do this. So I stay where I am.

"Hey, Player." Her eyes rove over me, taking in my jeans and plain black hoodie. "You look cute."

I bat my lashes at her. "Why, thank you."

Her sudden shyness seems to fade away when she rolls her eyes at me and climbs in.

I wait until she's buckled, then pull away from the curb. "You ready?"

Natalie folds her hands in her lap. "I have no idea what we're doing. So... maybe?"

"You're ready." I smirk.

The drive is about twenty minutes, and I take the time to ask her about her week.

We've texted every day, so I know the bulk of it, but she tells me about her big presentation to the board tomorrow and that she's a little nervous.

"Why are you nervous?"

Natalie sighs. "Because I'm a chicken."

"You are not a chicken, Green Eyes. You're the opposite of a chicken."

"What's the opposite of a chicken?" she asks me.

"Terrifying."

She lets out a startled laugh. "Terrifying? How so?"

I lift a shoulder. "It's hard to explain. Just that you know what you want, and you don't settle for less." She makes a small humming sound, but I can't tell if she agrees. "I get that they're a bunch of stuffy business nerds. But you're a business nerd too. They just have a hard time accepting that because you aren't stuffy too."

Natalie is silent for a long moment.

I glance at her when she doesn't reply. "What?"

"That's... accurate."

"Don't sound so surprised, Wife. I'm more than just a pretty face."

She huffs out a breath. "I wonder if I should wear a formal business suit tomorrow."

I shake my head. "Nah, they've already seen the real you. Wear what you would normally wear. Changing now would just look like an act of submission. Just be yourself, Princess."

"I hate when you're right." She sighs.

I laugh, but before I can reply, Natalie sits up straighter in her seat.

Because we're here.

Chapter 118

Natalie

I open my mouth, but I don't know if I want to laugh or scream. Because Luke brought me to an outdoor skating rink.

An ice-skating rink.

Like the one I fell on multiple times in the way too recent past.

Luke drives slowly through the gravel parking lot, the lot and rink brightly lit by large flood lights.

There are a handful of cars here and maybe a dozen people on the ice. A large field is situated next to the rink, with frames for soccer goals, so this must be some sort of public sports park. And between the rink and the field is a small wooden building with the words *Warming House* written on the side.

When Luke turns the ignition off, I finally look away from the death trap called an ice rink and make eye contact.

"Luke."

He holds up a hand. "Trust me."

My mouth shuts.

Trust me. Of course he'd go there.

"I do." I glance back at the rink. "But I don't think I can wear—"

"I said trust me, Princess." He cuts me off, then opens his car door and climbs out.

I stay in the car for an extra moment while I shove away the urge to whine.

When Luke said he had a surprise, I imagined he meant dinner out.

When Luke told me to dress comfortably and for the outdoors, I pictured some outdoor winter market that sold mulled wine and crocheted hats.

So this...

I look back at the ice.

This is not what I had in mind.

The far back door clicks open. "Come on, Natalie. We'll have fun, I promise."

"Promises, promises," I grumble and unbuckle myself.

With my feet on the ground, I adjust my layers and then pull my thick gray headband on over my ears and pull my ponytail free.

When I circle around to the back of the SUV, I pause.

Then I snort. "Pardon me, Mr. Bank Robber, I'm looking for Luke."

Luke blinks at me, his eyes the only thing visible on his face. "I don't want to be recognized."

I blink back. "You're going to scare the children."

"It's a balaclava," he huffs as he tugs the mask off his head. There's a slight crackle of static as he does it, leaving some of his hair standing on end.

I bite my lip. "I know what it is, but it's thirty degrees, not negative twenty." I nod to the duffel bag sitting in the back of his vehicle. "You have any other tricks in there?"

"Yes." Luke stares at my headband as he says it.

I narrow my eyes. "Why does it feel like you're lying?"

He lets out a groan—that shouldn't be sexy—then shoves his hand into the end pocket of the bag and pulls out two items.

The first is a black fleece neck warmer that he yanks down over his head until it's bunched around his neck, covering him from his chin to the collar of his hoodie, blocking out his recognizable neck tattoo.

The second item is a hat.

A pale yellow knit hat with a pink, white, and yellow pom-pom on top.

I press my lips together while he pulls it onto his head, then I continue to watch as he uses his fingertips to tuck any visible strands up under the hat.

When he's done, he drops his arms and looks at me.

"It's very pretty," I tell him, trying to keep a straight face.

"It's for you."

My brows go up, shifting my headband. "Really?"

Luke nods. "I wasn't sure if you'd have winter gear."

I look back up at the hat.

It really is pretty.

"Well, thank you. It's very nice." I reach up and run my pointer finger along the front of it. "Try not to stretch it out with your big head."

Luke makes a rumbling sound low in his throat, and I yank my hand away with a squeak before he can grab it.

A car crunches over gravel as it drives in our direction, stopping Luke from retaliating.

"So... you want me to watch you skate around?" I ask, changing the subject and trying not to read too much into him buying me a pretty winter hat.

Instead of answering, Luke grabs the duffel bag and swings it over his shoulder.

When the back door is shut, Luke holds his hand out to me,

and my stupid heart squeezes when I place my palm against his.

This is just a simple date.

He bought a hat because he's a good person and he doesn't want me to freeze.

I won't lose the rest of my heart tonight.

I expect him to lead me right to the ice rink, but instead, we head toward the warming house.

Before we reach the door, it's shoved open from the inside, and two small children come running out with skates on their feet.

Luke catches the door, holding it open, and gestures for me to go in first.

Warm is correct.

The room is maybe the size of a large bedroom. It's simple and bare, with benches along the walls and a double row of benches down the center of the room.

People are scattered inside, in different stages of resting or changing footwear. And tennis shoes and snow boots are shoved under the benches, along with some bags similar to the one Luke is holding.

The fluorescent lights overhead have yellowed plastic covers. And that, mixed with the heater in the corner of the ceiling blowing super-heated air, gives the room a hazy effect.

A familiar hand presses into the center of my back, guiding me to an open section of bench that doesn't have any shoes underneath it.

I sit, my back to the wall, but Luke doesn't join me on the bench.

Instead, he crouches before me and starts digging in the duffel bag.

The action puts his pom-pom right at eye level, so I reach out and squeeze it.

The yarn is so soft I squeeze it again.

"Get all your aggression out now, Princess. I don't need you trying to squash my other pom-poms later."

I roll my eyes. "Not my fault you have such a nice pom-pom." I give it another squeeze for good measure.

Luke sets a large pair of hockey skates off to the side, and then he starts to pull out the next set.

"Seriously, Luke. I don't—"

I stop talking because the next pair he pulls out is not the oversized pair I wore with the Blizz suit. They're hockey skates, same style as his, but instead of black and white, these are cream.

Cream leather. Cream laces. Pretty, just like the hat.

"If the sizing is wrong, I can get different ones." Luke sets them down, then begins untying the boots I'm wearing. "But I based it off the shoes you have by the front door. And I know you wear those pairs regularly, so I assume they must fit well."

"Oh." My voice comes out as a whisper. "That was really thoughtful of you."

Luke lifts his gaze from my skate and grins. "I'm not just a hot body."

I flick his pom-pom.

Luke laughs and pulls my boots off, clearly not having the same crisis of heart that I am.

He shoves my boots under the bench beneath me, then holds the first skate open.

I shove my foot in, wiggling my heel until everything feels like it's in place.

Luke's fingers brush the bare skin of my ankle as he rolls up the bottom hem of my jeans, and I feel the zip of his touch run all the way up my leg.

My eyes stay locked on his fingers as he laces the skate up.

It looks like a delicate task, but his large hands make quick work of it.

We repeat the process for the next foot, and when he rolls up the bottom of that pant leg, I swear his fingertips linger just a little longer, drag just a little farther around my ankle.

"I'm gonna have you stand up for me." Luke pats the top of my foot. "If you need to, keep a hand on the wall, but move your feet around. Make sure they feel okay."

He had me so distracted with his little touches that I totally forgot the reason he was putting ice skates on my feet.

Because we're about to go fucking ice-skating.

Resigned, I take his offered hands and let him pull me up.

Luke grins again.

"What?" I ask, getting my balance.

"I forgot that wearing skates puts you at the perfect height."

Heat fills my cheeks, but I still have the wherewithal to slap Luke's hand away when he lets go of mine and reaches for my side. "Luke, there are kids."

His grin doesn't fade as he moves to sit on the bench to put his own skates on.

Doing as he said, I walk in place, shifting my weight around to test the fit.

The skates are shockingly comfortable. They don't pinch anywhere, and the padding inside feels like it was made just for me.

I'm not saying I'll skate any better than I did before, but if I'd had these on during that stupid game, I bet my feet wouldn't have been killing me at the end of the night.

Finished with his laces, Luke stands, putting our height difference back to normal. "How do they feel?"

I take a few more steps in place. "They're really comfy."

"Too tight? Too loose?" He's asking me seriously, but his lemon-meringue hat ruins the effect.

So, even though I don't really want to skate, I can't stop my smile. "They're Goldilocks. Just right."

"Just right indeed." He trails his eyes down my body, then sighs and kicks his duffel under the bench. "Shall we?"

After I pull my mittens onto my hands, I take his offered one. "If we must."

My steps are still a little wobbly, but Luke's hold is steady, and we make it out of the warming house with ease.

The snowflakes have gotten even bigger, and I can hear the difference. That quiet of a heavy snow. And it helps calm my nerves.

The little path between the house and the rink is made of long rubber mats, and when a kid darts around us, making me sway, I suddenly feel like a crotchety old lady who wants to shout at all the neighborhood children to *keep it down*.

Then I see the kid trip and face-plant into the rubber mat.

He doesn't cry. Just gets back up and starts running again. But I still feel like a tiny bit of cosmic justice was doled out.

Except then I'm reminded of all the times I fell last time I was on the ice.

I tug on Luke's hand. "Did you bring any kneepads? Or wrist guards? Or... something?"

Luke shakes his head with a smirk. "Nah, Princess."

Then we're at the opening in the half wall that encircles the rink.

"Hope you have more of that stupid salve," I mutter as I try to push the aches and pains from last time out of my mind.

Luke steps onto the ice, turning to face me and offering me his second hand. "You're not gonna need it."

I grip his hand tightly so both my hands are palm to palm with his, and put my first skate onto the ice. "Why's that?"

Holding my breath, I put my second skate onto the ice.

"Because I won't let you fall."

His words are so simple.

So matter of fact.

So... everything I want.

I inhale, the ache in my heart intensifying with each second that passes, but I force it away. Force it down. Because I won't let my affection for this man be filled with dread.

Even my hummingbird is stepping in, jumping up and down, using her wings to add weight as she tramples on the bad feelings building in my chest, trying to make them disappear.

"Relax, Green Eyes. We'll start easy."

I lift my gaze from Luke's chest to meet his. "Okay."

He dips his chin. "Just hang on, alright?"

I nod.

Luke keeps his arms bent, his elbows tucked against his sides, so I do the same, leaving our hands clutched between us.

Then his feet start to move.

The ice is smooth under our skates, and the people skating around us fade from my awareness as I let him pull me across the rink.

We move faster.

"You okay?" Luke asks.

"I'm okay," I answer.

"Good. Now start skating."

His hands drop away from mine, and my arms automatically shoot out to catch my balance, but I'm moving fast enough that I'm already steady.

Luke is still moving backward, somehow aware of the people behind him, but he doesn't move away from me. He keeps pace, still within reach.

So I skate.

I know how. I've proven I can. But I've also proven I'm not good.

My first movement is jerky.

349

The second is smoother.

By the fourth, my arms are moving with my body, and I'm skating at the same speed we started at.

"There you go." Luke beams at me.

Then he does something with his feet because he's suddenly at my side, facing the same way I am.

"Ready to go faster?"

I start to shake my head, but Luke's hand is already pressing into my back.

He applies pressure, bringing me with him as he speeds up.

"One more time," Luke says. "Then we can have the hot chocolate I brought."

I put my fists on my hips. "Do you mean to tell me you've had hot chocolate this whole time?"

He nods. "And if you can spray me, you can have it."

I purse my lips, then shrug.

Either I accomplish it, or I crash into him, and he cushions my fall. Basically a win-win.

"Alright." I drop my fists.

We're about fifteen feet away from each other.

Luke is standing still, his pretty yellow hat covered in a layer of snow.

I start to skate.

It's just enough distance for me to get a bit of speed. And then, when he's only a couple feet in front of me, I do the maneuver he's been teaching me for the past half hour and skid to a stop, my blades perpendicular to his, sending a spray of shaven ice across his legs.

Luke lets out a whoop as I turn toward him.

"I did it!" Without thinking, I throw myself against him, wrapping my arms around his neck in a hug.

Luke doesn't fall. Of course he doesn't. He just wraps his arms around my waist and lifts me as he hugs me to his body.

My skates dangle above the ice as I bury my face against his fleece-covered neck.

"I'm proud of you, Little Royal," he murmurs as he holds me a little tighter.

And I squeeze my eyes shut a little harder.

Luke starts to skate with me still in his arms.

I cross my ankles and bend my knees, keeping my feet out of the way as we glide over the ice. And it feels like flying.

"Thank you, Player." My words are quiet, but I know he hears them.

Luke rubs his cheek against the top of my head. "You did so good."

Maybe this feeling inside me isn't doomed to loneliness.

I hold him tighter.

Maybe Luke is falling in love with me too.

Chapter 119

Natalie

"I'm gonna take a shower." He scratches his chin. "Probably trim the beard too. It's getting itchy."

I nod as I hang up my jacket in the entryway. "I might make some tea. Want any?"

Luke shakes his head. "I'm good."

He walks into the bedroom and leaves the door open. And I have to bite my lip when I see him start to strip as he crosses the room.

He drops his shirt to the floor, then he pauses before he kicks it into the bathroom.

When the bathroom door shuts, I drop onto the couch.

Tonight was nothing short of magical.

A fantasy.

And the final straw.

There's no denying it. I'm madly, deeply, truly in love with this man.

He's understanding, kind, funny, generous. Sexy to a fault. Stubborn. Demanding.

Luke is my match.

And he's given up so much for me—his lifestyle, his condo —while at the same time giving me even more.

He's come with me to public events.

He's encouraged me.

He's given me friendship.

I press my hand to my chest as I think about us sitting in the open back of his vehicle, drinking hot chocolate out of a thermos he must have brought straight from the airport.

He's done so much.

And I've...

My throat tightens. I've given him nothing.

I blackmailed him into this situation.

I moved into his condo.

I've forced him to lie to his teammates and the world.

I made him lie to his mom—the same way I lied to my dad.

I took what would have been a minor PR mess for Luke and turned his whole life upside down.

Guilt seeps into my lungs, suffocating me.

I need to do something for him. I need to give him... something.

My eyes drop to his laptop on the coffee table.

Maybe I can take us back to where it all started. I can take us back to Mexico, and we can relive the weekend, this time as husband and wife.

My laptop is on the chair in the bedroom, so I reach for Luke's.

He should be a while in the bathroom, but I want this to be a surprise. If he comes out and finds me on the computer, he'll ask what I'm doing. Because he's curious, not untrusting.

Plus, I think his practice and game calendar is saved on his computer. I know we can't leave until the season is over, which is a few months away, but if I have his schedule, then I can work out the whole thing while keeping it a surprise.

I prop the laptop on the couch armrest, then curl my legs to the side and open the browser.

It takes me a moment to remember the name of the resort we went to, but I find the site quickly.

The room I had was nice, but a higher floor with a view of the ocean would be even nicer.

I stop my scroll when I see something called the *Princess Suite*.

Well, that couldn't be more perfect.

As I click to see the photos, a text box pops up in the corner of the screen.

When I grabbed Luke's laptop, I hadn't considered that it would be synced to his phone. I'm not trying to snoop, but my eyes move on their own.

Jacob: What's up, dick?

I think that's his cousin. The one who got married the same day mine did.

I'm too far away to hear if the shower is going yet, but it's not like I need to reply and say Luke is busy. It's just a text. Luke can reply later.

I move the cursor to delete the text box.

Jacob: You squared away that mistake marriage yet?

My hand stills.

Mistake marriage.

Not accidental.

Mistake.

Luke: Not yet.

My eyes jerk up, looking down the hall, but Luke isn't there. He must be responding before getting in the shower.

Jacob: Well, if you need motivation, Molly is back in town. And I heard she asked about you.

A sick, heavy feeling settles across my chest.
Who is Molly?

Luke: Molly?

See, Jacob, no one cares about Molly.

Jacob: Molly... Your first love.

Your first love.
I press my lips together.
We weren't each other's firsts. That shouldn't hurt so much.
And I shouldn't be reading this.

Luke: Isn't she married?

I lean closer to the screen.
Please let her be married.
Please don't do this to me.

Jacob: Divorced.

Jacob: Just like you're going to be.

Disappointment.

S. J. Tilly

Disappointment in myself, like I've never felt before, washes over me.

It sucks the air from my lungs.

Fills my soul with wet, heavy concrete.

> Luke: You're the dick.
>
> Jacob: Have you told her?
>
> Luke: Not yet.
>
> Jacob: Waiting is only going to make it harder.
>
> Luke: I know.
>
> Luke: I'll tell her soon.
>
> Luke: ...

I grip the lid of the laptop and snap it shut.

Waiting is only going to make it harder.

I set the computer back on the coffee table.

Divorced.

Just like you're going to be.

That sick feeling intensifies.

I bend forward, and my vision blurs.

Mistake.

I feel so stupid.

So incredibly stupid.

My fingers tremble against the armrest as I push myself up to stand.

I can't believe I was such a fool.

This was never going to work.

I try not to blink.

Try not to free any of the tears dancing along my lashes.

But I fail.

I fail because while I was falling in love, Luke was planning his escape.

I'll tell her soon.

That phrase alone...

I press my hands to my stomach.

I can't have that conversation.

I can't stand in front of Luke when he tells me it's over.

I'm not strong enough. I won't survive it.

My hummingbird backs away from the awful feeling filling us and bumps into my spine. Her little legs buckle, and she slides down my vertebrae until she's sitting, her wings slumped at her sides as she blinks.

We were too hopeful.

Luke spreading his arms, blocking his cousins, and telling us to run.

Luke twirling his finger, sitting in the penalty box, wanting to see our jersey.

Luke keeping his arms around us as he introduced me to his friends.

The kiss on the red carpet.

The ice skates.

Luke... being himself.

He was just being himself.

And we got too confident.

I press my hands over my heart.

"We'll be okay," I whisper.

For me.

For my pretty little bird.

For the future.

My steps are unsteady as I hurry down the hall and into the bedroom.

The bathroom door is still shut, and I try my best to quickly gather a pair of pajamas while tears drip down my cheeks.

If I can be asleep before he gets out—if I can *pretend* to be asleep—then I won't need to face him.

And I can't face him.

Because right now, with my heart fracturing inside my ribs, I can't look at Luke and pretend I don't love him.

Chapter 120

Luke

TONIGHT WAS... more.

It felt different.

And as much as my cousin is an annoying dumbass, he's right.

I need to talk to Natalie.

But when I pull the bathroom door open, the condo is dark, with just my bedside lamp on.

Natalie's dark hair is the only part of her I can see. Her body is outlined under the covers, facing away from me, still with sleep.

We'll talk tomorrow.

Chapter 121

Natalie

My steps are quiet in the dark of the early morning.

My nerves are already shaky from packing in the dark.

I couldn't get all my things. Couldn't risk waking Luke.

But I have two suitcases ready. And I already retrieved the folder that was buried within one of them.

I try to steady my breathing. My heartbeat feels too loud in the silent condo.

My hands tremble as I smooth the papers out on Luke's dining table.

Luke's.

It was always his.

Never ours.

No matter what we said. No matter what I felt. We were just playing house.

Playing house in a condo that I wanted to be my home.

I wished it.

Willed it.

But none of that made it true.

I lower myself into the chair.

My ribs groan as my hummingbird strains to reach between them. Trying to swat the pen out of my grip. Trying to stop me, even though she knows this is our only choice.

My fingertips ache as I drag the ink across the paper. But I don't stop.

It's best to do this now.

Best to get it over with.

Even though it's making my heart fucking hurt.

Tightness curls around my throat as I close the folder.

None of this is Luke's fault.

He did nothing wrong.

And that makes this even worse.

It also makes it right.

Luke deserves happiness.

He doesn't deserve to be trapped.

This is the best option for both of us.

Luke doesn't have to find a nice way to tell me he doesn't want to make this permanent.

And I don't have to pretend I'm okay with it.

After closing the folder, I set the pen on top.

The truth always gets out. There's no beating it.

So it's time to control the narrative.

Time to face the board and tell them the truth.

I fucked up.

But I won't step aside.

I won't walk away from the company.

Everyone makes mistakes.

But my biggest mistake wasn't accidentally marrying a decent man.

It was falling in love with him.

When I stand, I place my palm over my hip. Over the inked

bird on my side, the mirror of the one that lives inside me. The familiar I've always wished was real. The friend who will never let me down.

And together, we walk out the door.

Chapter 122

Luke

SNOWFLAKES DANCE *around us as we spin.*

Natalie's hair spread across her shoulders. Her smile aimed at me.

I let go of her hand, wanting to touch her lips.

But when I let go, she starts to fall.

I lunge for her.

She reaches for me.

But my fingers only brush hers before she disappears.

My body jerks as I gasp awake.

Fuck.

I roll onto my back and slap a hand over my heart, trying to slow it.

I slowly inhale and push the nightmare out on the exhale.

Before I turn my head, I know what I'll find.

An empty bed.

I rub my palms over my eyes.

I'm going to make myself crazy with this.

I just need to talk to her.

Feeling ridiculous but not caring, I roll over to her side of the bed and press my nose into her pillow.

It smells like her shampoo.

Smells like her.

I should've set an alarm so I could've gotten up with her. But it's my sleep-in day. No practice. No game. So I didn't wake up early, and now I've missed her.

I lift my head and look at my clock.

Natalie's big meeting starts in an hour.

I sigh and accept that confronting her this morning would've been a bad idea.

With a groan, I push myself up and out of bed.

It's not that I expect our talk to go poorly, but I can't know for sure. So tonight will have to be soon enough.

I shuffle to the bathroom, going through the motions, but when I put my toothbrush in my mouth, a spot of color catches my eye.

I stare at it for a long moment before I reach out with my empty hand to grab it.

It's still in my palm when I spit the toothpaste out of my mouth, and I continue to stare at it.

Natalie's wedding ring.

She left it at home.

She never leaves it at home.

Chapter 123

Natalie

I PACE my office one last time.

This is my decision.

I take another deep breath.

It's my job to face the consequences of my actions.

My exhale is choppier than it should be.

I'm doing the right thing.

My heart gives a sad thud.

And I give it a moment. Because sometimes doing the right thing hurts.

Chapter 124

Luke

I YAWN as I pour myself a mug of coffee.

Then scroll through sports news on my phone as I pad over to the living room.

There's nothing I really have to do today, so I might as well catch up on emails.

Eyeing my full coffee mug, I snag my laptop off the coffee table in front of the couch and head to the dining table.

I feel a weird mix of tired and nervous, and I don't know why.

It's that fucking dream.

Lowering into a chair, I set my mug down and then use my laptop to nudge a folder out of the way.

I roll my neck out while I open my laptop.

Then I stare at the screen.

It's the page for a resort in Mexico.

The resort.

Was Natalie looking at this?

Does she want to go back?

I scroll the page and smile when I see the name of the suite she was looking at.

If she hasn't already booked this room for us, I'm going to.

When I move the cursor, something else catches my attention.

The text thread with my cousin.

That nervous feeling inside me transforms into dread.

Mistake marriage.

Divorce.

Talk to her.

I look from the texts to the website.

Natalie was on this computer.

I look at the browser, wondering if I can find out when she was using it.

Hoping that maybe she didn't see...

Divorce.

That word echoes in my mind. And I lift my eyes, looking past the computer screen to the folder on the table.

No.

She wouldn't.

I shove the laptop to the side and drag the folder in front of me.

It looks like the same folder that was on her desk that day.

The day I went to her office.

My hands feel unsteady as I lift the cover.

I expect a typed form, but the top page is a handwritten letter.

I know what's behind the letter, but I can't bring myself to lift the page.

Because the letter is written to me.

Luke,

I'm sorry I'm being a coward and not doing this in person.

And I'm sorry for pushing you into this whole marriage thing.

I never should have done it. Shouldn't have threatened you the way I did.

I'm sorry for making you flip your life upside down.

I know you didn't plan on being my husband, but you were great at it. Too great.

And I can't make you play along anymore. It's not fair to you.

~~And I can't pretend like I'm not~~

If you ever get married again, I can tell her you weren't in love with me. That it was all an accident. It won't take away from what you offer her.

I'm sorry, Luke.

When you find someone to love, she'll be a lucky girl.

Yours, Nat

I stare at the page.
Stare at the spots where the ink is smeared.
Look at the sentence she crossed out.
I can't pretend like I'm not...
Not what?
And *when you find someone to love.*

What the fuck is she talking about?

I love her.

I don't want to turn the page.

I don't want to see what I know is there.

But I do it.

I lift the letter and look down at the divorce papers.

I look at Natalie's signature, stark next to the blank space for mine.

Chapter 125

Natalie

"I WILL HANDLE the press on this," I tell the room, forcing myself not to shift on my feet as I continue to stand at the head of the table, opposite where my father is seated, surrounded by our board members.

"And that's supposed to make us feel better?" Arnold crosses his arms.

I make eye contact with the cranky old man. "Yes. I know what I'm doing."

He huffs. And I inhale, ready to snap at him.

"Wife!"

The shouted voice outside the conference room startles us all.

Before I can move, the double doors fling open.

And Luke walks in.

"Luke?" I breathe.

He's disheveled in jeans and a wrinkly T-shirt, fresh snow dusting his hair.

His eyes are locked on mine. "Natalie—"

"It's okay." I fight through the crack in my voice, my emotions finally breaking through. "I already told them."

He takes a step toward me. "Told them what?"

I swallow and force myself not to look away. "I told them the truth, Luke."

"The truth," he repeats, stepping closer. "That we met in Mexico. That the first time I saw you, laid out on the weight bench, reading a book, I knew I had to have you. Or did you tell them about the time you shoved me out through your balcony pool so your dad wouldn't catch us?"

Murmurs dance around the previously silent room.

Luke takes a step closer.

"Did you tell them about all the text messages? All the phone calls?" Luke is only a few feet away now. "Did you tell them about the dance party, how we didn't know it was a wedding ceremony, but how it was the best thing I've ever done?"

I press my hands to my chest, my heart beating wildly beneath my palms.

"Did you tell them how fucking perfect we are together?" His tone is... passionate.

And then I see it, the folder in his hand.

"What?" I whisper.

"You heard me, Princess." He closes the rest of the distance between us, pulling the papers out of the folder. "I'm not getting married again." He drops the folder to the floor, then rips the papers in half. "Neither of us is." He tears them again. "Because we're not getting a fucking divorce."

Luke tears the papers again before tossing them onto the conference table.

Then he lowers to one knee.

"I love you, Green Eyes." Luke lifts his left hand and pulls a pink silicone ring off his pinky finger, leaving the other one in place on his hand. "My Little Royal." He holds the ring up between us. "I haven't done a good job of showing it, but I think I loved you long before I accidentally made you my wife." He reaches out with his free hand. "Please put this twelve-dollar ring back on your hand and tell me you'll give me a chance."

Instead of reaching for the ring, I reach for his shoulders.

My legs can no longer support me, and I lower to my knees.

Chairs creak around the room.

"Are you serious?" I whisper.

Luke nods. "I looked them up online. Only twelve dollars."

A small laugh bubbles out of me, but it's followed by a sob.

"Don't cry." Luke slides the ring back on his pinky and cups my cheeks with his palms.

"But I saw—" I think of those damn text messages.

Luke brings his face closer to mine. "My cousin is an idiot. He's known all along that I never wanted to leave you. That I didn't want to lose you. He was trying to motivate me to tell you. If I'd have known you saw..."

"You really love me?" My hummingbird leans forward with me. Needing to hear him say it again too.

"You should never have to ask me that. And that's my fault. You should feel it." He lowers one hand to press against my chest. "You should know it. Because yes, Natalie. I love you. So fucking much."

I blink, but it doesn't stop the tears from falling.

He brushes one away with his thumb. "Now tell me what you crossed out, Princess. Tell me what you can't pretend."

The doubts drop away, crumbling into nothingness as they hit the floor.

Because I believe him.

I feel it.

I grip his forearms, balancing myself against his strength so I can tell him what I was too afraid to write in that letter.

"I can't pretend like I'm not in love with you." My grip on him tightens. "And I thought... I couldn't stay if you didn't love me too."

Luke swallows. "Will you tell me again?"

I know what he's asking.

So I nod. And I tell him.

"Luke, I love you. And that night in Vegas was the best thing that ever happened to me too."

Someone sniffs.

Someone clears their throat.

But I don't know who because my eyes are closing, and Luke is pulling me closer.

When our lips meet, something inside me shifts.

It's like we've been waiting a lifetime for this.

Because maybe we have.

He kisses me with all the emotion I saw in his eyes.

And I do the same.

I let him taste how much he means to me.

I push all my love toward him.

Chapter 126

Luke

Natalie's love drapes over me like a blanket, like a physical weight I'll be able to take with me no matter where I go.

I press my lips to hers one more time, then pull back.

Her green eyes sparkle at me, hope and happiness filling them. The worry and sadness I saw when I stormed into the room are nowhere to be seen.

"Will you please wear your ring?" I ask, my face still only inches from hers. "I didn't like seeing it on the counter."

She nods and lets go of me with her left hand.

I have to pull both my hands away from her body, but I use my right to slide her ring back off my pinky and onto her ring finger.

"I'm sorry for not talking to you." She looks from her ring back up to my face.

I shake my head. "I should have too. But no more apologies."

"Just love," Natalie whispers.

"What did she say?" A stranger's voice cuts through the room.

"She said just love," someone else replies.

Natalie widens her eyes. And I widen mine back.

I sorta forgot about the audience.

Together, we turn our heads and find everyone standing from their chairs, huddled around this end of the table, looking down at us. And apparently listening to every word we've said.

And as we kneel on the floor together, half of the people applaud.

The other half look skeptical but still interested.

Natalie drops her forehead to my shoulder with a groan, and I fight the urge to start laughing.

I've played in front of thousands, but I've never felt more on display.

One clapper is louder than the rest, and he steps around the crowd to stand behind us.

"This is the sort of leadership I want to see." Natalie's dad beams down at us with tears in his eyes. "Owning your actions and moving forward."

Natalie lifts her head and looks up. "Thanks, Dad."

I grip her hands, and we get to our feet, turning to face her father.

"You're welcome." Mr. Wagner wipes at his cheek. "You have six months to work your current position and enjoy being newlyweds. Then I'll start the transition of making the company yours."

Pride slams into my chest.

Natalie's mouth drops open, but mine pulls into a grin.

My Princess is about to take on her dream. And I'm going to be behind her every step of the way.

Epilogue One

Luke

"I'm proud of you, Lucas." Mom pats my arm before taking it. "This is a beautiful spot to marry a beautiful girl."

I smile down at my mom.

She knows this is a renewal, but since she wasn't at the real wedding, she insists on treating this as one. Natalie insists it's cute, so I'm prone to agree.

"Thanks, Mom."

She squeezes my arm. "She's a wonderful woman, a good person. But so are you. You're a good boy, and you deserve her."

"Thanks, Mom," I say, quieter this time.

Mom flew up to Minnesota three weeks ago, renting an apartment a few blocks down from our place for the month.

She did it because she wanted to get to know Natalie before our *wedding*. And I should have seen it coming. Their connection. The instant feeling of family.

It only took two dinners before my mom told Natalie she could call her Mom if she felt like it.

And it only took another week before Natalie did it.

It was simple.

Our own Sunday brunch, as we were all having seconds.

"Would you like some more coffee, Mom?"

Natalie said it, and then all three of us burst into tears.

And now I'm pretty sure Mom is going to go back to Colorado and try to convince my aunt that they need to move back up here.

I take a deep breath of the floral-scented air.

Next to me, Mom straightens her shoulders and takes a deep breath. "I'm ready."

Ash

Luke and his mom appear at the end of the aisle, stepping out from behind the wall of blooming flowers.

I pull Meghan into my side. "You did a good job, Banshee."

She wiggles against me, causing her sequin dress to sparkle in the afternoon summer sun.

"I've always wanted to do something here," she says, referring to the hummingbird garden in the arboretum. And I can see why.

It's full of life.

Full of vibrancy.

I kiss the top of Meghan's head. "Love you, Baby."

She tips her head back, a soft smile on her mouth. "Don't call me Baby."

I press my lips to hers.

Jackson

Katelyn sets her hand on my thigh as Luke and his mom reach the front row.

"I know." My wife's voice is quiet.

I place my hand over hers and squeeze.

Luke has been my best friend for... so long.

He's one of the best men I know. And he's wanted to find love for... so long.

And now he's found it.

I shift my grip and lift Katelyn's hand to my mouth, pressing my lips against her soft skin.

Everything is changing.

Luke and Natalie met last fall, so it's been less than a year, but it already feels like forever.

She's about to take over the corporate world while us guys are starting to think about our own careers and how they're nearing their end.

And then there's my sister.

I glance across the aisle to where Steph is sitting with my

brother-in-law. Who I'm sure will be my brother-in-law twice over once they take the time to get married.

I still can't believe she hid her relationship with Alex for so long. I never would have pictured them together, but seeing them with each other, I get it. And in a couple of weeks, they'll be moving in together in a cute little house out on Darling Lake where Alex is going to work as a fourth grade teacher.

My gaze moves up a row to my mom.

She's already crying, reaching out to pat Luke's mom on the shoulder.

When she sits back, Coach puts his arm around Mom's shoulders and hands her a tissue.

This spring, after the season was over, Mom sat me and Steph down to tell us that she was moving in with Coach. She told us that she'll always love our father and that she would never remarry, but that she loves Coach too.

They leave on a cruise tomorrow. And I couldn't be happier for her.

Dad passed away a long time ago, and we will always miss him, but I'm glad she has someone to spend her days with.

And in my mind, they only hold hands. The noises Ash and Meghan heard in that closet at my wedding were just them holding fucking hands.

"Oh," Katelyn breathes, and I turn my head.

Then we all stand to face the bride.

Flowers dot Natalie's dark hair, and her light pink dress reminds me of Katelyn's wedding dress.

I wrap my arms around my wife, pulling her back to my front.

Then I lean down so my lips are next to her ear and tell her the truth that will never change. "I love you, Kitten."

Natalie

My dad's arm trembles a little under my touch, and I hold on to him tighter.

It's always been just the two of us. Me and him. And now, in an instant, our family has turned into four.

After our honeymoon, I'm going to become the CEO of Wag Corp.

I'm excited to start. Excited to be in charge of something good.

It's what I worked so hard for. But even though it was always the goal, it still terrified me. Because I never really wanted to face down the world alone.

I look up the aisle. At the man in the black suit, standing in front of the ribbon-covered gazebo. And I smile.

He's the reason the world doesn't seem so scary anymore. Because he's the reason I won't have to face it alone.

I know I'll always have him at my side.

The grass is soft under my steps, and when my dad hands me off, I decide I don't want to wait until the end.

Instead of taking Luke's hand, I grip the front of his suit and pull Luke down toward me.

He goes willingly, and I feel his grin against my lips as he kisses me back.

The crowd cheers, and someone whistles loudly.

And it's perfect.

Luke pulls back, his shining eyes locked on mine. "I love you, Princess."

Epilogue Two

Natalie

My cheeks are burning, so I cover them by pulling the head into place. My new crystal tiara is secured on the very top. Between the ears.

"Natalie, get your ass in here," Luke calls from the bedroom.

I look at myself in the mirror of the Princess Suite bathroom and wonder if I can really go through with this.

Then I yank the front flap open, the newly added magnets pulling apart silently, and let the section of white furry material drape down, exposing my bare breasts.

"Wife. What is—"

I step out of the bathroom.

And Luke falls off the edge of the bed.

Luke

"What... How..."

In front of me is Natalie. Dressed up in a Blizz suit. White fur. Yeti head. But it's not the old suit. Because in the old suit, Blizz was wearing a jersey, and Natalie's tits weren't hanging out.

I shuffle toward her on my knees in nothing but straining boxer briefs.

"Fuck me. Why do I like this?" I reach for her hips, balancing myself.

"No idea," Natalie replies as her paws grip at my hair. "But I like the way you like it."

I trace the hole in the fabric.

"Fuck, I like it a lot." I pull a nipple into my mouth.

Natalie grips my hair tighter, and I move to the other peak, sucking harder, making her moan.

I finally pull back and look at her nipples glistening before me while running my hands up and down her soft, fuzzy sides.

Natalie lets go of my hair and grips the piece of fabric

hanging below her tits. "Let me show you how it works." She lifts the fabric, and I hear the small metallic sounds of a dozen little magnets snapping into place, covering her bare flesh and hiding the seam completely.

I tip my head back and look into her comically large eyes.

Those are different too.

The eyes have been painted green to match Natalie's and lined with swooshing black lashes.

"Princess Blizzy, please tell me you have these snaps in other places too."

Natalie gives me a slow nod, and I notice the sparkly crown on top of her head.

I open my mouth to comment, but then she lifts her leg onto the bed beside us.

The stretch of the fabric causes another round of little snicks as magnets release.

Mouth still open, I watch the seams between her legs pop open. The fur spreading to reveal my wife's bare pussy.

"Fucking hell," I growl a second before I lean in and bury my face against her slit.

She's already slick.

And warm.

And delicious.

I grip her furry butt cheeks and pull her harder against my mouth.

Eating.

Devouring.

I pull back just enough to take a breath.

"I want to fuck you from behind, like my submissive little pet." I slide a finger inside her as I flatten my tongue over her clit.

My Princess moans.

"But I also want you on top of me," I admit, adding a second finger. "I want to feel your claws squeezing my throat, like the predator you really are."

Natalie tugs my hair to pull my head back. "Let's do both."

Then she crawls onto the bed. On all fours.

Epilogue Three

The Group Text Messages

Banshee: Okay, girls, I know I just asked this in *our* group text, but Ash will not shut the fuck up asking me what our plans are, so I'm resending the question here.

Banshee: When the guys win that big shiny cup next week, who is going to host the celebration party?

Ash: Sue me for being interested in your life.

Banshee: You are overbearing and you know it. Go chat up your own group text.

Zach: Ours isn't as fun as yours.

Banshee: And how would you know that?

Sugar: Lucky guess?

Banshee: Izzy!

Sugar: What? If we're cuddling when you guys message me, he's going to see it.

Zach: Yeah, Ash, maybe you should cuddle more.

Jackson: I just have Katelyn read them to me.

Banshee: Katelyn!

Kitten: Jackson, can I talk to you outside for a moment?

Jackson: Was that supposed to be a secret?

Banshee: Apparently nothing is sacred.

Ash: Am I the only one who hasn't been spying on the wives?

Ash: Luke, where the fuck are you?

Banshee: Probably tied up in a bear suit.

Princess: Meghan!

Banshee: LoL Why are you responding? Is Luke... occupied?

Ash: When you release your husband, will you tell me where you got that tailoring done? I have a few things I want snaps added to.

Sugar: What snaps?

Princess: Meghan, I'm going to end you.

Banshee: I thought everyone knew!

Princess: You make a big deal about our texts but tell him that?

Sugar: Tell him what?

Sugar: What are you guys talking about?

Princess: Nothing! We are talking about nothing!

Banshee: Izz, I'll text you.

Princess: I hate you.

Banshee: No you don't.

Sugar: You put secret snap cutouts in the Blizz suit?!

Kitten: Hold up, what?

Princess: How do I leave this friend group?

Banshee: You can't. It's pretty much a blood-in, blood-out situation.

Princess: So if I throw a tampon at you, I can get out?

Sugar: Ew.

Princess: I'm not talking to you guys anymore.

Banshee: Luke can just answer for you. When you untie him.

Kitten: How do you know so much about their sex life?

Princess: Oh. My. God. She doesn't.

Banshee: So are you saying you've never tied Luke up?

Jackson: I don't think I want to know the answer to this question.

Ash: I do.

Zach: We're in too deep now, Jacky Boy.

Jackson: I'm handing my phone to Katelyn. She'll tell me when I can look again.

Ash: Prude.

Banshee: So...

Sugar: Natalie is taking an awfully long time to answer.

Banshee: Two blinks for yes. No blinks for no.

Kitten: How is she supposed to blink through a text?

Banshee: Logistics aren't my problem.

Sugar: So when you say tie up… Is that like a rope? Or is it just a different way to say handcuffs?

Banshee: What do you know about handcuffs, Little Miss Izzy?

Sugar: Nothing.

Kitten: The lady doth reply too fast.

Banshee: Ash is the one who demanded this chat, and now he's off on his laptop googling "sex ropes."

Luke: *sends link for beginner restraint kit*

Epilogue Four

Ten Years Later

Zach

"Wilder!" Coach Noah calls out.

Both of Jackson's kids start skating toward Noah, away from their goal.

"No." Noah waves his hand. "Number thirty-three Wilder."

I snicker.

Then I see Jackson a few yards down, face to the glass like I am, waving his hands for the younger of his sons to turn around.

Katelyn is sitting on the bench a few rows behind him, smothering a smile with her mitten.

My snicker turns into a laugh.

The indoor practice arena is large but empty, save for the players and their parents, so sound travels.

Jackson jerks his head in my direction. "Knock it off, Hunt."

My daughter skids to a stop on the ice. "What?"

"Sorry." Jackson gestures for her to keep going. "Talking to your dad."

Her blond curls stick out around her helmet, reminding me so much of her mother. But then she jumps into her little seven-year-old sprint and knocks over one of her opponents, reminding me of me.

Coach Noah blows his whistle and skates into the fray, resetting the group of six- to eight-year-olds.

Izzy sighs as she steps up next to me, cup of hot cocoa in hand. "She's gonna be trouble."

I grin as I drape my arm over her shoulder. "It's good for her to get it out of her system in summer league."

"Get it out of her system, or learn bad behavior?" Izzy shakes her head and hands me her hot chocolate.

Before I take a sip, I lean down and press a quick kiss to her temple. "I love you, Sugar."

Luke

Two years after winning the cup, I retired. So did the rest of the guys. And now, this is our routine.

Jackson and Zach stand at attention, playing assistant coach —even though Noah does just fine. And why wouldn't he? He's a starter on the Sleet now. He doesn't need help.

Ash and I just enjoy sitting here, watching the chaos, then going home to our child-free, wife-centered lives.

"Ash." Meghan turns to face us from her spot with Natalie a few rows ahead. "Can you go get the extra marshmallows from the car?"

Ash groans, but we all know he's going to do it.

He'd do anything for her. Just like how he's facilitated the girls' illegal hot chocolate distribution.

Sitting between Meghan and Natalie is a two-gallon thermos with a spout. Accompanied by paper cups, sprinkles, and a dwindling bag of marshmallows.

I get up with Ash and move down to sit next to my wife.

My shoulder bumps hers. "What's the flavor this week?"

Natalie smiles at me. "Snickerdoodle."

I hold out my hand. "Load me up."

As she pours my cup, I take a deep breath, enjoying the scent of chocolate and cinnamon mixed with the nostalgic scent of a hockey rink.

There's something about it.

The ice.

The chilled air.

It's always going to feel like home.

No matter where life takes us.

No matter what we accomplish.

No matter where we go.

This will always feel like home.

Taking the cup from Natalie, I move it to my far hand so I can pull her into my side.

I turn my head, pressing my lips to her hair. "I'm so fucking proud of you."

My wife tips her gaze up to meet mine. "Because of the flavor?"

Her green eyes are full of soft humor.

But she knows.

She knows that the world is better with her in it.

I hold her tighter. "Because of everything."

Natalie

This life of mine.

I wouldn't change it for the world.

It's wild to look back. To see all we've been through. All we've done.

Luke rests his head against mine.

I fill my lungs with his warmth. And I feel the peace in the center of my chest. Where my hummingbird is splayed out on a pile of fluffy love.

Love that Luke has given us.

Love that he's spoiled us with.

And even after all these years, I fall asleep every night knowing that the softness inside my chest is only going to keep growing.

Because Luke is mine.

And because no matter how much time goes by, I'll always be his Princess.

The End of the Sleet Series

Acknowledgments

Thank you so much to all of my Sleet Sluts. I adore you so damn much.

This series has been years in the making. I started daydreaming in 2019 about this *kiss cam scene*, and my mind just couldn't let it go. So I didn't. And then *Sleet Kitten* was born. Then *Sleet Sugar*, and *Sleet Banshee*, and as I was writing the epilogue of *Banshee*, I was like... I think Luke needs a book. And he did. And now, finally, in 2024, he has his story.

So thank you to everyone who was patient, and thank you to everyone who made this possible.

Mom, thank you for all of your help with edits and alpha reading and putting up with my crazy timelines.

Kerissa, thank you for being the best friend and assistant a girl could ask for. I know I'm the worst to work with, but you're the best, so it evens out.

Thank you to Gabby and Nikki and Elaine for joining me in this Airbnb in St. Louis so I could finally finish these edits.

Thank you, Lily of the Light for all the glorious sessions to clear my head and get my energy in the right place to make this happen.

Thank you, Mr. Tilly, for feeding me and feeding the dogs and understanding that I do my best work at 2 a.m.

Thank you to all of my BeanBaggers. I love having the safe space of the BeanBag Book Club. (If you're not in my Facebook reader group and you've gotten this far, then it's time to join.)

Thank you to my ARC readers. I adore you and appreciate you.

There are so many more people to thank, but my brain is mush, and I'm still sitting in my emotions about the end of the Sleet. So just know that I love you, and I appreciate you.

Now go forth and be good.

And if you can't be good, have fun.

About the Author

S. J. enjoys burying her head in books, whether to read them or write them or listen to them.

When she's not busy writing her contemporary smut, she can be found lounging with her husband and their herd of rescue boxers.

To stay up to date on all things Tilly, make sure to follow her on her socials, join her newsletter, and interact whenever you feel like it! Links to everything on her website www.sjtilly.com

Also by S. J. Tilly

Love Letters Series

Contemporary Romance

Coming Soon...

Alliance Series

Dark Mafia Romance

NERO

Payton

Running away from home at seventeen wasn't easy. Let's face it, though, nothing before, or in the ten years since, has ever been easy for me.

And I'm doing okay. Sorta. I just need to keep scraping by, living under the radar. Staying out of people's way, off people's minds.

So when a man walks through my open patio door, stepping boldly into my home and my life, I should be scared. Frightened. Terrified.

But I must be more broken than I realized because I'm none of those things.

I'm intrigued.

And I'm wondering if the way to take control of my life is by giving in to him.

Nero

The first time I took a man's life, I knew there'd be no going back. No normal existence in the cards for me.

So instead of walking away, I climbed a mountain of bodies and created my own destiny. By forming The Alliance.

And I was fine with that. Content enough to carry on.

Until I stepped through those open doors and into her life.

I should've walked away. Should've gone right back out the door I came through. But I didn't.

And now her life is in danger.

But that's the thing about being a bad man. I'll happily paint the streets red to protect what's mine.

And Payton is mine. Whether she knows it or not.

KING

Okay, so, my bad for assuming the guy I was going on a date with *wasn't* married. And my bad for taking him to a friend's house for dinner, only to find out my friend is also friends with *his* wife. Because, in fact, he *is* married. And she happens to be at my friend's house because her husband was *busy working*.

Confused? So am I.

Unsurprisingly, my date's wife is super angry about finding out that her husband is a cheating asshole.

Girl, I get it.

Then, to make matters more convoluted, there is the man sitting next to my date's wife. A man named King, who is apparently her brother and who lives up to his name.

And since my *date* is a two-timing prick, I'm not going to feel bad about drooling over King,

especially since I'll never see him again.

Or at least I don't plan to.

I plan to take an Uber to the cheater's apartment to get my car keys.

I plan for it to be quick.

And if I had to list a thousand possible outcomes… witnessing my date's murder, being kidnapped by his killer, and then being forced to marry the super attractive but clearly

deranged crime lord would not have been on my Bingo card.

But alas, here I am.

DOM

VAL

When I was nine, I went to my first funeral. Along with accepting my father's death, I had to accept new and awful truths I wasn't prepared for.

When I was nineteen, I went to my mother's funeral. We weren't close, but with her gone, I became more alone than ever before.

Sure, I have a half brother who runs The Alliance. And yeah, he's given me his protection—in the form of a bodyguard and chauffeur. But I don't have anyone that really knows me. No one to really love me.

Until I meet him. The man in the airport.

And when one chance meeting turns into something hotter, something more serious, I let myself believe that maybe he's the one. Maybe this man is the one who will finally save me from my loneliness. The one to give me the family I've always craved.

DOM

The Mafia is in my blood. It's what I do.

So when that blood is spilled and one funeral turns into three, drastic measures need to be taken.

And when this battle turns into a war, I'm going to need more men. More power.

I'm going to need The Alliance.

And I'll become a member. By any means necessary.

HANS

Cassie

How to make the handsome, brooding man across the street notice me.

Step one: Deliver baked goods to his front porch, even though he never answers his door and always returns the containers when I'm not home.

Step two: Slowly lose my mind as a whole year passes without ever running into him, no matter how hard I try.

Step three: Have my boudoir photos accidentally delivered to his mailbox instead of mine. Have him open the package. Then have him storm into my home for the most panty-melting scolding of my life.

Step four: Still figuring out step four.

Hans

I'm a dangerous man.

A man who has spent the last two decades removing so many souls from this earth that it's a miracle my hands aren't permanently stained red.

I'm a man who belongs in the shadows.

I certainly don't belong in my pretty little neighbor's bedroom when she's not home, touching her things and inhaling her scent.

I shouldn't follow her. Shouldn't watch her. Because no number of cookies on my doorstep will change the fact that love isn't an option for me.

The only option left for me is violence.

Sin Series

Romantic Suspense

Mr. Sin

I should have run the other way. Paid my tab and gone back to my room. But he was there. And he was... everything. I figured, what's the harm in letting passion rule my decisions for one night? So what if he looks like the Devil in a suit? I'd be leaving in the morning. Flying home, back to my pleasant but predictable life. I'd never see him again.

Except I do. In the last place I expected. And now everything I've worked so hard for is in jeopardy.

We can't stop what we've started, but this is bigger than the two of us.

And when his past comes back to haunt him, love might not be enough to save me.

Sin Too

Beth

It started with tragedy.

And secrets.

Hidden truths that refused to stay buried have come out to chase me. Now I'm on the run, living under a blanket of constant fear, pretending to be someone I'm not. And if I'm not really me, how am I supposed to know what's real?

Angelo

Watch the girl.

It was supposed to be a simple assignment. But like everything else in this family, there's nothing simple about it. Not my task. Not her fake name. And not my feelings for her.

But Beth is mine now.

So when the monsters from her past come out to play, they'll have to get through me first.

Miss Sin

I'm so sick of watching the world spin by. Of letting people think I'm plain and boring, too afraid to just be myself.

Then I see *him*.

John.

He's strength and fury and unapologetic.

He's everything I want. And everything I wish I was.

He won't want me, but that doesn't matter. The sight of him is all the inspiration I need to finally shatter this glass house I've built around myself.

Only he does want me. And when our worlds collide, details we can't see become tangled, twisting together, ensnaring us in an invisible trap.

When it all goes wrong, I don't know if I'll be able to break free of the chains binding us or if I'll suffocate in the process.

Sleet Series

Hockey Romantic Comedy

Sleet Kitten

There are a few things that life doesn't prepare you for. Like what to do when a super-hot guy catches you sneaking around in his basement. Or what to do when a mysterious package shows up with tickets to a hockey game, because apparently, he's a professional athlete. Or how to handle it when you get to the game and realize he's freaking famous since half of the 20,000 people in the stands are wearing his jersey.

I thought I was a well-adjusted adult, reasonably prepared for life. But one date with Jackson Wilder, a viral video, and a "I didn't know she was your mom" incident, and I'm suddenly questioning everything I thought I knew.

But he's fun. And great. And I think I might be falling for him. But I don't know if he's falling for me too, or if he's as much of a player off the ice as on.

Sleet Sugar

My friends have convinced me. No more hockey players.

With a dad who is the head coach for the Minnesota Sleet, it seemed like an easy decision.

My friends have also convinced me that the best way to boost my fragile self-esteem is through a one-night stand.

A dating app. A hotel bar. A sexy-as-hell man, who's sweet and funny, and did I mention, sexy as hell... I fortified my courage and invited myself up to his room.

Assumptions. There's a rule about them.

I assumed he was passing through town. I assumed he was a businessman or maybe an investor or accountant or literally anything other than a professional hockey player. I assumed I'd never see him again.

I assumed wrong.

Sleet Banshee

Mother-freaking hockey players. My friends found their happily ever afters with a couple of sweet, doting, over-the-top, in-love athletes. They got nicknames like *Kitten* and *Sugar*. But me? I got stuck with a dickhead who riles me up on purpose and calls me *Banshee*. Yeah, he might have a voice made specifically for wet dreams. And he might have a body and face carved by the gods. And he might have a level of Alpha-hole that gets me all hot and bothered.

But when he presses my buttons, he presses ALL of my buttons. And I'm not the type of girl who takes things sitting down. And I only got caught on my knees that one time. In the museum.

But when one of my decisions gets one of my friends hurt... I can't stop blaming myself. And him.

Except he can't take a hint. And I can't keep my panties on.

Sleet Princess

My trip to Mexico for my cousin's wedding was only supposed to be a few days of obligation and oceanside.

I wasn't expecting Luke.

Wasn't expecting the hot hockey player, with the smirks and the tattoos, who kept *bumping into me.*

And I certainly wasn't expecting to spend a night on the beach, under the stars, underneath *him.*

It was magical, but I thought it would end there.

Instead, we exchanged numbers and stayed in touch.

So when Luke invited me to watch him play in Vegas, I went.

And it was great.

Until we woke up the next morning and found the wedding certificate in my pocket.

Turns out that dance party we snuck into was actually a group wedding ceremony.

And now we're married.

Which is bad.

Because I think our wedding was actually our first date. And if my dad finds out, he'll cut me out of the family business.

So when footage leaks of Luke and me hot and heavy in an elevator, I have to make up a new plan to save my reputation and career.

Now, all I need is for Luke Anders to act like he's madly in love with me.

Should be easy.

Right?

Darling Series

Contemporary Small Town Romance

Smoky Darling

Elouise

I fell in love with Beckett when I was seven.

He broke my heart when I was fifteen.

When I was eighteen, I promised myself I'd forget about him.

And I did. For a dozen years.

But now he's back home. Here. In Darling Lake. And I don't know if I should give in to the temptation swirling between us or run the other way.

Beckett

She had a crush on me when she was a kid. But she was my brother's best friend's little sister. I didn't see her like that. And even if I had, she was too young. Our age difference was too great.

But now I'm back home. And she's here. And she's all the way grown up.

It wouldn't have worked back then. But I'll be damned if I won't get a taste of her now.

Latte Darling

I have a nice life—living in my hometown, owning the coffee shop I've worked at since I was sixteen.

It's comfortable.

On paper.

But I'm tired of doing everything by myself. Tired of being in charge of every decision in my life.

I want someone to lean on. Someone to spend time with. Sit with. Hug.

And I really don't want to go to my best friend's wedding alone.

So, I signed up for a dating app and agreed to meet with the first guy who messaged me.

And now here I am, at the bar.

Only it's not my date that just sat down in the chair across from me. It's his dad.

And holy hell, he's the definition of silver fox. If a silver fox can be thick as a house, have piercing blue eyes and tattoos from his neck down to his fingertips.

He's giving me *big bad wolf* vibes. Only instead of running, I'm blushing. And he looks like he might just want to eat me whole.

Tilly World Holiday Novellas

Second Bite

When a holiday baking competition goes incredibly wrong. Or right...

Michael

I'm starting to think I've been doing this for too long. The screaming fans. The constant media attention. The fat paychecks. None of it brings me the happiness I yearn for.

Yet here I am. Another year. Another holiday special. Another Christmas spent alone in a hotel room.

But then the lights go up. And I see *her*.

Alice

It's an honor to be a contestant, I know that. But right now, it feels a little like punishment. Because any second, Chef Michael Kesso, the man I've been in love with for years, the man who doesn't even know I exist, is going to walk onto the set, and it will be a miracle if I don't pass out at the sight of him.

But the time for doubts is over. Because *Second Bite* is about to start "in three... two... one..."